A SCIENCE FICT...

URSA MAJOR

CYBORG SHIFTERS
BOOK VII

NAOMI LUCAS

URSA MAJOR

CYBORG SHIFTERS #7

NAOMI LUCAS

CONTENTS

 Created   with   Vellum

To Justin, my husband, for convincing me that I needed a Cyborg Bear in my Shifter series. If it wasn't for him, Cypher may have been a walrus, a snooty house cat, or worse, another bug!

Terraform Zero, a virtual reality colonization game, has swept the galaxy by storm. The Champions are household names that give humanity hope. Vee Miles believes she is good enough to compete amongst them, but the costly entrance fee is holding her back.

Enter the Earthian Planetary Exploration Division.

Still reeling from a publicity nightmare named Zeph, the corporation is desperate to change the public's opinions toward Cyborgs. They offer to sponsor Vee. The EPED gets the PR boost, and she gets to keep the prize money. The EPED's deal comes with strings though, and she has to pretend to be a made-up Cyborg shifting bear named Cypher.

A male that had the look of a Viking space warrior, with enough scars and otherworldly brawn to make any woman swoon. An imaginary male that makes her heart race…

Little does she know she's being used as bait to lure the real Cypher from his den.

He's out now.

He's coming for her, and there's no place virtual or otherwise for her to hide.

$\mathcal{V}$ee wiped her hands on her faded jeans and focused on the sleek black business suit worn by the man in front of her. It was the kind of suit that a woman like her didn't normally see, and it clearly defined the gap in status between her and this man.

Not so much a man. A Cyborg.

The first Cyborg she'd ever laid eyes on in her life. She knew all about them—she'd been obsessing over their heroics since she could crawl. They filled the fantasies of men and women across the known universe, practically gods among them.

The power, prestige, the fear and awe they generated were felt by every human being. Even their domineering beauty. And Cyborgs were beautiful, even in their *I want to kill you*, and rugged way. Danger had its allure.

It must be easy, being born into status.

But sitting in front of one now, all she knew was intimidation. That dangerous side they harbored really made itself apparent.

Nightheart. He told her to call him Nightheart. *What kind of name is Nightheart?*

Unlike Nightheart, Vee was a gutter rat city dweller. Nightheart's suit alone cost enough to cover her rent for months, not counting the shoes, belt and other accessories.

To be sitting across from a Cyborg, one who silently stared at her, judging her, seeing into her soul, was different than worshiping them from afar. Being in the same room put her firmly inside the blast radius if anything went wrong.

He's not going to choose me…

She waited for him to speak, to do anything but stare at her in such an uncanny way that it made her skin crawl.

Is there something wrong with me?

Of course there's a lot wrong with me.

She didn't look like the average young woman. At least not the type of woman to be in an office like this one, in front of a man like *him*. There were clean chrome walls and holographic screens everywhere, exaggerating his power and his wealth. Not to mention the vast view of New America City sprawling out from the floor-to-ceiling windows on three sides of them. The sight dizzied her.

She had one window in her apartment, and it faced the dull metal wall of another skyscraper apartment building. Not only that, she was a *woman*, average or not. Very few women were given these opportunities… and if they were, it was because they had the backing of a big corporation or the government.

No. Vee didn't belong here. Not with her hair a vibrant dyed-red that shimmered in the light, her makeup to match, and the loose-fitting clothing that hung from her frame, vintage and bright. What corporation would back her? It was a one-in-a-million chance.

She may have proven her talent, but the rest of her left much to be desired.

Vee worked hard to keep the disappointment from her showing on her face. *Perhaps I still have a chance to convince him?*

But as the minutes ticked by, she feared this may be the entire interview. *Him* staring at her.

Him judging her.

Him second-guessing why he happened to pick her application out of a sea of them.

"I—"

"You'll do," he finally said.

She frowned. "I'll… do?" Had she heard him correctly?

"I said, you'll do."

Excitement surged through her. *I'll do!* She nearly jumped from her seat.

But the Cyborg was already focused on something else, ignoring her, as if the long, awkward stare never happened. As if he had no idea what he had just done for her. That he hadn't judged her solely based on being a solo player.

Still, just because he said she'd *do,* didn't mean she had the sponsorship yet. Vee sobered.

Another holographic screen rose beside him, and her gaze snapped to it.

My media site. And with it, her bio, her blog, and her videos appeared.

"Vee Miles," he said offhandedly. Coldly. Deliberately.

Vee shivered at the sound of her name on his lips.

"We reviewed your resume on our sponsorship program site. It appears you qualify for the Terraform Zero Championship, but you lack the funds to participate. Am I correct?"

She straightened when the words *sponsorship* and *championship* came out of his mouth. "Yes," she answered a little too quickly. "I've been training every day since I was six to compete at an interstellar level. I want to be on the front lines colonizing a new planet."

I want to give hope to the human race. She kept that part to herself.

Nightheart waved his hand, cutting her off. "You have a seventy-eight percent average for planetary habitation success. That's impressive."

He was impressed with her? Her toes wiggled. "Yes."

"You have competed in local tournaments since you were twelve, even winning many against veterans in the field."

She nodded.

"Do you have a partner you work with?"

"No. I work alone." Most Terraform Zero players played with others. Not her. She never had the friends to form an alliance nor had the means to buy her way into one. When she was younger, she desperately wanted to be a part of a team. But as the years went on, finding one became harder as she became more isolated, and she realized that she worked better alone.

She learned so much more that way.

Now she was known for being a soloer. *Making all my opponents' teams look bad.* She liked that.

Nightheart's brow fell. "Hmm."

Please don't let that be a problem.

"We can give you three million credits to get you to the championship."

Her mind went blank at the offered amount.

She barely had enough credits to cover her rent and food each month. Three million would not only get her to the championship, but it'd get her there in style. *I could buy all new equipment and still live like a queen after the tournament!*

"And guarantee you a job if you win," he continued, turning back to her with his unnerving eyes. Dull yellow eyes, to be exact. Yellow eyes that seemed more fitting for a monster or a demonic fiend. "The Earthian Planetary Exploration Division has partners—friends—in that field."

"I don't know what to say except why? Why me?"

He threaded his long fingers and placed them on the desk. "You're young. You have a fairly large following, and there is nothing in your past that would hold you back or reflect badly on the EPED."

His lips twitched. She could've sworn she saw lines of numbers flick over his pupils, but he blinked, and they were gone before she could decide.

"We've reviewed countless applications in the last few months, Vee Miles, and not one has looked as good as yours. One that has everything we want. Although—" the Cyborg cocked his head "—there are several others we are considering."

She bit down on her tongue, knowing his meaning. *If I don't accept and accept soon, I'll lose this chance.*

"Are you still interested?" he asked.

"I am. Where do I sign?"

Nightheart's lips twitched again. "That easily?" He lifted his hands from the desk. Big, pale hands. The kind that could wring her neck or break her spine before she blinked—or both.

Why am I thinking this?

He handed her a folder.

She opened it to find two paper contracts and a pen. "I wouldn't have applied if I wasn't serious. I read the terms and conditions prior. I'll read them again now." Though, literally, she really had nothing to lose. No money, no prospects, not even real freedom. She couldn't afford it.

And those who worked for, or affiliated with a corporation like the EPED, were known for being taken care of. *Perhaps…because it's run by a Cyborg that'll change.* People flocked to work for a place like the EPED because it was at least something, a way to improve one's life.

"You don't want a lawyer present?" he asked.

"I can't afford a lawyer."

"Ah. There is one caveat though, Vee Miles. One you must follow without exception that was not advertised on our site."

Vee glanced up from the contract. "A caveat?"

She lowered the folder into her lap as he explained.

---

*T*hat night, Vee lay on her bed while the day rushed through her mind. Hours had gone by, signing page after page. A digital copy was sent to her personal IP identification immediately after.

Nightheart explained everything. That if she won the Terraform Zero Championship, she would get to keep the prize. That if she didn't win or receive a high-profile job from the event, she would be given one at the EPED.

They're better than the military, she mused. Workers were hard to come by, and right now, one of the freedoms she did have was that she was able to work for herself… for the time being.

Vee made sure to add a clause in the contract that if she placed second or third, even if she worked for the EPED afterward, she would be allowed to participate in next year's championship if she qualified. Sponsorship or not.

Details were hashed out.

In one week, the three million credits would be in her account.

She grabbed her pillow, pressed it to her face, and screamed with heart-thundering excitement. Every fiber, every muscle seized with disbelief. She screamed a little more until her neighbor banged on the wall and yelled at her to shut up.

I may have signed away some of my freedom, but who wouldn't in my circumstances?

Rolling over, she gazed at her apartment's ceiling and wiped happy tears from her eyes.

She'd never had more than a couple hundred credits in her account at any given time. Not since she moved out of her parents' apartment and into her own. The moment she'd turned eighteen and refused to go to college and get a higher education, her relationship with them became strained.

'If you want to make it in this universe without a degree, then go and try. Prove us wrong.'

Despite their differences, she still had a relationship with her parents and understood their reasoning.

They never understood her love for the game, or that she was already pursuing her life's goals through it. Or that she was working for a bigger dream: making the game into a reality.

It was a way to get off of Earth and explore the wilds of the untamed universe. To be one of the first people on a new planet.

Terraform Zero had everything, taught everything one needed to play it well. Playing the game as a child, she was learning methodology, statistics, advanced math, interpreting algorithms, vocabulary, history, meteorology, zoology, ethics, and the list goes on and on. There were levels of course, and courses offered within the game, starting beginners with a simple point-and-click game. But for those who really loved it, they could advance deep into the wholesale logistics of colonizing a new world. The game never went deeper than the player wanted.

Though the game's eighteenth edition came out five years ago, the game had been around for the past two hundred, perfected and re-perfected by the best scholars in the known universe. It was used as a simulation for potentially habitable planets, moons, and asteroids. Oftentimes, the location became a multi-year challenge for those who took the game seriously.

This year, the Terraform Zero Championship was releasing a real, new, potential spot in the Andromeda Galaxy that could be colonized, and those who competed would be the only ones to get the planet to their game's systems.

Even if I don't win, I need to be there.

Vee snagged her wristcon, swiped her fingerprints, and logged on to the network. She brought up the contract and saw her signature at the bottom of each page.

But the caveat...

It was really strange.

Nightheart came to mind. She shivered. The caveat *was* a bizarre one and hard to wrap her mind around, though it wasn't unreasonable.

She scrolled through the pages until the part where *Cypher* filled her hologram screen and stared at his picture.

A lump formed in her throat. Vee swallowed thickly.

'We want you to have a partner, and not just any partner, but one unique enough to draw the crowds.'

'A partner? But I'm known for not having a partner...'

'A Cyborg. One we produced, named Cypher.'

Her mouth dropped open. 'What?'

'Consider it a marketing ploy, a way to represent my kind in a good light while you get to achieve your dreams. People see Cyborgs as nothing more than war heroes, cold machines. We need to show them that we're more.' He sighed. 'Again.'

And that explained why Nightheart and the EPED cared at all about her and the championship.

Vee suspected she knew why he wanted positive PR.

Cyborgs had come under attack after a rogue one—one who worked directly for the EPED—kidnapped a human woman and child from the planet Kepler. It was all over the interstellar news. Public opinion on the once-great heroes has since been at an all-time low, the lowest since their first emergence during the Great Galactic War.

Terraform championships were watched by hundreds of millions, and not just hundreds of millions, but by Trentian aliens as well, scholars, politicians, and industry experts. People who had a voice, who could sway public opinion. A Cyborg player would look good for them.

Now she was going to be thrust into the political mess by impersonating a made-up one. Confidentially of course.

Three million credits. Three million credits, and my dreams.

When she asked Nightheart what she was going to do during the championship—because she couldn't be two people at once—he told her:

'We'll take care of it.'

Ooookay. Were they going to create an android lookalike?

Was that cheating? She had no idea, but there weren't human and machine stipulations on who could compete, and androids have been on teams before. As long as the android wasn't the team leader and not the decision-maker, it was okay.

Only Trentians and half-breeds couldn't compete.

She inhaled and studied this Cypher some more.

Could he look any more like a Viking? Vee rolled her eyes. Still, he was handsome—this made-up man—and that made her uncomfortable. *At least he's not real. They probably couldn't pay a Cyborg enough to accompany me to the championship.*

Or play in the championship at all.

Even with their current tenuous reputation, they were still fabled war heroes. Fantasies made flesh. Only a thousand or so existed throughout the universe. Not only were they otherworldly with superhero-like abilities, but they were also incredibly rare.

And incredibly strong and incredibly deadly. They lived long lives, were exceptionally hard to kill, and were enhanced with the finest technology humans had ever created.

We made gods.

Literal, breathing gods.

Hecking heroes.

Meeting one was an honor… *A scary honor.* Nightheart unnerved her, but the one in the image—Cypher—appeared way more intense.

Vee sighed. Not having experience with men in the slightest, how was she going to pretend to be a burly, badass-looking, should-be-in-a-romantic-movie power-wielding giant? She rubbed her lips in thought. The digital specs didn't say how tall he was, but he appeared to be tall…

He had long, messy brown hair, scruffy facial hair, and pale beige eyes, so bright they were inhuman. His frame was big and brawny, and muscles hinted at beneath his tight clothes were large enough to tear the fabric if he flexed too hard. He could've been a warrior berserker or a bodybuilder.

Whoever came up with his design must've been a woman. Her throat tightened at the thought. Heat fluttered in her belly. A woman with a singular, raw fantasy: the need for a man that was more than one of those stringy alley dwellers in the city below. Something better than those wearing old leather and rusty facial piercings. A man that didn't reek of smog and dried sweat, or had the cool aura of the military.

And then there was the fact that he was a Cyborg. What was she going to do? How was she going to pretend to be *this*, even on the network?

Vee glimpsed the time on her screen. *7 p.m.*

She closed the contract file and squeezed her eyes shut. *I can do this. It won't even be that hard.* All of Cypher's information was in the packet Nightheart had given her. She had one week to add his profile onto her media site and introduce him to her followers.

But not tonight.

Tonight, she was going to celebrate, make margherita pizza, and play her game.

Today was a good day. She inhaled. *Tomorrow,* Vee decided. She'd become a man. *Play* at being a man. Roleplaying can be fun, right? People have been playing at being other genders for millennia, many becoming them entirely.

Her lips curled into a smile.

What   could   possibly   go   wrong?

*eep... beep... beep...*

Cypher ignored the sound and continued watching the numbers of Ghost City, the specs, the programs and the city ship's security modules. Blips happened often and usually weren't his to take care of.

Numbers ran through his head like an endless stream, and he was always aware when there was a blip in the system, or when there was an incoming or outgoing ship.

He was Ghost City's watcher, after all.

There were others who ran Ghost, and *those* Cyborgs were as much loners as he was. It was easier that way when you ran the Cyborg mecca—when every Cyborg you dealt with was an independent asshole who disliked answering to anyone. When dealing with a group of highly adverse men and several women, distance was key.

Cyborgs especially didn't enjoy secrets.

That's why those who ran Ghost City remained away from the general population. Most knew one or two on the council, and the rest were all authoritative shadows. To deal with those on the council directly was difficult, even for his kind. The closest to a spokesperson Ghost had was Breco, and even Breco was a shifting shadow in a sea of other, more prominent shadows.

Cypher worked for the council. He knew who they were and couldn't care less about their elusiveness as long as they left him alone.

Solitude was the way of this bear. He stretched out his fingers as Ghost City's numbers ran through him in waves.

When the council formed nearly sixty years ago after the Great Galactic War, Cypher was among the leading group. He was there when the city ship, now known as Ghost, was acquired. He even had a say in the retired military ship's procurement. His commission went towards it.

He'd helped in rebuilding it, updating it, securing it. Ripping out the guts and making it into what it was today. A ghost.

A dangerous, silent, shielded machine that could be likened to a Cyborg in many ways, all except the organic components. It slipped through the darkness of space without a sound, vanished in a blink of an eye. Ghost was the closest thing Cyborgs had to mysticism.

Part of him *was* Ghost City. He was the data hound and security expert, but he also relayed information to his brethren seeking entry. It was a needed haven for a people who had no real home, no real place to go after the war. Without war, or a common enemy, Cyborgs had little else to focus on. Many of his kind struggled to find their way.

Cypher joined most of his brethren in the exodus from an exhausted and used-up human military, though some 'borgs remained behind.

Staying with the military, taking commands from lesser men, wasn't for most of his brethren, especially not him. Not all men were lesser, but many were by the end of the war. Too much pain, hopelessness, bitterness, and death had a way of twisting one's mind.

And human men were too tired to care after enduring so much suffering.

So Ghost got its system.

Me.

Everyone had access to Cypher when seeking— unlike the council—and were given the city ship's coordinates when needed.

Gatekeeper. Stabilizer. Watcher. Even bouncer.

Motherfucking werebear.

He cracked his knuckles. *No one could do my job.*

He was great at it because of what he was. Bears hibernated. It was easy for him to deactivate and spend hours, days, even weeks in his head, hooked up to machinery. He could power down at a moment's notice and stay that way for an exceedingly long time. Years if he had to. His hardware and systems were built for such a feat.

While others needed the occasional protein intake, his body would self-maintain. All Cyborgs could self-maintain… for a time. But unlike the rest, Cypher could go near indefinitely.

And there'd been times where he didn't emerge for months, or no more than several times a year, losing himself in the endless miasma of running numbers, systems updates, and the occasional *blip*.

Scanning the streams one final time, Cypher rose and unhooked the wires attached to his arms.

His time of intermittent hibernation ended six months ago. Leaning back, he cracked his neck and lower back and then turned to the bench and weights stacked in the corner of his room.

Zeph—or Hector, some might call him—put his kind on alert throughout the universe for unprecedented actions. Like kidnapping a woman and child from a renowned client of the EPED, a division run by one of their own.

Since then, Cypher had something else to focus on: the intergalactic media.

What with protests popping up and distrust for his kind at an all-time high, a sect of humans—those with small dicks—wanted them herded up and destroyed. Small-dick men wanted their power back.

Not like we ever really took it from them. Cypher grunted. Not even those tiniest of dicks could find a way to slide in and penetrate his defenses. Cypher's cyber fortress would stand forever.

Go big, or go die.

Rumors abounded of the existence of Ghost. *Some jackass spilled the beans.* The Cyborg city ship had always been a well-kept secret until recently.

The workout bench creaked when he lay onto it. Leveling his eyes with the bar, he gripped it and lifted all two-thousand pounds without heaving.

Every day since Zeph's blunder, Cypher had spent hours working out. It was a way to get the aggression out of his systems. And he was fucking aggressive. Joining Ghost's team and remaining in hibernation most of the last sixty years hadn't just been a job to him; it was an escape from his beast.

A beast that loved to gore his enemies and tear them to shredded bits at the drop of a hat.

Beep.

Security alert.

He frowned, lowered the bar to his chest, and turned his head to his systems setup.

Beep. Beep. Beep. Security alert!

Cypher popped the bar back in place and moved to the panel, plugging himself back into Ghost. It took him a moment to realize the beeping wasn't coming from Ghost at all, but from his internal systems.

What the fuck? He jerked out the wires.

Behind his eyes, a neon red webpage emerged with bold black text.

Flinching from the assault, he swiped it from his mind to project on a screen before him, enlarging it, tensing.

Several pop-ups for virtual reality gaming gear flooded the sides of the page. A thunderdome tune hit his ears, and right at the very top, front and center, was a picture of him on the page.

Little bunnies hopped across the top of his image, shooting each other with laser guns. The lasers bounced around in myriad neon colors.

Stunned, he stared at his image.

How?

Above the murderous bunnies was his name in bigger black letters.

*W*elcome Cyborg Cypher

My first partner!

*M*y *name?* Not only was there an image of

him on this site, but his name as well. Two things that shouldn't exist anywhere on the network.

Below it, messages started popping up from people responding to the announcement.

'Oh my god, Miles, a real Cyborg? Or just a pretender?'

'No way.'

'A partner!'

'Does that mean you're going to the championships!?'

They kept coming.

Beep. Beep. Beep. Security alert!

He shut down the alarm with a virtual slam. But then the beeping restarted, and another blog post with another image of him hit the top of the page. *What the fuck?* His fists clenched. This one was him in his military uniform. There was a rifle under his arm, a rifle he still had today.

A picture he'd never seen before, never even knew had been taken, was now posted on this site.

A holographic bunny hopped off his screen and shot at him with virtual lasers, dancing all the while.

He grabbed the fucker and squashed it, and the other bunnies fled. They didn't return.

Information pooled onto the media page in real time. His eyes darted to the posting, reading it in seconds. To his horror, it was all about him, things he'd never shared with anyone else, specs even, and configurations of his makeup.

His honors in battle.

Even my fucking animal.

Along with numerous other attributes and personal preferences, like a fondness for sleep. *It's not sleep, motherfucker. It's hibernation.*

Cypher read over the information several times, still in disbelief. It just wasn't possible. But as details about him continued to leak, his mind went to the poster. He didn't know how much time had passed. Three minutes, two hours? It continued to his abject horror.

Hundreds of ways to seek out the poster, Miles— V. Miles to be exact—and destroy them shot through his head. His muscles vibrated with rage, and tension built inside his systems. His metal plates shifted, urging him to release his bear.

All thoughts of Ghost and his duties vanished from his mind.

Sharp silver claws shot out of his fingers, and he swiped out in fury. They struck part of his paneling, slicing through it. His body grew.

Messages continued to pop up on the holographic screen, and as he took in the information being released, the rage built. Someone began to answer the messages, and answer those about *him* accurately while using *his* name.

Someone had dared to steal his identity.

Someone was pretending to be him.

V. Miles had gotten a hold of his information and leaked it onto the network.

And somehow, someway, they thought they could get away with it. A dark rumble sounded from his throat.

Without waiting any longer, Cypher hacked into the site's mainframe and found his target.

Vengeance   took   over.

 *t's done.*

Vee slipped into the hover train and found an empty seat. She licked her lips, studied the other passengers around her, and wondered if they smelled new money in the air. Was that possible? Her paranoia said it was.

Stop it. No one knows but you.

She shook her head.

The EPED had wired the funds to her account this morning, and she left the bank with her wristcon clutched in one hand and the other supporting it. The train zipped through the skyport and into the airways above the city, and she settled into her seat with an exhale.

Now that she had money, it seemed like everyone around her somehow knew. Loosening her hold on her wristcon, she put her earplugs in and looked out the dirty window to her side. Smog peered back at her.

She tapped her finger on her wristcon to the music blaring in her ears and tried to relax. When she didn't think she could take her unease anymore, she glanced once more at the people around her and slipped on her glasses. Her media site popped up, and her glasses scanned her pupils, logging her in.

And there it was, right at the top.

Another new message from Cypher. A guy who contacted her hours after her first post on her page a week ago.

Her 'real' fake Cyborg teammate.

Or so he claimed.

Every day, a new message waited for her, and though she hadn't yet responded—trolls will be trolls—her worry increased with each one. What started off as merely requiring an eye roll, a delete, and a block turned into something more sinister. Not blatant harassment, but something uncomfortable and subtle, building more each day.

She didn't know why he targeted her, but she had her suspicions. Some of her followers were anti-cyborg, artificial intelligence, and mecha. She'd lost a few after her announcement, so it might have been one of them.

But this…was a little extreme.

The block should've worked. Vee stared at the new message notification. She didn't understand it. An IP block to another IP block was absolute. In this day and age, one's IP was like your secondary social security number. You only had one. Any more and you needed special privileges… or you worked for the government.

One's IP was as sacred as your thumbprint and eye scan. It was your virtual personal identity.

But the guy came back. She blocked him the next day, and he came back again.

It shouldn't have been possible.

She contacted the server her site ran on, and they said they didn't know what she was talking about. There'd been no blocks coming from her end, and this 'other Cypher' wasn't reading on their end either. She took screenshots and sent the images to them. But they claimed they never received them, and when she went to load the images again on her page, they were gone from her computer.

She contacted the EPED after several days of fighting with the site's server but couldn't get through to Nightheart. A woman, Mia, gave her a half-assed response saying not to worry about it, and that *they* would look into it.

As the smoggy city zipped past her, the others on the train fell from her mind.

Sweat slickened her brow.

Vee stared at the message notification for the rest of the ride, only stopping when it was her time to disembark and take the railway home. She didn't stop for groceries or to check on her elderly neighbor down the hall, but went straight to her apartment and locked herself in with a shudder.

Perhaps she wasn't paranoid about having money. *Perhaps I'm nervous because of him.* The stranger on the network.

Bees, her tabby cat, came sauntering up to her and rubbed his face against her leg. She scratched her baby behind the ears and went to her mini kitchen to feed him. After making herself a sandwich, she slipped off her shoes and settled on her bed, looking around.

Nothing had been moved, nothing was out of place, but she remained tense.

She lived in a five-hundred-square-foot studio. From the entryway, her bed was in the back left-hand corner, her kitchen in an alcove to the right, opposite her bed. There was a detached bathroom with a cleansing stall next to the kitchen, the only space fully partitioned except for a closet between her bed and the kitchen on the back wall.

With only one window, she bought a giant mirror to stand next to the door to the right, giving the illusion of more space. And in the open space between her bed and the door was her equipment—a giant square box without walls.

Straps hung from the corner poles to keep her anchored when she played standing. But there was a chair positioned in the middle—currently plugged in—that could be moved in and out of the box at will. The top was made of metal and plastic, with projector tech and additional outlets for add-ons attached. It ran parallel to the ceiling.

There was a big old chair in the front corner on the left that'd seen better days. But it was her favorite place to study, with Bee's cat tree beside it. Her walls were decorated in cheap cloth tapestries, most depicting outer space, some with whimsical designs. It was cramped but clean, and best of all, it was hers.

She moved in several years ago, and so far, it had served her well. Paper-thin walls and old appliances included.

With three million, I can finally move into a bigger place. One with better security. Yet the thought only made her tired. Her eyes dragged to the floor.

I have no time to move, not until after the game.

Which meant she couldn't invest in new equipment yet, either. There would be no room for it.

Vee ate her sandwich and set her plate aside.

She glanced down at her wristcon and petted it with a finger. She turned to Cypher's file on the bed next to her and then to her Terraform Zero equipment.

The championship was two months away. She had three separate simulations running, each testing her abilities in the hardest way possible.

Yria, a predominantly water planet with primitive sentient life.

Then there was Okran, a planet much like Earth but with hostile giant carnivorous beasts, three suns, and low gravity.

And finally, Juntao, a desert planet with constant sandstorms and tornadoes but with enough fossil fuel and minerals to be a goldmine for any extraction company.

There was much more to each of them—ethics, environment, economics, and industry—but she wasn't going to get into that now.

Vee flopped back onto her bed with a sigh. *The last thing I can focus on right now.* She chewed her lip, spinning her network bracelet on her wrist. She kept glancing at the door. A paper-thin door that wouldn't protect her for long if someone wanted to get in.

Cypher.

A shiver ran up her back.

She needed to get him out of her head—the fake freaking troll, not the one she roleplayed now for her fans. Sucking her lip into her mouth, she loaded up her site, eyes darting straight to the top of the screen where her messages were.

Her brow furrowed. Two messages waited for her now in her inbox.

I've never gotten two before. All of her fan mail came to her through less personal ways.

She kept her identity hidden because it was safer that way.

Most of her followers assumed she was a boy—though some insisted she was a girl. Some thought she was an AI. *They'll all find out soon.* Her true identity would be on millions of screens in several days.

If I can't deal with one creeper, then how can I deal with many? Ugh.

She clicked the first message and swallowed, preparing for the worst.

I don't know who gave you my information, or if you stole it for yourself, but you will pay for this. - Cypher

Go away! Vee deleted it.

She opened the second.

1803-B345 Webber Rise, New America, NV 89100. I'm coming.

Her heart plummeted into her stomach. *He knows my address.*

A bang sounded outside her door and startled her out of bed.

She dove for her phone and called the EPED but was put into a queue. Ending the comm, she tried for the security office of her building but no one answered. A chime filled the space, and she jumped again before pivoting back to sit before her holograms. Another message.

Not a message, a call. *Unknown number.*

It rang and rang, and she just stared at it.

It stopped, and she wrenched her hands into her bedding in relief. But then it started again.

Heckfire! She swiped the receiving line and answered.

Silence met her on the other end. Vee bit down on her tongue to keep from speaking first. She wasn't going to give the fucker the satisfaction.

And then she heard his voice.

"You've pissed off the wrong Cyborg, Miles. I'm coming, and there's no place in the universe you can hide."

Her soul slammed into her stomach. She imagined a lot of people and voices on the other end, but not this one... This voice was raw and gruff, and even if a threat hadn't been issued, she would've still heard one in his voice.

She glanced at Cypher's image on the screen. The giant hulk of a man.

The voice sounded like *him.*

Deep and haunting, powerful enough to thrum her nerves. She didn't like it at all.

Her throat tightened, but then she took in a shaky breath, mustering courage.

"Your threats don't scare me, creeper. I don't know who or what you are. I don't care if you're one of those anti-cyborg activists, and even if you were, I surely don't give a damn. And you better listen carefully because I'm only gonna say this once!" Anger replaced her nervousness. "Get help. Because if you come for me, I'll make sure everyone in the damn stratosphere knows who and what you really are. A deranged freak, seeking his one minute of fame by harassing a girl who's only trying to make a difference in the universe."

She ended the call with more fury than she thought she had in her, got off her bed, shoved her big chair in front of her door loud enough to piss off her neighbors, and found her metal bat. When she was set, she glared at her barricaded door.

Sitting down with a huff in her Terraform chair, she slapped the bat in her hand.

Come for me, freak. I'll be waiting.

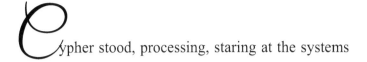

ypher stood, processing, staring at the systems

powering on in his ship's bridge. He tried fruitlessly to open communication with Miles again. But unlike Cypher before all this, Miles had basic personal information on the network.

Gender hadn't been something Cypher had paid attention to, assuming Miles was a male.

But Miles wasn't a man. Miles was a woman.

"You okay, man?" Jayce mused from behind him.

Jayce was a long-term resident of Ghost like him. But where Cypher worked for those in charge, Jayce spent his days being unofficial security for Ghost's shipping port. The silver-haired, silver and golden-skinned, piercings-obsessed Cyborg knew everyone who came and went on a personal level. A watchdog who exhaled fire. An anime character who drank and smoked—a lot.

Jayce wasn't Shifter class like Cypher was. Still, he and Jayce went way back. In a way, the two of them held parts of the same job, just different sides of the same coin.

V. Miles is female. No, Vee Miles. He scanned her files a little more thoroughly. Cypher's lips twisted into a frown. It didn't matter. Female or not, she was going to pay dearly.

A twenty-three-year-old female. So damn young.

He delved back into her files for an image of her. The only one he had was of a male and female laughing and embracing. He had assumed Miles was the male.

The female in the image… Half her face was obscured, hiding her features. But she had bright red hair, though it was pulled back into a tight ponytail. And she was tiny next to the young man.

"Yo!" Jayce snapped his fingers in front of Cypher's face. "You know I hate it when you ignore me."

"Deal with it."

Jayce lit up a cig. Honeyed tobacco and something akin to artificial mint pervaded Cypher's nostrils.

"So how long will you be gone?" Jayce asked.

"I don't know. Why are you here?"

"To see you off, perhaps slip my fingers through the years of dust on your consoles. Maybe I'm curious why you're leaving us so suddenly. I'm sure you have some great stuff squirreled away in your den. I can't wait to paw through it."

Cypher grunted, watching Jayce do exactly as he said—slide his fingers over his bridge's systems.

They needed cleaning. "Breco sent you," he accused. His direct contact to the council wasn't thrilled with this new development.

"Perhaps that's why I'm here." Jayce shrugged. "If you leave, he's threatening me that I'll have to fill in for you." He sighed and took a puff. "I don't want to." Jayce ended on a whine. "I hate everything you do. That's why I like you so much, you make my life easier."

Cypher initiated his ship's cleaning bots just as the thrusters under him reverberated to life. "I don't have a choice."

"So why are you leaving?"

Cypher tangled his hands into his hair, closing his eyes. Cyborgs hated secrets. His brethren who cared wanted to know. "It's a security matter. One I can't fix remotely. I tried. Trust me, I'd rather not leave either." For a week, he'd tried.

"Doesn't happen to do with you going to compete in the Terraform Zero Championship this year, does it?" Jayce grinned.

Cypher leveled Jayce a glare. "You looked me up?"

"Oh, come on, we all know. We're just waiting for you to come out, Cypher. Come out of the closet, please—" Jayce's grin grew "—the big bad closet you've made your home, Cypher. Come out. Pretty please."

Cypher pushed Jayce out of his way, and the other Cyborg stumbled back, dropping his cig. Cypher was one of the biggest there was, only eclipsed by a mere handful of his peers. Jayce cackled and righted himself, picking up his cig.

"Get off my ship, Jayce."

"I knew it! So that was who you were talking to when I came in. Your partner! I'm going to tell everyone!" Jayce spun to the exit, his piercings flickering from the neon lights from the consoles. "Holy hell. Looks like Jayce has the inside scoop. I'll be drinking for free all week."

"That's not…"

But Jayce was already out of his bridge. Cypher gritted his teeth as he listened to Jayce laugh his way down the corridor. He ordered the doors closed to his vessel when Jayce was gone. *Fire-breathing motherfucker.*

More images of Vee Miles were waiting for him when he turned back to the task at hand.

'Your threats don't scare me, creeper.'

Her voice still sounded in his ears.

My threats should, little girl. They really should.

He sat heavily in his captain's seat and requested allowance for take-off. He loaded the pictures in his head while he waited, knowing somewhere Jayce was laughing while Breco demanded answers from him. Cypher's fingers twitched.

Not my problem now.

He leaned back, cracked his neck, and projected the images. There were several dozen. He flipped through the ones of her from her childhood, noting Vee's hair color hadn't always been red but at one point was a light brown. When he got to her more recent images, he studied each one a little longer than the last.

His brow furrowed.

Vee Miles was cute. Not like a child or a kitten but a woman who had all the features to be adorable. Chubby cheeks, heart-shaped face, wide eyes. And her hair was red. Gleaming neon red. *Like her media site. Makes sense. Females like to match.* Her hair fell just a little past her shoulders in waves.

She stood smiling in a navy blue skin-tight suit with retro earbuds hanging around her neck.

Cypher leaned back and rubbed a hand over his mouth. Was this really the culprit who stole his identity? It didn't make sense.

Scrolling through the data in his head, he delved deeper into her past.

Vee had no higher education in information technology, nor did she belong to any shady organization. She didn't have a degree at all. There were no arrests or dealings with the law. She was born and raised on Earth and lived in a studio apartment in New America City, where she had resided alone for the past four years.

She owned a cat.

Instead, everything in her file indicated she was a gamer, an avid Terraform Zero player, and a rising star in the field of planetary colonization—according to leaderboards. That's how she made her money. There was nothing that indicated a skilled hacker or a master network manipulator.

Riffraff, juvenile. Cypher grumbled. That's what she was. She hadn't yet learned the universe wasn't a game, at least not the kind anyone wanted to play. Even her clothes were either too loose or too tight, too grungy and sometimes way too revealing. She didn't even know how to dress properly.

Who the hell was this woman? And how did she get her hands on classified information about him?

He couldn't stop studying her picture.

Vee looked like someone in need of a handler, to give her a hard lesson in life. She was beautiful when she smiled. Innocent, fresh. The antithesis of everything his kind was and represented; hard, battle-worn space warriors with a penchant for alien blood and *ultimate* control.

She's small enough to be crushed by my hand. Far too small, and too young for the likes of him.

Cypher ran a hand over his face. How long had it been since he had a woman? Years? Decades even? It was sometime right after the war ended. Since then, he only had the urge to pump his dick a few times over the years, and it'd been more like maintenance than anything else. A release of seed his organics made, only to be replaced by fresh cum. Purging the lines, nothing more.

And he never looked at pictures of women while he did it, knowing the urgency that could be built if his bear went into a rut. He avoided women in general, even those on Ghost. Even Rose Cagley, Ghost's treasured doctor.

It wasn't worth it. Ruts were dangerous, and he was already an aggressor for his kind without it.

But here was a picture of a pretty, clean, female, unclaimed by another Cyborg, with a bright smile and hair he wanted to sniff. His cock urged him to grip it.

She wouldn't be clean once he got through with her.

A crackle on his ship's communication channel pricked his ears. Cypher cursed, forced his metal dick to recede, and shoved Vee's images to the back of his mind. He wasn't traveling the universe to fuck her.

He was traveling to bring her down and fix the mess she made.

A voice sounded. "You're leaving for a goddamned game?"

Breco.

Cypher sighed. "No."

"Then what is Jayce fucking talking about? What is this shit on the network?"

"A security issue, Brickman. One I'm about to take care of. Do I have permission to leave? I'm going either way."

Cypher heard something bang and break in the background.

"What's Ghost going to do without you?" Breco asked.

"What it's always done, I assume? All my shit will continue running while I'm gone, and whoever you put in charge will have access to Ghost's servers and feeds. My AI is set up to listen to the council's commands—if they're reasonable. If they're not, he'll shut you guys out. Do I have permission or not?"

"This reeks of entrapment."

Entrapment?

Cypher growled, growing impatient. "Well?"

"When are you coming back?"

Hell. "As soon as I take care of this. Fuck man, someone out there stole classified information—

information about me—and posted for all to see on the network. I'll be back as soon as that person is dead or silenced." Vee's image surged to the forefront of his mind. "No one gets away crossing one of us, especially not with me," he warned, clenching his hand. "You'd do the same."

"*Fuck!*"

"Don't let the universe find our city in the meantime. I'd recommend a no Cyborgs policy while I'm gone. No one comes in or goes. Run dark." Cypher angled his ship off port anyway, typing in coordinates for Earth. "They're looking for us."

"Get back here soon."

Planning on it.

He ended the comm.

Cypher double-checked his supplies, his weapons, and his ship's tech once more, making sure he had everything he needed for battle, gripping his laser pistol poised at his belt. Despite knowing he had more firearms and weapon attachments to his body stored in his cruiser than most Cyborgs did on a normal mission, nothing seemed to lessen the tension rampaging through him.

It doesn't matter who ended up on the other side, he told himself. He ran his tongue across his teeth.

Go big, or go die.

He hadn't had the taste of fresh blood in his mouth in ages.

The barriers lifted where his ship had been stored, pulling his eyes forward.

Space. Big, black, beautiful space with a billion stars filled his view. Seen for the first time in decades from the seat of his captain's chair, one that still managed to carry his massive weight.

But as Cypher surged his thrusters forward, leaving Ghost in his dust, space wasn't what he gazed at. Vee's smile invaded his head again, her cherub features practically shorting out the wires of his mind. His mind's eye trailed down over her body in its skin-tight clothes in his now-favourite image of her, over her outrageous curves and back up to her innocently happy dark eyes.

His jaw ticked. Anger and something else he couldn't quite place surged through him.

No   one   crosses   me   and   lives.

$\mathcal{V}$ee wrung her hands. The calls from Cypher had gone off the deep end. What she hoped would be a stern warning on her end had only made things worse. Now he was leaving her messages, voicemails.

'Answer the comm, Vee.'

'This will go easier for you if you submitted.'

'I'm coming.'

I'm coming. Cypher's voice ran through her head again and again.

Yet no one showed up at her door. No one had snuck up on her when she went out. None of her neighbors had seen or heard anything out of the ordinary. Several days had gone by with nothing but her nerves keeping her on edge.

She paced the floor, glancing around at the enormous glass windows and white walls—the high-definition pictures of different planets and expensive paintings—while she waited anxiously. The giant foyer to the EPED building offered some comfort. People in suits and androids passed through constantly.

Shouts filled her ears, and she tried to ignore them. Right outside, there were dozens of protestors and even some reporters trying their best to get their voices heard among those coming and going.

Several had yelled out her name when she'd scurried in this morning. She wiped her palms on the side of her pants.

It was only a matter of time…

When she signed the contract a week and a half ago, she knew what it meant. But this…this harassment wasn't something she expected. Not so personally, not at this level.

My site only has twenty thousand fans, not twenty million.

Her wristcon buzzed and she glanced down. Another comm was coming in from *Cypher*.

"Vee Miles, Mia is ready to see you," a well-dressed android said, striding up to her.

"I'm here to see Nightheart, not Mia."

"Nightheart is unavailable right now. Mia is waiting. Would you like to wait for Nightheart? I really can't give an estimate on when he will be available."

"No, no. I want to speak to someone now, please." After numerous comm calls, she had yet to get a hold of him. Why would it be any different now? He was a powerful Cyborg, after all.

Vee wasn't a fan of the woman who worked for him.

The android smiled, took her hand, and scanned her fingerprints. "Head for the elevator, Vee Miles. It will take you to the appropriate floor."

She strode toward where the android indicated, and the doors slid open for her. Moments later, she was on a different floor, and a gorgeous blonde woman waited for her.

"Miss Miles?" the woman asked, checking a tablet in her hand.

Vee stepped off the elevator. "Yes."

"I'm Mia. Come this way."

Mia led her down a short hall and into a conference room, which had the same decor as the foyer. When they were seated across from each other, the woman set down her tablet.

"You're being attacked?" Mia asked.

"Yes." Vee licked her lips. "By a man who claims he's the real Cypher."

Mia cocked her head. "Has he approached you? Hurt you?"

"No… it's all been online. Look." Vee loaded up her wristcon and projected her site. There, in the corner, eight missed calls. Not an unknown number anymore, but with the name Cypher attached. As if he and Vee were friends…

"Ah. Has he made any mention he's coming?"

Vee frowned. "Yes." *Strange question.*

Mia picked up her tablet and typed something in.

"Why?" Vee asked.

The woman didn't answer until she set her tablet back down. Vee tried to peer at it, but the screen was shielded for privacy. *Figures.*

"We need to be sure of the extent of his threat to you."

"The extent of his threat? He's done things that shouldn't be possible on my site and within the boundaries of my IP and network domain. Isn't this going to cause a rift for the game? If I can't control what my followers see?"

Mia held up her hand. "Don't worry. We're taking care of it. Now, about the announcement, are you ready?"

Vee sat back, confused. It was like no one but her was worried. *They didn't hear his raspy, deep voice...* The same voice she heard every time in her sleep now. It was in her dreams.

"Announcement?" she asked slowly.

"The announcement from the Terraform Zero coordinators about this year's participants. It's tonight."

Vee's eyes widened. How could she have forgotten? *Oh, god, maybe that's why some of the people outside knew my name. My picture is going to be everywhere, everywhere tomorrow!*

She surged to her feet. "I've gotta go."

"Are you okay?" Mia rose with her and followed Vee as she started for the elevator.

She hadn't even told her parents yet. "I'm fine." The elevator zipped open and she stepped in.

"Vee!" Mia called after her.

Vee pivoted to face her.

"Don't worry about Cypher. He won't hurt you," she said.

Vee's brow furrowed. "What?" But the doors slipped closed and Mia was gone. The next moment, the foyer was before her.

Wait, what?

Confusion overtook her anxiety.

He won't hurt me? Vee shook her head as she made her way to the exit, toward the rabble of upset voices outside. They couldn't see her through the glass, but in the time she'd arrived earlier, more had gathered. Was the animosity that bad?

I need to get home.

I need to prepare. The last place she wanted to be was out in the city when her picture was broadcasted everywhere.

She gazed at the protestors outside blankly, catching a glimpse of Nightheart's face in the glass reflection behind her. When she turned, he wasn't there.

A twitch of unease gripped her chest.

Mia said it like she knew him, Cypher.

That he really did exist. That… no…

Her wristcon buzzed, and Vee jumped. Her eyes flew to her wrist. Another call.

Cypher.

They wouldn't… Would they? Could Cypher be real? What was the point of telling her otherwise? Vee chewed on her lower lip. What if he was real and that's the reason it was impossible to block him, because whoever heard of someone blocking a Cyborg?

She raised her shaky finger. The buzzing continued.She swiped her bracelet and answered.

"You picked up," a deep voice said. *His* deep voice.

The image of the hulking, ancient-looking warrior, with long, dark hair, thick stubble over his sharp jaw, and light brown eyes punctured her thoughts. A being who transformed into a giant metal bear. A man-made creation that could smite her entire existence.

Oh. My. God. Her chest constricted.

"Vee Miles?" the voice asked, prompting her to speak. Was that a hint of worry?

She cleared her throat. "Are you… are you really Cypher?" *Please laugh, please say no. Say anything*

50

that a stupid troll would say and a Cyborg never would.

There was a short pause before he answered. "Yes."

Vee wrenched her eyes shut before she had a meltdown. "Can you prove it?"

Something akin to a growl reached her ears. "Of all the classified information you've shared about me to the universe, what haven't you shared yet?"

"Your model number," she whispered.

Someone opened the large doors and walked into the EPED foyer. Vee snapped her eyes open. She shifted out of the way to let them pass.

"865, group five, shifter class. What's that noise?"

Her heart fell. "It's nothing. Just a few protestors."

The number was the same in her documents. *Fucking hell.*

She was a pawn. Vee glanced behind her to the elevators, but then decided it wasn't worth it. The damage had been done. It was a caveat, after all, and a powerful Cyborg had lied to her. The last thing she wanted was to have two godly beings pissed off at her. One could wipe out her existence, but two?

"Protestors?" Cypher asked.

I need to make it right.

First, she needed to get out of here. She couldn't deal with the real Cypher now, not when she was on a timer.

"I'm so sorry," she said, returning her attention to him. "I'll call you back. Tonight. Please, please believe me. I can explain."

"Fucking hell, wai—"

Vee ended the call and ran out of the doors. She dodged the protesters outside even though some of them tried to stop her. When she was at the spaceway, she checked the time. It was after three in the afternoon, and peering up at the projections around her, there was nothing but advertisements on them.

She laughed mutely as she wiped her damp hands on her pants. Going to the Terraform Zero Championship was her dream, and seeing herself everywhere had been part of it—a big screw you to all the men who dominated the game.

She kept her image off her media site, certain she would get a lot of flak for being a female.

It was part of the reason she was so shocked the EPED chose to sponsor her.

Now she was beginning to figure out why. *Is it because they think they could easily control me?* The desperation of her situation and gender status screamed *yes*.

There were far fewer women than there were men. Everywhere. The equality her sex enjoyed before the Galactic War vanished when humans released a virus into the Trentian alien homeworld that essentially neutered their species. Now the aliens sought human women to continue their race.

Women should stay on Earth. Women shouldn't seek intergalactic fame.

Do your duty and breed more humans. Do you want the attention of Trentian men? They'll send their Space Lords and their smugglers and steal you.

None of it mattered right now until she was back safe at home.

Ugh.

Her wristcon buzzed again but she ignored it. It kept buzzing until she got home, pushed her chair back in front of her door. After she fed and loved on Bees, took a shower, ate, and brought up her network to ready a post for when the announcement hit.

She called her parents and told them the news—they were at least happy on her behalf. All the while, she stared at the picture of Cypher on her screen, feeling his deep voice penetrate her flesh and the paranoia that any minute he could come crashing through her door.

And then it happened. The speakers for the tournament aired. The twelve competitors were listed.

Flux, Agent Smith, Future Future, Pulse of Life, Leene Salty, Beautiful Horizon, The Brandons, Sunsets and Dawns, Halo Grail, Space Dogs, and one that surprised her, Deadly Dearest. One of the first and only woman-run teams since even before the war.

Then her name was announced and her image, with her Terraform black suit, set against her neon red and black gamer tag she sent in when she qualified aired. So did an image of Cypher.

Vee smiled despite everything, surging to her feet to jump up and down. Music played, posts on her page flooded her media site, and she beamed.

Congratulations!

For a moment, everything else that happened in the last week faded away.

She grabbed her pillow and screamed her excitement into it, even ignored her neighbors banging on the walls. Bees jumped up onto his cat tree to get out of the way.

This moment—this moment was going to stay with her for the rest of her life, bad stuff be damned. She wasn't going to let anything ruin it for her. She'd worked too damned hard for it. Even if she lost two months from now, she would always know she earned her place—above thousands of others to compete.

She'd earned it, no one else. Vee swiped away the happy tears gathering on her lashes.

No matter what happened between now and then, nothing would take this from her, Cyborgs, politics, or otherwise.

An hour passed before she settled. Lying back onto her bed, she gazed at the glow-in-the-dark star stickers on her ceiling.

Vee lifted her hand into the air and looked at her wristcon. Other calls were waiting for her, but she ignored them, going to Cypher's most recent one.

Do it now before you lose your nerve.

She swallowed the lump in her throat, curled her toes, and finally sent a transmission to Cypher's source.

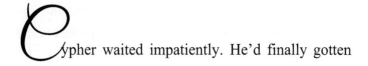

ypher waited impatiently. He'd finally gotten

through to her, only for the call to end right when she seemed to believe him.

Protestors? Where was she? Was she also protesting? It hadn't seemed like it, just based on their short conversation. She seemed winded, aloof… And if she was protesting, what was so important to her to risk her safety? It didn't sit well with him.

Is she safe?

And, somehow, he was involved. In all of this. Without having a clue as to how or why.

Cypher punched the wall, and his fist went right through the plated metal.

Why do I even care? I'm putting an end to all of this. And Vee was nothing but his first stop. He jerked his arm back and shook out his hand.

Vee didn't matter, he told himself. Whether she was out and unprotected made no difference to him. *She's just a hiccup. A damned bump.* Nothing more than something he can squash under his boot.

A goddamned thorn in my side.

Cypher wiped his mouth on the back of his hand. He readied his ship to warp to the Milky Way Galaxy and tried to focus on the task at hand, shutting out everything else. In the last couple of days, he'd gone through Sagittarius Dwarf and Canis Major, having left Andromeda where Ghost currently traveled half a week ago.

As his ship moved into commercial warp space, he paced the bridge, unable to sit still. He was accustomed to long periods where nothing happened besides systems updating, but for some reason, the patience he'd honed all these years wasn't helping him now.

His AI sounded. *Incoming transmission.* He paused and looked at the source.

Vee.

Fucking Vee. The bane of his existence. She was finally calling him.

He halted his warp preparations and rushed to accept it.

"Hello?" Her voice came through and filled his audio tech.

"Vee," he said roughly, unable to find the right words. He didn't want to lose her again. Not when he finally had her. Making conversation didn't come naturally to him. He couldn't remember the last time he spoke directly to a human.

"I need to know. Are—are you really Cypher? Please tell me honestly."

"Haven't we already established this?" he snapped.

A lengthy inhale sounded through the comm. "I don't understand. I'm so confused," she whispered.

That makes two of us. Though, against his better judgment, be believed the worry in her voice was genuine. He sat heavily in his captain's chair. No matter the circumstances, he wasn't going to allow himself to feel sympathy. He lowered his voice. "Understand or not, the information you released is classified. Take it off your site. Better yet, take down your fucking site, and vanish. Stay off the network entirely. If you do that, I may let you live."

Fuck. He palmed his mouth. He shouldn't have said that to keep her comm open.

Vee's breathing grew ragged. He bet if he were next to her, her heart would be racing. Would her chest rise and fall along with it?

Is her blood pumping?

He pictured her in distress, skin flushed, lips parted, hair a mess, and found he rather enjoyed the image.

"I can't!" she said.

"What do you mean you can't?"

"You didn't see…?"

"See what?" he asked but was already inputting his name and Vee's into the network while loading up her site. Within seconds, a new picture of him loaded into his headspace, and with it the broadcasted announcement that he was participating in the Terraform Zero Championships this year. Site after site appeared with him and Vee, increasing by the second.

Cypher let out a string of curses.

"Please don't kill me," Vee begged through the comm. "I'm not ready to die."

He continued to curse, moving to her media page to read all the congratulatory comments, pausing when a slew of threatening ones appeared as well. The comments grew worse as his visual tech scanned them.

His gut twisted with anger.

She was his to deal with, no one else's.

Vee may have been naïve, may have been young, but to receive this kind of animosity? At least he had a reason to exact his revenge, a personal, private reason, unlike the masses.

His opinion of humanity plummeted.

"I can fix this," she continued to plead. "I'll fix this. Just give me a chance. I only found out you were even real a couple of hours ago. You see, I've always worked alone. I'm known for being a loner, and the contract—"

"What contract?"

"The one I signed with my sponsor to fund my trip to the championships," she answered.

"Who?" he demanded.

"I don't know if I should tell you. I don't even know who you really are."

"You have all my information. What do you mean you don't know who I am? A fucking Cyborg! Vee, who the fuck is sponsoring you?"

"That's akin to telling me you're a human. And what will you do if I tell you? You already promised to make me pay!"

He was going to rip out his hair. "Can't you see you're being used? We both are?"

"Hasn't the damage been done? He asked me to pretend to be you, to add you to my team, that's all. He'd take care of the rest. You weren't supposed to be real."

"Vee, so help me Satan, if you don't tell me, I'll force it out of you one way or the other," he warned. Somehow, imagining his hands on Vee's flesh made his groin tense. He reached down and adjusted his cock. She was too small for him, too young. "You could be in danger."

She sighed, and he literally heard the anger rush out of her. "Aren't I *already* with you? And why do you care? I can take care of myself. I'm a woman, Cypher, and used or not, I'm being paid to achieve my dreams." Her voice had ended with a whisper. "But even so," she continued before he could say something, "I signed the contract, not you. You not being real was a part of it. I'll go back tomorrow and—"

"No."

"No?"

He didn't want her near anyone who might be using her, not before he could get to her first.

"Where are you now?" he asked.

"Home…"

"Stay there until I arrive. You're not to leave." The threatening messages on her site unnerved him.

"You just told me to vanish…"

"I'm not going to hurt you," Cypher barked.

"…that's what she said before I left. Cyborgs don't hurt humans, not unless they deserve it."

"For fuck's sake, who?"

"The EPED."

Cypher let out a roar. He grabbed his armrests and shattered them.

Nightheart. Of course it was Nightheart. The piece of shit was ruthless in getting what he wanted. Cypher should've known. Nightheart had been trying to recruit him for years as a Retriever for his Exploration Division, but Cypher refused to leave Ghost.

He didn't think the other Cyborg would stoop so low as this though. *Perhaps I don't know him as well as I thought.*

He turned on Zeph. Couldn't keep the bull shark. And Nightheart's best Monster Hunter is Gunner, one of the worst Cyborgs among us.

Cypher should've suspected Nightheart.

Cypher was one of the strongest shifters amongst them. A prime candidate for Nightheart, a perfect addition to his team. What could a spider, a snake, even a dog do when up against a bear? No offense to Dommik, Stryker, or Netto, who he respected. But what could Nightheart do if Cypher went up against him?

Nightheart was terrifying to any Cyborg, but Cypher?

No.

Cypher was made of pure, rippling muscle and metal stacked upon each other. His ancestors were some of the largest carnivorous mammals that roamed Earth, and though he took traits from the grizzly and kodiak clan, he did not possess the DNA of those who were the primordials of his species.

It made no difference.

But his body was large to contain his animal, and the metal plates within him were perfectly infused with nanobots of the Ursidae gene line. When he shifted full mecha, he was larger than any bear in existence, a pure powerhouse of might. His grip was strong, his jaws made of rare pyrizian metal, and he not only had the brawn of his body but also had claws that cut clean through metal. No expense was spared when it came to his creation long ago. Apparently, some doctor favored him.

If his claws didn't immediately tear his prey in two, his teeth would. If neither worked, Cypher could crush his prey beneath his weight.

Right now, he wanted so badly to use both on Nightheart.

"C-Cypher?" Vee's voice cut through his rage. Cypher unclenched his fists and let the pieces of metal and leather of his armrests fall to the floor.

Why her?

Why bring Vee into all this? How the hell did she get into Nightheart's path?

"Nightheart," he said.

Her breath shuddered. It was all the answer he needed. She'd met the fucker.

His body tensed with animosity. And something else, something that made him want to punch the wall of his bridge again.

"You're scaring me," she whispered. "Is there something wrong with Nightheart?"

Cypher growled, hating the Cyborg's name coming from her. "Don't leave your home, Vee. I'll be there soon. I'm warping."

He cut off the comm between them and put his ship back into action.

Milky   Way,   here   I   come.

7

*T*wo days passed without a message from Cypher.

She wanted to tell him she couldn't adhere to his request to stay put. At least not much longer. For a day and a half, she'd stayed indoors. And not just because Cypher commanded she do so, Vee argued, but because she'd already planned to stay inside anyway.

He had beef with Nightheart; that was evident. Not her. *Once he's here and realizes that I can't help him in his quest for revenge, he'll leave.*

So why can't I get him out of my head?

It's because he's a Cyborg. A freaking hero. A one-in-a-hundred-million man.

Alpha men weren't her thing. At least she thought they weren't. But the way her throat tightened whenever her wristcon buzzed made her wonder. She never paid attention to boys growing up. None had caught her attention or held it long enough for her to care. She'd always been preoccupied.

Vee grumped, threading her fingers together. She pictured Cypher's super alpha-self barging in, pushing her up against the wall, and throwing all his military dominance her way.

Her bracelet buzzed, and she jumped. Checking it, disappointment filled her when Mia's name showed up on the screen.

"Hello," Vee answered.

"You ready?"

No 'hello' back. Mia was business and nothing else. Vee pitied her. She couldn't imagine a life like Mia's.

She straightened her shirt out. She kept it simple, wearing a tight faded black tee and torn jeans. "Yeah."

"Good. We're waiting outside your building. Look for the black hovercraft with tinted windows."

"I'll be right there."

She was scheduled for an interview on Intergalactic Entertainment. Vee chewed on her lip. She and Cypher both were. But somehow, she didn't think Cypher had any intention of playing the role of her partner.

Nor did she want him too.

I work alone. Always have, always will. The sponsorship contract was nothing but a means to an end. She didn't need anyone else to win.

And I can't forget he threatened me. Still, she believed him and everything he told her—how could she not? She was more afraid of disappointment than anything else.

He's most likely going to make me back out of the championship.

Her heart hurt at the thought.

She petted Bees goodbye and walked through her doorway, checking the hallway both ways before going to the elevator.

The sooner Cypher comes for me, the sooner he'll leave me be. That's all she could hope for now.

OMG, get out of my head.

But I'm actively disobeying him.

Vee frowned as the elevator went down. *He doesn't own me.* She pursed her lips. When the grungy foyer of her apartment building revealed itself, she let out a relieved sigh.

But a questionable thought invaded her mind. Cypher could own her if he truly wanted, she realized. He was now an obstacle to her dreams. Her stomach clenched.

Pushing the thoughts aside, she scurried for the entrance and stepped outside—only for a huge crowd of people to swarm her, screaming her name. Vee recoiled, stunned, as lights flashed in her face.

"Ms. Miles, are you excited to be going to the championships?"

"What made you team up with a Cyborg?"

"Did you pay your way in?"

She brought her hands up to her face to cover her eyes from the lights.

But right before she did, she saw *him*—Cypher— across the street, wearing a dark brown military-grade uniform with his long hair tied back at his nape.

Her skin prickled and her throat closed up. She dropped her hands to get a better look, but several people crowded in front of her. When she shoved them aside, he was gone.

Where'd he go? Her pulse quickened. *He's here.* Vee scanned the smoggy rust-metal streets.

"Over here!" Mia yelled, waving from the seat of a black flyer. Two security guards came out and headed for Vee. They pushed the reporters away and escorted her to the hovercraft. She let them lead as she searched for the Cyborg.

Something wet hit her back just as she ducked in.

When the door shut and the hovercraft shot into the air, she twisted to gaze out the window at the scene below. But it quickly became a mass of unrecognizable people. *I must have been mistaken.*

She rubbed the chill from her arms and turned to face Mia.

She sat across from Vee wearing another tight, black pencil skirt suit. Her perfect blonde hair—no strand out of place—emphasized those icy gray eyes. Corporate princess.

Vee pushed her loose hair back uncomfortably and tugged her shirt to the side to see what had hit her.

"Someone spit on you," Mia said.

Vee made a face and released her shirt. "Assholes."

"What did you expect? You're entering a man's universe, and with a Cyborg no less."

"Maybe a little common decency? They don't even know me."

Mia smiled stiffly. "They know you're now famous and have a following. Not to mention, they're humans—emotional and ignorant. What can you expect?"

"Does that mean you're not human?" Vee cocked her head, studying Mia a little more thoroughly. *Mia could be a high-tech android, or a Cyborg.* The woman, though beautiful, was a little too scarily perfect.

Mia crossed her legs. "I spend the majority of my time dealing with Cyborgs. It's hard not to see the difference between humans and nonhumans with a job like mine."

Mia must be the envy of millions of women everywhere. Though envy was the last thing Vee felt toward the cold woman. "You must have some amazing stories…"

"Yes."

She waited to hear them but Mia didn't elaborate.

"Cypher is here," Vee announced, studying her. She didn't know if it was true but she said it anyway.

"Is he now?" Mia picked up her tablet and typed something in.

"He's real."

"I never said he wasn't," Mia said.

"But Nightheart…"

"Did he explicitly say Cypher wasn't real?"

Vee sat back, but then the wet spot on her shirt made her cringe and lean forward. "I…"

She couldn't remember if he ever said fake, but it was clearly stated she would need to play Cypher's part. That she needed to pretend to be him, act like him, respond as him on her site. That the addition of this Cyborg personality was essential to her contract. That besides doing such things was part of the deal, everything else would be taken care of, and not for her to worry about. "No."

God, she felt like an idiot.

"Don't worry, Ms. Miles. Nightheart would never lie to you. Lying is beneath him."

That didn't make Vee feel better at all. "So," she licked her lips, not expecting a straight answer, "what was the point of it? Why bring me into this?"

"The point of what?"

"Having me pretend to be him, why was it part of the contract at all?"

"Ah. I'm not at liberty to say."

"But I'm not in danger? You're not going to jerk the rug out from under me, are you?" Vee asked, wishing she could find the excitement she experienced several days ago. Uncertainty plagued her much of the time now.

Mia laughed. "No, Ms. Miles, you are not in any danger. Your dreams are also not in any danger. At least from us. You are, essentially an employee now, after all. Looks like we've arrived."

The hovercraft lowered from the sky and landed on a private airpad before Vee could ask anything more. Moments later, their security guards let them out of the vehicle. Crisp, clean air filled Vee's nose. Far cleaner than the air in her part of the city.

She glanced at the buildings around her. Some were gothic, some industrial, some merely chrome and glass. The one thing they all had in common though... They were beautiful and well maintained. *Must be near the EPED headquarters.*

She and Mia were led inside by an assistant to Intergalactic Entertainment and brought to a quiet room with drinks and food waiting for them.

"Make yourself comfortable. Someone will come for you through those doors there when they're ready," the assistant said, handing a tablet to Vee. "Here are the questions you'll be asked if you want to review them beforehand." The assistant left them shortly after.

Vee sat and looked around. Mia was sitting further down the couch from her, working on her screen. Vee's eyes went to the giant televised projection to the right of her. On it was the host of the gaming sports show, and next to him was Deadly Dearest's frontrunner, Diatrix Greer, and several of her teammates. Her lips parted in awe.

She'd followed DD for years, was a fan of theirs. She'd even once competed against them in a local competition when she was first starting. That was a long time ago, back when she dreamed of once joining the all-female team. But that was before Vee realized that it was a polyamorous group with no men allowed, virtually unjoinable unless she wanted to change her whole lifestyle.

Cypher popped into her head. *Ugh.* She pressed her face into her palms.

The doors to the studio opened. Vee surged to her feet, expecting to see him. But it was Deadly Dearest who walked through, all smiles and swagger. Tall, sexy, and confident, the women had a particular look with skin-tight red suits and long ponytails atop their heads.

Her gaze met Diatrix's. The bombshell with black hair headed straight for her, scanning Vee up and down.

What was with it and all the beautiful women around her lately? She was beginning to believe she was more out of her league than she realized.

"Diatrix Greer," Vee exhaled the other woman's name almost reverently. "I—I'm honored to meet you."

"Vee Miles," Diatrix cooed back, glancing about. "Where's your Cyborg?"

"He's"—Vee peered at Mia who wasn't paying attention—"not here."

"That's too bad. He is the reason why you're here, right?"

Vee's brow furrowed. "No?"

"Oh, come on, Miles, no one thought you could be competing alone all these years. Interesting that you had a Cyborg helping you. How'd you manage that?"

"I—"

Diatrix shrugged. "No matter. You'll never win anyway." She pressed her finger to Vee's forehead. "You don't have the capacity for such an endeavor, and even if you did, everyone will think it's because of him." She pushed her finger in, making Vee's head lean back before dropping it.

Vee's mouth opened and closed. But before she could say anything, Diatrix walked away with her teammates and out the door.

Bitch. Vee bristled. She wanted to chase after her, grab her ridiculous ponytail, snap her head back, and slap her in the face. Instead, she balled her hands into fists. *I don't need to prove anything to them.*

She turned away when the studio door opened again.

"Ms. Miles, we're ready for you," a different assistant announced.

Without a backward glance, Vee stormed to the stage.

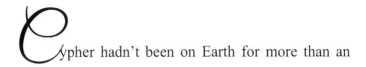

ypher hadn't been on Earth for more than an

hour before he was racing through the skies of New America City in a stolen hovercraft, headed for Vee's address in the slum district.

He hadn't stopped once since their last conversation. After flying through space at breakneck speeds, his cruiser was in bad need of repairs. He wasn't leaving Earth anytime soon.

When he touched down near her scraper—which looked like it was built a thousand years prior and hadn't been maintained—his body went rigid. He surged out of his vehicle and threaded through the grimy streets to her home.

Humanity. It disgusted him. Industrial waste clogged his nose.

When he arrived at Vee's apartment building, there was a crowd loitering outside. He scanned each human and analyzed their intent. Protestors and reporters. They, like him, were there for Vee.

Some held holograms above their heads calling Vee a filthy cyslut and machine fucker.

If they only knew a Cyborg was right behind them. He'd pummel some of these scrawny humans, to know how many comrades they'd seen die in the war, if he could still keep a low-profile afterwards.

With murder on his mind, he searched for a way to get inside the apartment building without anyone noticing, hacking remotely into its poor security system and finding old blueprints. He uploaded them, and was studying the layout when the crowd rushed the scraper's poorly-lit entryway.

He caught sight of red hair.

"Vee! Are you truly a Cyborg sympathizer?" Questions streamed through the air, filling up his audio. Lights flashed, cameras rolled.

Cypher stepped closer for a better look. He needed to see Vee, really see her. The crowd parted for a moment, and there she was. His hand settled on the gun at his hip as their eyes caught. Everything else vanished.

His systems faltered, the wires in his chest thrummed to life. The rest of his body stuttered to a full stop as the real her took over his mind. She was so small. He took another step forward, but the crowd shifted, and he lost sight of her.

"Whoa, are you that Cyborg, Cypher?" a kid next to him asked.

"No," he said when others turned his way. He scanned the crowd, trying to catch another glimpse of Vee, but there were too many people. He threw up the hood on his jacket. *I can't stay here.* He slipped back into the smoggy alleyway before anyone else noticed his presence. But when he glanced up to search for Vee again he found her and several men in suits helping her into a black hovercraft.

No! He rushed forward. *Fuck plans.* But the vehicle shot into the air right before he reached it, disappearing into the clouds above.

"Stupid cyslut has to go and ruin my favorite game, making it fucking political."

"What's with girls wanting to fuck them? They too afraid to have a real warm-blooded man between their legs? First androids and now them?"

Cypher snarled, turning to see who was speaking. Several men in grunge-wear, carrying fake AK47s and signs, wearing faded shawls around their shoulders and commercial military boots stood beside him. One lit up a smoke as a female reporter approached them.

"Who the fuck cares what the twat fucks?" the first man spat. "Cyborgs aren't human. They shouldn't have rights. They're mindless battlebots that should've all been decommissioned after the war, not running our space programs, military, and now in our fucking games."

The men noticed the reporter and turned to her. She smiled. "Care to give a statement to the press?"

The second man took a puff of his cig, looking to reporter up and down. "Sure. Would you fuck a Cyborg, bitch?"

Cypher unclenched his fists and strode to the men before she could answer. *Fucking human scum.* He grabbed their necks simultaneously and slammed them to the ground. The reporter gasped.

"What the fuc—" The first man's eyes widened.

Cypher held them pinned to the pavement as they flopped around like fish trying to claw off his hands.

"You think you know everything," he said, his voice low. His grip tightened, and the men finally looked at him. "I could snap your necks without a thought."

The men stopped struggling.

"*It's Cypher!*" someone yelled.

Cypher's eyes flicked back and forth between the two miscreants, furious. "Tell me, what do you really think of me and my kind?"

One man tried to answer, but only spittle came out.

"What was that?" Cypher goaded. "I didn't catch it."

The other man stared at him with horror.

Cypher's mouth shifted into a muzzle, and he extended his claws, scraping the backs of the men's necks. The smell of urine filled his nose. "That's

78

right, fuckers. The next time you shit yourself, remember this, the only reason you can shit at all is because *we* won the war for you."

Cypher stood, transforming back, dragging the men up with him. He released them with a shove, and they stumbled back. Choking in ragged gulps of air, they turned and fled.

He wiped his palms on his pants only to find the crowd had returned. Cameras flashed. He dusted off his uniform as questions bombarded him.

Without giving humanity's dregs a second thought, he strode away, went back to his stolen vehicle, and began tracking Vee's wristcon again. He lost any of those who dared to follow him in the skyways.

Numbers lit up his mind, coordinates shifting in real time. Vee was headed toward the glittering high-rises in the distance. He knew the moment she came to a stop. Zipping around over hovercrafts, he made his way toward her location.

His body buzzed. A comm came through his internal feeds, and he didn't need to check it to know the EPED was now aware of his arrival. *Fuck off, Nightheart. I'll deal with you soon.* The aggression in him mounted. It was a small miracle he hadn't killed the imbeciles outside Vee's apartment building.

I should've. He sneered. *Should've killed them for all to see. And then really shove my gun down Nightheart's throat.*

His mind teetered between finding Vee and murder as he neared.

Intergalactic Entertainment. The words appeared in blue and gold across an Elyrian-style glass scraper. As he neared, building security came out to greet him. They warned him to turn around. Ignoring them, he went straight for the landing pad. Before his vehicle touched the ground, he shot out the door and made his way to the entrance.

Those who tried to stop him were shoved away. Ripping the door off its handles, Cypher entered the building and threaded through the hallways. Within minutes, he found himself at the back of a studio audience.

And there she was, unobscured, under clear lights, on the stage before him. He came to a stop.

Vee was tense, her arms curled over her chest. It made her breasts appear far too big for her petite frame under the tight shirt she wore.

Seeing her like this was worth the stress of the trip. *Spitfire.*

His eyes trailed from her chest to her vibrant fiery hair around her shoulders. It glowed radioactively, so much he was afraid it would burst into flames and burn her skin. Yet at the same time, he wanted to thread his fingers through it and see if it held heat at all. To see if he could withstand it.

She stared at the interviewee, her face tight with annoyance.

"I don't know, Tim," she snapped. "Cypher and I haven't worked together for long."

Lies. We haven't worked together at all, he thought.

"I earned my place in the championships by myself, through countless hours of hard work," she continued. "Since I was six years old, I've been obsessed. Cypher is only going to help me transition to a higher class of planetary colonization, seeing as he has real experience where all I have are simulations."

Cypher's lips twitched. *She's such a liar.* He could read it all over her face. It was almost cute.

If the lies didn't include him.

Tim set down his notecard. "Ah, so he won't be in the rings with you like the other teams?"

"We haven't figured that out yet."

Several security guards flanked him, zappers in their hands. One grabbed his arm. Cypher ignored them.

Tim smiled. "You did earn your way to the championship, Ms. Miles." He waved his notecard.

"But I also have it on authority you didn't accept the offer until the EPED sponsored you." Tim's smile widened. "Could it be you're being paid to propagandize Cyborgs? They are under attack for being run by one. Nightheart, is it? And employing many more."

Vee stiffened. "That's not true."

"What are your thoughts on the Zeph scandal, and the abduction of a woman and a child?"

Cypher frowned, seeing the worry on Vee's face. Part of him wanted to let her suffer the questions, to deal with the choices she made taking a contract from Nightheart, but a stronger part sympathized with her.

She didn't know who she was getting involved with.

Seeing her now only confirmed she was a victim in a bigger scheme. A scheme to get to *him*.

Cypher cleared his throat and jerked his arm out of the grip of one of the security guards. Vee and Tim looked his way as the audience twisted around. A collective gasp sounded as he strode to the front of the audience and onto the stage. Cameras turned his way, and Tim waved his hand to stop the security guards from following.

Cypher stared at Tim—who looked giddy with this turn of events—all while knowing Vee's eyes were on *him*, taking *him* in.

Cypher settled next to her on the couch, and she had to shuffle down to make room for him. It wasn't quite enough.

He pressed his thigh against hers. It'd been a long time since he was so close to a woman, to be able to touch one even in such an innocent way. He draped his arm across the back in case she leaned enough so that he could touch her hair.

There would never be enough space from him.

"Well, isn't this a surprise!" Tim exclaimed. "I guess the Cyborg *is* in the house." The audience laughed, and the host held out his hand toward Cypher. "It's an honor to meet you. A real war hero."

Cypher stared at the man's hand until Tim awkwardly drew it away, laughing it off. "I'm not here to answer questions. I'm only here to collect Vee. She's needed elsewhere."

"Is that so?" Tim rubbed his chin. "I'm pretty sure she accepted this interview."

"Plans change." He moved to stand.

"Wait!" Tim turned to Vee, who hadn't said a word since Cypher sat down. "One more question, Ms. Miles, if you will."

Cypher growled.

Vee fidgeted next to him. It was as if any frustration she had disappeared upon his arrival. *She's scared—intimidated.*

For some reason, he enjoyed it and moved a little closer to her. It brought back memories of all the times humans avoided him for his size and ever-present scowl.

"Sure," she said.

"If there is one thing you wanted your fans to know, one thing you wanted to say to them, what would it be?"

Cypher shifted to look at her. Vee straightened and uncrossed her arms, placing her palms on her knees. She wetted her lips. He took note of every little action she made, storing it away inside his hard drives.

"I would like everyone to know, fan or not, that if you have a dream, the kind of dream that consumes you, that fills your mind to the brink—until there's no room for anything else—to do everything to achieve it. This game isn't about fame or politics for me. It isn't even about money or notoriety. It's about finding freedom in a universe where freedom is only granted if hard won." She exhaled slowly and glanced his way.

"Thank you, Ms. Miles. We appreciate you coming on the show, and bringing your partner with you," Tim said. The audience clapped.

With Cypher's eyes still locked with Vee's, he stood and took her hand, finding it clammy. Pulling her to her feet, he escorted her from the stage, tugging her along after him.

Everyone they encountered gave them a wide berth as they moved through the building and back to the rooftop airpad. Maybe it was because he kept one hand poised on the handle of his gun. After he had Vee settled in the passenger seat and he'd entered the vehicle, he hacked the system, locking the doors so they wouldn't open without his acceptance, and guided the hovercraft into the sky. She remained stiff and quiet the whole way.

This time, no one gave chase.

He had her. She was his.

He drove them out of the city and into the miles of wastelands surrounding it. Out here lived the poor, the junkies, and anarchists. Middle America, once farmland, was nothing more than a sprawling desert. The East Coast was still green, and the oceans still existed but were highly polluted. Several national parks remained, but America was industrialized to death and back several times over.

There were far greener, far more beautiful worlds out in space. Even Ghost City's city ship was clean compared to everything he saw around him.

No wonder humans were desperate to leave.

Cypher glanced at Vee, who stared out the hovercraft's window, still stiff. His audio picked up the rapid pounding of her heart. Her scent invaded his systems, replacing the toxins that his body constantly cleared.

Bubblegum. No, vanilla… No. Cypher frowned. *Fresh-brewed coffee and honeysuckle. Chocolate?* She smelled of a variety of sweets, all too innocent for the likes of him. And too many to be a single one. He liked it. It made her harder to read.

He breathed her in, letting his systems be overtaken with her fragrance.

His groin shifted, hardened.

Fuck. It's been way too long since I've had a woman.

He was pent up, hard and revving to go. If he didn't find release soon, he didn't know how long he could go before doing something he'd regret. The memory of her gamer suit alone made his mouth water. Combining that with her smell and the time of year it was—spring—his body was more than ready to rut. His solitary existence had come to an abrupt end.

Vee's wristcon buzzed. He intercepted its signal—it came from a number owned by the EPED. Vee raised her wrist to her eyes.

"Don't answer it," he warned. He wanted to talk to her first before he involved the EPED.

"It's Mia."

"I don't care."

Vee lowered her arm back to her lap with a sigh.

Grumbling under his breath, he found an empty clearing to land his vehicle. When the hovercraft turned off, Vee sighed again. His eyes moved to her.

"So what now? Are you going to hurt me? Torture me? Kill me?" she asked, turning toward him.

"What? No," Cypher barked. "I'd never hurt a woman."

"How unequal. What would you do if I were a man?"

"Punch you in the fucking face, drag you by your nape to Nightheart, and demand retribution."

She crossed her arms under her breasts, making them rise. His gaze dashed to them unwittingly. Hellfire, they were too big for her. Vee couldn't be more than two or three inches over five feet at most, but she was shaped like sin. Now that he was this close to her, it didn't seem like she should be real.

She licked her lips. "Well then… what are you going to do to me?"

His jaw ticked. "What am I going to do to you...?"

"I—" She shifted uncomfortably. "I think I've been so nervous about everything happening, and now that it's finally happened, I can finally breathe. Almost."

"I'm not going to do anything to you," Cypher groused. He'd made her that nervous? *Of course I did.*

She sagged a little in her seat.

What did she think I was going to do to her?

Vee's eyes darted to his legs before she looked back out the window. "Good…"

Cypher frowned, realizing his hard-on was pushing his pants taut at his crotch. Did she think he was going to molest her?

Fucking hell. His mood soured, and his anger rose. The worst part was that he did want to touch her, to peel off her clothes and reveal those curves… "I only want answers," he gritted, shifting in his seat. "I'll make a deal with you, Vee Miles. One I think we can both agree on."

She glanced his way, hope in her eyes. "A deal?"

"You tell me everything you know, and in turn, I'll let you go. And you'll never see or hear from me again."

"D-deal!"

Cypher's stomach twisted, and his bear snarled. Vee's excitement at having him gone burned more than he wanted to admit. Whether it was the male part of him or the beast, he didn't like it at all. Regardless, he had her now, and with her cooperation, this would all be over soon. He anticipated having all this burning to ashes behind him.

Whether his bear wanted something more or not, didn't matter at all.

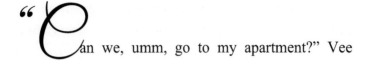

9

"**C**an we, umm, go to my apartment?" Vee asked when the Cyborg next to her went quiet. She threaded her fingers together. *Stop twitching.*

Her anxiety built again the longer his silence continued. She couldn't help noticing his build—too big for the hovercraft—and the tension in his hands that palmed and clutched his knees. The dark brown leather of his suit was taut over his frame, growing tauter by the minute.

She couldn't help noticing his gun either. Nor the bulge between his legs—was he well hung or hard? She tried not to think about it. The more she did, the more she wanted an answer.

She also couldn't help noticing the fact that even though he was a man, he screamed Cyborg. Reeked of it, maybe? The smell of heated metal was everywhere. Heat came off his body in waves, consuming her, enveloping her in *him*.

Though this was the second time she'd been in a Cyborg's presence, Vee could tell Cypher was angry. She wiped her palms on her jeans, her heart thumping hard, refusing to slow down.

Since the moment her eyes landed on him at the studio, her belly had filled with butterflies, and her throat felt tight. He *was* the warrior she pictured. So fantastical among the technology surrounding him. Nearly what she expected... That's what she told herself to keep from running away.

Intimidated. She was incredibly intimidated.

But she didn't think he was going to hurt her. Even when he'd taken her from the building, she followed willingly. He just didn't give her the impression of a bad man. Vee pursed her lips. *Or I'm an idiot...*

"Why?" he asked.

She flinched and answered quickly. "It's dinner time, and my cat gets noisy when he's hungry. My neighbors don't like it." Did she want Cypher in her home? Did she have a choice even if she didn't?

Vee glanced around at the shadowy wasteland and the dilapidated buildings, all darkening as the sun lowered in the distance. *I'd rather be home than out here.* Even if it meant having a Cyborg invading it...

He grumbled and started the hovercraft. When they started back for the metropolis, she exhaled in relief.

"You said you contracted with Nightheart. I want to read your contract," he demanded.

"I contracted with the EPED, not Nightheart specifically."

"Nightheart is the EPED."

Vee rolled her eyes. "Sure, you can read the contract. I have it digitally, and I have a paper copy. Do you have a preference?"

"Digitally," he barked.

"Of course." Viking and Cyborg weren't a good mix, she decided. The crankinesswas extreme. At least it was something to take her focus off her situation. Mild irritation was easier to deal with than nervousness. "Anything else, sir?"

The hovercraft lurched forward, and Cypher cleared his throat. She glanced his way.

"Clear your schedule tomorrow," he said.

"Yes, sir."

"Don't call me that."

"Why?" *I'm playing with fire.*

Or a bear. I'm playing with a bear.

"I'm not your fucking boss, that's why!"

"Are you sure about that?"

He turned his head and caught her eyes. She wanted to look away but couldn't.

"Absolutely," he finally answered.

Vee pursed her lips and wiped her palms on her pants again. "Why do I need my schedule empty tomorrow?" she whispered.

Cypher kept his eyes locked on her, heating her under his stare, foregoing the skyroads entirely. "Unless you want to be interrogated all night, I'll need tomorrow to get everything I want out of you."

She managed to tear her gaze from his. "Yes…you're right…" Vee stared ahead until he turned away.

The golden twilight vanished behind them under the smog and city lights, but the lights weakened the closer they got to the slums. When the rusted skyscrapers became familiar, she knew they were close. "Of course you know how to get to my place," she mumbled.

"I'm a Cyborg."

"I know…"

It was full dark by the time they parked, and she couldn't get out of the hovercraft fast enough to shake off Cypher's heat. But the door didn't give the first time and when she tried it again, it opened swiftly. The smell of industrial waste was a small relief. She'd been drowning in his scent without being aware of it.

He came around the vehicle and took her arm. "Come on. It's not safe."

"You care about my safety now?"

He stopped and turned toward her, nostrils flaring. "You are under my protection until our deal is ended."

"I keep pepper spray in my pocket."

His nostrils flared further. "Fucking hell." He pivoted back with another rumble and pulled her after him into the alleyways.

Vee decided there was no point in arguing.

When they reached her apartment building, there was a group of people still gathered out front. She and Cypher stopped a building away. He pulled her into his side.

"How are we going to get through them?" she asked, pushing away. "I don't think my pepper spray will work on all of them."

"Give me a moment."

She glimpsed his face under the smoky streetlight, seeing his pupils glaze over with numbers. Awed, she stared when a buzzing filled her ears and all the lights on the street shut off. Darkness flooded the area. She blinked and Cypher tugged her forward.

"Cypher?" she questioned, stumbling after him.

"Hold onto me," he ordered.

She clasped the side of his jacket.

Gasps sounded as they neared her building, and she squinted at the dark figures around them. Scurrying every which way, the people fumbled with the lights on their cameras and wristcons. Cypher pushed through until they were safely in her building.

The streetlights zinged back on when the elevator opened. He pushed her inside.

She jerked her arm out from his grip. "Stop manhandling me! We're inside now. I can walk."

He bypassed the elevator's keycard system and tapped her floor's number. "I will once I know you're safe."

"I've lived here for years. I assure you I'm fine. I don't need your protection."

"A female of your stature will never be fine," he snapped.

Now her nostrils flared. Vee rounded on him. "I don't know who you think you are—"

"A Cyborg."

"I know that! You've only mentioned it several times in the last two hours. You have no right to try and dictate my life, even if it's only for a short time. I said I would answer your questions, not give myself over to you. I can take care of myself. Always have, always will." How had this male ever made her nervous? Godly or not, he was exasperating.

"You're the one who was calling me sir not long ago, little girl."

"Because in the few freaking minutes you've been in my life, all you've been is grumpy! You're an easy target!"

"An easy target?"

"To tease." The elevator shot open, and Vee stepped out. "Have you ever talked to another human before? Dealt with a human? You don't know me. I'm resilient."

Cypher narrowed his eyes on her.

Bees greeted them, rubbing against her leg. Brows furrowing, she reached down to scratch behind his ears when her hand stopped. "Bees?" He meowed, and she picked him up, holding him to her chest, turning to look down the hallway toward her apartment. "Why are you in the hallway…"

Cypher stormed past her and pulled the gun out from his belt. The click of the safety turning off had her springing forward to follow him. Her door was ajar up ahead. Cypher pushed her door the rest of the way open. She stopped at the threshold behind him as he entered, her heart dropping into her stomach.

Her apartment was trashed. Clothes had been torn from the closet, the walls were spray painted with words calling her everything from a bitch to a metal dick eater to a betrayer of mankind. All her food was spilled out across the floor.

Bees jumped out of her arms as Cypher walked the small space twice over.

A cry tore from her throat as she took a step towards her Terraform Zero machine. It'd been destroyed. Vee clutched the pole.

Everything…

The seat had been shredded, the straps sliced apart. Her screens had been shattered, and her suit… her suit lay wet and in tatters at her feet. The reek of urine filled her nose. Not even her goggles had made it—the ones she'd had since she was thirteen, given to her by her parents. She reached down to pick them up.

A hand clamped down on her shoulder.

"Don't," she whispered, blinking back tears.

His grip on her shoulder tightened. From the corner of her eye, she saw that he still held his gun in his other hand.

Bees meowed up at her. Vee wiped her eyes, dropped the goggles, and picked her cat back up. She pressed her face into his fur and wrenched her eyes shut.

Cypher's hand dropped from her shoulder. "Gather anything you want to keep. We're not staying here tonight."

She nodded into Bees's fur and inhaled shakily. It was too hard to speak, to say anything.

Suddenly, she was happy Cypher was here with her after all.

Everything   was   gone.

$\mathcal{V}$ee slowly packed a duffle bag with the few clothes and toiletries that survived. Cypher watched as he waited by the door, standing guard. All the fire in her had burned out, and had transferred to him instead. But seeing her spark diminished also sat ill with him. He couldn't help but blame himself. It was a Cyborg's job to protect humans—even if they sucked. Vee was a bystander to Nightheart's game, and Cypher thought he should be between them to keep her safe. She was innocent.

He'd never seen such a downward shift in a person so suddenly. It made him feel helpless to respond. Even more so since it was obvious Vee was trying hard to hold it in.

His concern for her safety had been justified. *Fucking hellfire.* His hands clenched.

Each item she lifted from the floor to check over, only for it to be dropped with a whimper soon after, infuriated him further. Was there anything in her home that the criminals hadn't wrecked?

If he'd arrived here sooner, perhaps he could've stopped the destruction. He couldn't help but wonder if his attack on the men outside earlier had anything to do with this. But simply sniffing the air, it was obvious the scents within Vee's apartment were different than those of the miscreants. Whoever did this wasn't them.

While he waited, he scanned all her belongings and calculated their market prices, intent on replacing everything Vee had lost. Even if it wasn't his fault, it was the least he could do.

He soon discovered that everything Vee owned cost less than some of his better guns. Cypher scowled. He could pay off her sad excuse of an apartment with less money than he paid to run his ship's thrusters to start his cruiser. Far less money.

Vee gathered her cat's food as he turned his attention to the pathetic security of her apartment building. His scowl deepened. What few cameras still worked within the building, he downloaded their feed into his systems to check later.

When she approached him, he took her duffle from her arm. She picked up her cat in turn, and they left. Her soft footsteps followed behind him without hesitation. When they made it back down to the foyer, the street was deserted and dark.

"Where are we going?" she asked.

"My ship," he said.

She didn't say another word as they made their way to his hovercraft and shot into the sky. Bees howled and hissed, crawling all over the interior. Cypher aimed for the airfield and a short time later, he was leading her to where his cruiser was parked, once again bypassing security measures and blanking out any feeds that caught sight of them.

He didn't want anyone to know where she was, or that she was with him.

Cypher helped Vee up the ramp of his docking bay, grabbing her hips and lifting her onto the ledge before she could climb it on her own. Vee pulled out of his grip and ducked her head, heading in quietly. His fingers twitched off the warm feel of her.

He closed up his ship behind them, locking it while powering on the interior lights.

Vee released her cat, and Bees tore down the hallway and into the bridge on the far end. It was just the two of them now surrounded by walls of metal, and in the dark part of his heart, he understood Zeph's motivations. Now that he had Vee in his space, a sense of calm overcame him. She was safe here.

Even if she was trapped.

His eyes trailed over her. Vee rubbed her arms and looked around. She looked everywhere but at him.

Why wouldn't she look at him?

"Come," he said at last, frowning. He headed toward the bridge but stopped and turned to a closed panel door to the right. "You'll stay here." The door zipped open, revealing the only quarters his cruiser had. He moved to the side to allow Vee entry.

Inside to the left was a sturdy queen-sized bed—one that could hold his weight—and a chair across from it on the right. Straps and wires hung from the chair where it faced a series of screens—a crude version of his quarters in Ghost City. It was a place he could hibernate indefinitely. Along the same wall as the chair was the door to the lavatory.

Vee stepped inside and moved around his room, checking it out.

It was small and crappy and would be considered old compared to most of the ships his brethren now owned. Seeing Vee within his space only emphasized this and how out of touch with reality he truly was.

I should've upgraded my ship. Why didn't I?

He waited for her to say something.

"It's clean," he ground out when she didn't speak. *I'm not good at this.*

She finally turned to him. "Thank you, Cypher."

Exhaustion marred her face, and a stab of guilt pierced his chest. *She just lost her sense of safety and everything she owned and all I care about is what she thinks of my piece of shit ship?* His jaw clenched.

Bees scurried past his feet and jumped up on the bed.

101

Cypher fumbled. "Will you be okay?" he asked, eyeing the cat pawing his mattress.

Vee shifted on her feet. "I don't know. I want to be alone right now. Is that okay?"

"All right…" He awkwardly peered around once more. He wanted to do more, to say something to alleviate her pain—to get her to talk to him further—but he realized he had no idea how to do that. It's not like he could hold a gun to her head and force her. This wasn't war. She wasn't his enemy. "I'll leave the door ajar if you need anything. I'll be down the passageway in the bridge." He moved to leave.

"Can you leave my bag?"

Her bag. It was still on his shoulder. "Right." He moved and placed it on the bed beside the cat. He flexed his shoulders when the weight of it was gone. When he turned around, Vee shuffled back away from him.

Cypher's hands twitched at his sides. "Goodnight," he rasped.

"Goodnight."

He stared at her for a moment longer, wanting more but not getting it. Giving up, he strode to the panel door and closed it partially behind him, leaving several inches open.

What the hell had come over him?

His audio picked up Vee exhaling heavily, and his hands fisted at his sides.

Cypher growled and stormed into the bridge. *Fucking confused is what I am.* He stopped himself from punching another hole in the wall or letting his bear come out so he could roar at the top of his lungs. Females confused him. Distance from this situation was what he needed to get his head on straight. Maybe he needed a full-on head transplant. He had one waiting in storage...

He settled for calling Nightheart instead.

Seconds later, Nightheart's IP attached to his. *The fucker's nearby.*

Cypher wasn't surprised. With bugs turning up on many of his brethren's ships, him rooting out and finding most of them, he had his suspicions on who had been planting them.

That, and he knew Nightheart better than any other Cyborg.

He and Nightheart fought side by side for a time during the war, and during that god-awful time, he witnessed Nightheart transform only once—and saw his frightening shifter side go up against unbeatable odds that no one else possibly could, not even another shifter class Cyborg. Seeing Nightheart in action was enough to put the pieces together about the bugs. No one else had ever seen the president and CEO of the

EPED release his creature except Cypher. And for that, the two of them were bonded in a messed-up way. At least according to Nightheart.

Keep your friends close but your enemies closer.

"Nightheart," Cypher snarled.

"Welcome to Earth, buddy," Nightheart responded.

"Why are you doing this?"

"You know why."

"It's not going to work," Cypher warned. "I won't join you."

"But you've considered it, haven't you?" Nightheart mused coldly. "Don't tell me you haven't. Your abilities are wasted on Ghost, sorely wasted. Imagine what it would be like to have boundless freedom, money, and power—and the chance to let your animal roam again. To be savage, primal, and strong. To answer to no one…but me."

Cypher dropped into his captain's seat and palmed his face. Of course he'd considered Nightheart's offer. Nightheart had been trying to get Cypher to join his team of Monster Hunters and Retrievers for decades. More so now due to Nightheart losing half his employees in the last few years.

Without requisitions coming in, without the badly needed resources spread throughout some of the most dangerously known planets and moons coming in, without heroes stomping out threats that no one else had the power or abilities to handle, Nightheart and the EPED were losing vast sums of money and influence.

"I could do all of that already if I wanted to. I could have all of that if I wanted. Have you ever thought about that? I don't need you." Cypher countered. "No one needs you. Especially not me. I could crush your metal skull in without breaking a sweat. And for fuck's sake, Nightheart, why did you bring her into it? You posted my information all over the fucking network!" Knowing Vee was closeby, despairing, had him baring his fangs.

"I didn't post it. She did. How do you like her, by the way? I think I chose well."

"But you gave it to her, told her to do so," Cypher snapped, his anger rising. He wanted Nightheart's thick skull between his hands.

"You were trapped on Ghost. It was for your own good."

"My own good!? God, you're delusional. I've told you this once, but I'll tell you again: my bear is a solitary beast, and when it's around others for too long, it lashes out. Remaining on Ghost was for me as much as it was for the protection of everyone else.

Don't you know anything about the animal I'm spliced with?"

Nightheart chuckled. "Excuses."

"I'm going to kill you."

Nightheart laughed louder. "I don't doubt that, friend. No doubt at all. I wouldn't have it any other way. So you want me to send you the contract?"

Ignoring him, Cypher hissed, "Vee's apartment was ransacked this evening."

Nightheart's laughter halted.

"Was it you?" Cypher asked.

"No."

"Did you realize bringing an innocent into your schemes would cost them, or was your selfishness enough for you to not care?"

"Zeph fucked us over. I'll send a team out tonight to follow Ms. Miles and ensure her safety."

"Zeph fucked *you* over. And don't bother, she's with me."

"If you can't think of Cyborgs as a collective, where one action by an individual affects us all, you don't deserve to call yourself one." Nightheart's voice chilled over the line.

Cypher's muscles contracted, the tendons in his body strained. "And what does that make you, you piece of shit? When you're willing to betray one of us to serve your own whims? I won't work for you. If you leave Vee alone and fix this problem you caused, I won't come after you—"

"You know I won't do that. I like you too much."

"Why?" he roared, his bear claws shooting out from his fingers.

"Because a deal is a deal, Cypher, and Ms. Miles signed a binding contract. The whole universe knows now."

"She's innocent!"

"And *you* threatened her for over a week."

"I won't rest until this is over! I can make your problems so much worse that Zeph's indiscretion will look like child's play. I will ruin everything you're striving to build and burn it to the ground. And I will laugh the entire time."

Nightheart went quiet.

"You know I can destroy you," Cypher continued.

Something rubbed against his leg, and his eyes dropped to find Vee's cat nuzzling against his shin. He frowned at the small creature and some of his fury dissipated.

"Come to my office tomorrow," Nightheart muttered. "We'll talk on the subject further."

"Already fucking planning on it." Cypher ended the comm call in his head, breaking the connection with Nightheart's IP. He reached down with one hand

and scooped Bees into his lap. The cat arched its back as Cypher petted it.

Vee's scent tickled his nose, sweet and strange. He calmed further as Bees settled. Cats loved his kind, and he likened it to the warmth his interior parts generated. Despite all the tech in the universe at their reach, Cyborgs ran hot.

"Why aren't you with your mom?" Cypher mumbled. Bees answered with a purr.

Cypher leaned back wearily in his chair and kicked his legs up on the console. He toyed with turning on his security system and checking on Vee, and after warring with himself for a minute, he decided checking wouldn't do any harm.

He was an advocate for privacy, but Vee wasn't well.

A screen popped up, illuminating the bridge, showing him the entirety of his room. He found her lying with her back to the wall on his bed. His heart thrummed. Tucked under the old threadbare covers, her hands were cupped in front of her mouth, and her legs curled up into a fetal position. The fire of her hair streaked across his pillow.

Her eyes were shut tight, and her brow was creased.

Cypher's throat tightened. He hadn't lain in that bed in years—not even once during this past week he'd traveled from Ghost—but he sorely wanted to now. The bed had been made for his size, and Vee was tiny within it.

I'd fit.

She's perfect. We'd fit together. There's enough room for both of us.

Not once had he ever thought about having a woman of his own. When he encountered women in the past, they were colleagues and professionals, those he worked with during the war. Back then, there were stringent rules about fraternization, even more so with Cyborgs and humans because the effects of such unions had unknown variables. Some Cyborgs ignored the rules, but he always followed them.

It wasn't only that there were rules, he and his brethren were 'young' during the war, and they'd been created for a specified purpose: to win. To destroy the Trentian empire at all costs, and with as few loss of human lives as possible.

Even if travesty was left in their wake.

Women didn't factor in when it came to winning. Bed sport wasn't going to lead anyone to victory. With the kinds of dominant kill-commands running through a Cyborg's head, basic needs like sex took a backseat. And with shifters like Cypher, grappling with being part animal, it made everything that much more difficult, codes or not.

The animal had needs. The man had needs. The machine almost always won between the three.

And for him, letting the machine win out was the safest course. His bear was vicious when threatened, indiscriminately so, and it wasn't clean. His kills were brutal and gory, and often left many to suffer long agonizing deaths. When he let the ursine out, he relished the sobs and howls of pain from his victims. They were justified to Cypher, for having gone against him.

For having gone against the codes deep in his head...

He scowled, staring at the woman in his bed, suddenly hating her as much as he hated Nightheart.

They'd upended his life, and out here, away from the cold confines of Ghost, there was nothing to distract him from the parts of him he kept buried deep.

His bear tasted freedom, and it tasted wicked. It tasted like what he'd imagined Vee's cunt tasted like. The primitive male inside him wholeheartedly agreed. That same male fantasized about it.

Vee had taken up all the open areas of his mind, and she refused to leave.

His cock hardened, and he removed Bees from his lap. Still scowling, he shut off the security feed and replaced it with his favorite picture of her—the one that emphasized her curves and small waist, completely wrapped up in a skin-tight gaming suit. A man's fantasy.

A wild fairy waiting to be plucked. A bright red cherry on top of vanilla ice cream, but with the added allure of rainbow sprinkles.

He would lick the picture if he knew it could somehow help.

Angry and bristling with pent-up lust, he barely restrained himself from storming back to his quarters and demanding answers from her. It would have been a poor excuse to be near her.

Cypher opened the buckle of his pants and released his cock. His booted feet hit the floor.

I'm not a good man. Behind his eyes, he roved his gaze over Vee's image. *A good man wouldn't do this.* He grasped his hard shaft and squeezed it. *A good man would respect her privacy.*

I'm not a good man.

His dick bulged under the added pressure. Pumping it hard from base to tip, Cypher didn't waste any time, savagely seeking release. There was only one way to get the heaviness out of him without hurting anyone, and this was it.

He zeroed in on Vee's ass. He had no idea if she was a virgin or experienced. It didn't matter; he'd take her anyway. He wanted her body opened for his dominance, wanted to be inside her, thrusting hard and fast, claiming every part of her. He wanted her fiery hair pulled taut in his grip as he tugged her head to the side so he could press his nose to her neck and breathe in her sweet scent.

He wanted to hear the sounds she'd make when she reached her peak.

Cypher came hard. Heated cum spurted into the air and landed on his consol. A guttural noise tore from his throat as he continued pumping his hand, needing more relief, needing more of the pressure inside to dissipate.

Most of all, he wanted to ruin her.

But his cum stopped spilling too soon, and the heaviness in his groin remained. He released his cock with a sneer before his skin went raw from his violence. He looked down at himself and the mess he made. *Fucking menace.* His shaft was still stiff but not as tight—his tip leaked. His pants were a mess. Cypher lifted his hand to peer at the cum sticking to his fingers. *Disgusting.*

In the back of his mind, he ordered his cleaning bots to sanitize the scene. Off to the side, Bees watched him suspiciously.

"Oh, screw off, cat," he grated. "You'd do the same thing if there were a female feline in heat."

Bees licked his paw.

Vee wasn't in heat. *Thank the devil humans don't have mating seasons.* Male bears, though… The rut was hard within him.

Was that what Nightheart was hoping for? Putting a pretty female in Cypher's sights that he had no other option but to seek out? Had the other Cyborg known that the moment Cypher focused on something besides Ghost's security systems, his rut would finally happen?

Cypher grumbled and dropped his hand, leaning forward to rest his elbows on his knees.

What would Vee think if she saw me like this?

I'm not a good Cyborg at all.

He grabbed his cock again and pumped.

11

*V*ee didn't leave Cypher's room for two days.

The first day was unsettling. She'd woken up disoriented and confused, but when she'd realized where she was, she'd slumped back into bed and pulled the covers high around her. She was in Cypher's ship—a strange man's ship—and it made her nervous. Despite what happened to her apartment, she faced much more than that now. She faced *him*, and barricading herself off seemed like the best course of action while she tried to figure *him* out.

This was the first time she'd been inside a spaceship of any kind. And though everything was clean, she could smell Cypher everywhere, even beyond the bedding. Metal and man, spicy, wild, and untamed—almost. *Almost untamed.*

He'd checked up on her several times, even bringing her buttered toast, and letting Bees out to roam the ship… Shame settled inside her, and an unsettling patter in her chest she couldn't shake came with each visit. Where was her courage?

She only knew it was the end of the first day because he brought her dinner and offered to show her his ship. There'd been a dandelion on her tray.

Vee sniffed the weedy flower and smiled. It stayed with her on the pillow next to her that night. The flower relaxed her nerves.

The second day was better.

She'd woken to Cypher bringing her breakfast, grumbling about restocking the food replicator machines and not having enough choices. But she'd devoured the foamy waffles and eggs, forgetting about everything outside for a few wonderful minutes. Cypher had awkwardly gazed around the room, tangling his fingers into his hair while asking her benign questions and offering to let the cleaning bots sanitize the bedding.

For some reason, he couldn't look at her for long before his eyes darted away. It made her smile.

His presence steadily became less intimidating.

That day, she'd logged onto her media site and gave updates to her followers. Even managed to message a few of them back, ignoring the increasing amount of mean-spirited notifications.

When she'd seen clips of her interview and clips of Cypher getting into a brawl with some assholes outside her apartment, she shut her wristcon off and closed her eyes. It was clear to her he held back his strength. She knew a Cyborg could easily kill whatever they came up against but Cypher... Cypher was huge, even in comparison to the other one she'd met.

She pulled up Cypher's file and read over all his information again for the hundredth time, trying to learn all she could about him.

Before she knew it, hours had gone by.

A long shower later, her desire to join the world of the living returned, despite the big, burly Cyborg in her path. *If he's going to harm me, he would have done it by now.*

I need to repay him…

But when she approached the door late that night, it didn't open for her. Her nerves threatened to return but she talked herself down and went to bed instead.

Vee woke the third morning with Cypher staring daggers at her from the doorway.

She scooted back. "Wha—"

"Time to get up. It's almost noon," Cypher groused. "We have work to do today." He pivoted and shut the door behind him.

Bees nuzzled her arm, and she pushed down the covers, sliding her feet to the floor.

She went to her bag of supplies. Pulling out a dress—one of the few articles of clothing that hadn't been destroyed—and a pair of underwear, she set them aside. Besides some toiletries, there was nothing else. Vee rubbed her face.

She scratched Bees' scruff.

When he licked his paws, she pulled his fluffy body into her lap and pushed her nose into his fur. "They didn't hurt you," she whispered. "That's all that matters."

Bees wiggled out of her hold and jumped back on the bed.

She picked up her clothes and stood. A few minutes later, after stuffing her grimy shirt and yesterday's underwear at the bottom of her duffle, she was as ready as she'd ever be, running her fingers through her tangled hair.

She headed for the door but stopped short. Had the last few days been mere hours? No...

I slept in Cypher's room.

I slept in Cypher's bed.

She inhaled sharply.

Her belly fluttered.

Ugh.

Vee squeezed her eyes shut and scrunched her face. Cypher wouldn't want someone like her when there were probably thousands of beautiful— experienced—women willing to do anything for a night with him.

The door zipped opened. She started.

A growl sounded. "What's wrong?" he asked.

Cypher stood directly in front of her.

"I—Nothing is wrong," she said quickly, trying not to cower. "Nothing that hasn't already been wrong."

Vee took a step back. He was way too big, way too tall for her to meet directly two feet away. And way too intimidating. The awkward, grumpy Viking from the last few days was well and gone.

She blushed and fluffed her hair forward to hide it.

But his uncanny eyes fell from her face. A beige glow erupted from his pupils as they landed on her red dress, and she brought her arms up to cover her chest. He scanned her over slowly. And not subtly.

He doesn't have those kinds of eyes that can see through clothing, right?

Right?

Oh, god. She tightened her arms around herself.

"Why are you wearing that?" he asked.

She straightened. "I don't have many choices. Most of my clothes were ruined."

He grumped, and his gaze met hers, darkening. He ran his fingers through his long hair, pulling it away from his face. It was then she realized how odd he appeared this morning.

Scruffy, tired, and—dare she think it?—worn out.

Had he gotten enough electricity in his systems last night? Oil? she mused. What did Cyborgs need to sustain themselves anyway?

Bears need meat. Vee pursed her lips. *Oil? Gasoline? Ice cream and fairy dust?* Or was it just meat?

Still, his hair was a mess, his face sunken—as if he was only a human male who hadn't slept in days. Cypher looked how she felt. Had he looked like this the whole time?

"You okay?" she asked, brow furrowing.

Another grumble, even lower this time. His eyes dove back down to her body for a split second, and she stiffened.

"Come, we have a lot to do today." He turned on his heel and strode down the ship's passageway.

Bees slipped from the room and followed closely behind.

With a sigh, she lowered her arms and did the same.

She glanced around the ship as she followed Cypher to the room he entered, stopping on the threshold. She hadn't given the ship much thought before now…

It was small but not cramped, and nothing like she imagined a spaceship would look like inside. The walls were a smooth, dark, dull gray. A sad, bleak color. There were grates on the sides that she avoided with her socked feet. Above, there were streaks of light, more grates, and some external piping.

There was a faint smell of rust in the air.

She could see straight into the bridge, down the hall, toward where her room was. There were several closed doors between her and the room, and she could only imagine that storage, medical equipment, and whatnot laid within them. Perhaps a secondary quarters for a crew member? At the other end was one more door and the hatch she climbed through last night. Still, though small, the ship was at least four times bigger than her apartment. At least she guessed it was about that big.

There was no one else on the ship but her and Cypher. She knew that without investigating.

He screamed loner, and the ship was quiet, lifeless.

Overall, Cypher's ship was cold. Well lived in but relatively out of date.

Shuffling and the sounds of machines buzzing pricked her ears. She turned back to the room. He was on the opposite side toying with several hologram screens.

Between them was a small lounge area with a single table against the wall to the left. Three empty bottles of alcohol were atop it.

So that's why he's grim.

The rest of the room was floor-to-ceiling state of the art replicators and high-level food prep machinery. Vee took a seat at the table and pulled one of the empty bottles toward her, sniffing it.

She wrinkled her nose. "I can't believe you drink this stuff."

He answered with a grumble. Vee pushed the bottles away. Cypher joined her at the table and placed a plate of food, some utensils, and a coffee cup in front of her. There was toast, jam, scrambled eggs. Her belly growled—sounding very similar to a certain Cyborg—and she picked up her fork.

"Thank yo— You can sit down, you know?" She peered up at him where he stood over her, staring holes. Any chill from the ship's starkness vanished.

"Send me your contract," he snapped.

"Oh, okay." She turned on her wristcon and opened the encrypted files. She swiped them in his direction, and his eyes flashed once. "Did you get them?"

He sat down across from her. "Hmm."

She wiped her palms on her dress. *Grouch.*

Cypher stared blankly at the table before him, and she went back to her food.

"I wanted to thank you," she began, swallowing, "for letting me stay here."

His eyes shot up. Anger suddenly etched his features. "You signed this?"

"Y-yes?"

His shoulders visibly strained against his brown leather jacket. "Did you even read it?"

Vee's face scrunched, and she sat back as he grew bigger. "Of course I did."

"You signed away your fucking life—*your fucking life*—and for what? Three million and the chance to play a game before a crowd? Can you be so stupid? Are you worth so little?"

Her mouth dropped. "How dare you," she whispered. *Major grouch.* All his softness disappeared. She'd read the contract. She wasn't signing away her life. She agreed to what Nightheart offered, and had been happy to do it. "I'm not stupid, you asshole—"

"Nightheart owns you!"

"—I'm worth so little? That's precious coming from you, who's literally made up of priceless technology and metals. Who threatened me before you even knew what was going on. He doesn't own me. No one does."

Cypher laughed. "What? Because you don't have a bill of ownership pinned to your ass? You do realize what reading between the lines mean, don't you?"

Hurt ripped through her. Her face reddened, but her eyes narrowed. "Of course I do."

"You're promised a job after the championship, you know that, right?"

"Yes!"

"That if you aren't offered one by one of the private or government-owned colonizing corps, that the EPED will provide you a job on one of their teams? Non-negotiable. A matter of loyalty to the cause, it states."

She remembered. She and Nightheart discussed it. A job like that was what this was all about, after all. A way to freedom, a way to do what she loved doing best, a way to use the skills she'd honed for years to good use…

"I read the contract, Cypher," she said. "I know what it says. Why do you even care?" Vee slammed her fork onto the table. *What is with this guy?*

He surged to his feet. "No one's colonizing anything, Vee! No one."

She jerked up, but he leaned over her, trapping her. Her mouth parted. The beating of her heart thrummed fast.

His heat, his smell, filled her nose. It was so much more potent than before.

"Have you heard of Axone?" he asked.

"It's a planet like old Earth. It's been playable on the Terraform games for years." What did Axone have to do with any of this? It was one of the first planets she played as a child, but one she quickly gave up on.

"It's not just in your game. It's a real place. It was the next planet slated for the Earth's government to colonize."

Thinking back, she recalled Axone on the news when she first started out. It'd been many, many years since she last heard about it, though.

He continued. "Everyone, Vee, everyone who was sent there died horrible deaths. Everyone but a single scientist, and only because one of my brethren happened to intercept her distress call and answer it. He almost died too during the extraction, several times over."

"I didn't know…"

"You wouldn't. The project, funded by EonMed, went dark. No one knows what happened except those who were a part of it. The Cyborg who rescued the lone survivor worked for Nightheart, the very same 'borg you contracted with. Trillions of credits were lost, and billions more to cover it up. Who paid for that? EonMed and the EPED. Since then, all colonizing efforts have been halted. It was the only planet slated for human settlement—the only planet still to this day."

"What about Gliese, Elyria, Kepler? They're colonized but still have people like me there as the colonies grow bigger, into uncharted territories."

"And what are the odds of you being sent there over residents that already live planetside, over those who've been in the business and know those planets better than Earth? You're a dime a dozen. You Terraform players are expendable. No, they'll send you to Axone, if anywhere at all."

She bristled. "You can't know that for sure."

Cypher's lips twisted. "No one lets trillions go to waste—for a simple monstrous outbreak. From a few unexplainable deaths."

He was too close to her to think straight. Still, she'd forgotten all about Axone. Even if EPED and EonMed now worked together on the planet—even if it was to get their investment back—that didn't mean she'd end up there. "There are moons and asteroids, smaller places owned by other private corporations where I could go. Not every place is regulated by the EPED or the government," she argued. There were mining planets, prison moons, and much more. "You're only trying to scare me. It won't work."

Cypher laughed, his face turning mean. She scooted back as far as she could go.

He leaned closer. "You forget one small thing, little human…"

Her eyes narrowed. "Which is?"

"You're already contracted with the EPED."

"How would you know all of this?"

"Know? For the very reason Nightheart had you pretend to be me to get me out of… It doesn't matter. I know because the Cyborg who went to Axone is a… friend. But mainly because Nightheart has been trying to recruit me since the beginning. And you, Vee, are nothing but a pawn to get what he wants. Once he's finished with you, you won't matter anymore."

She tore her eyes away from him and stared at the half-eaten food on her plate. Anger and worry swirled within her. How did it get to this? She was caught up in something that had nothing to do with her, and even if she tried to deny it, she couldn't deny what happened to her apartment, or that she was on a Cyborg's spaceship with him looming over her.

She couldn't deny the angry comments on her media site or the protestors outside her building.

Vee wanted to dive back into Cypher's bed and hide again—until she came up with a plan.

Was her lifelong dream worth all of this? She clasped her fingers together. Then it finally dawned on her…

I'm never going to have a normal life again.

"I don't know what to do," she whispered. "What should I do?" It hurt to feel so vulnerable. She hated it. And to be that way in front of Cypher... All she'd ever wanted was to help her kind and to find freedom in the process. But this?

None of what Cypher said had anything to do with helping her kind or finding freedom. In fact, it seemed like the opposite. Money, control, corporations...

The silence lingered, and she pulled her eyes back to him, her throat tightening. *He probably thinks I'm an idiot, a naïve little girl.* That pained her as much as everything else, Vee realized.

But as her gaze met his, she found him right beside her, mere inches away.

She jerked her head back.

He stared at her lips. Vee's body strained under his perusal. Her fingers shifted against each other, her toes curled, and most damning of all, her core clenched.

Cypher's shallow breath fanned her face. There was a hint of whiskey.

He moved a little closer.

Is he...is he going to kiss me?

Or is he going to strangle me?

"Cypher?" she said, saying his name so quietly she barely heard it herself.

He surged away from her, and the moment was lost. The anger returned to his face, and her heart dropped into her stomach.

"We confront Nightheart," he growled. "That's what we do. We're already two days late." He stormed out of the room. She heard his heavy footsteps resound down the hallway.

Vee stared at the space he recently inhabited and licked her lips.

Oh my god, he was going to kiss me. She was sure of it. *And I was going to let him.* A shiver rocked her, her hands were clammy where they were still clamped together.

But he didn't.

He hadn't kissed her.

The sound of the ship's hatch opening prickled her ears. "Vee!" he roared. "Come."

She jerked out of her seat and ran after him before she let her embarrassment take over. She couldn't let the fantasy in, not with everything else. She hurt enough   already.

128

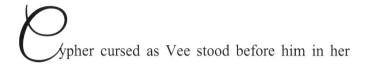ypher cursed as Vee stood before him in her

little red dress while they waited in the EPED's corporate foyer. His dick was hard as metal. The skirt fell to the middle of her pale thighs, and it just about killed him. Her legs were a little toned like he thought they would be. He wanted to grasp them in his hands and rub his palms all over them. He wanted to pull up her skirt, little by little, and discover what treasure was hidden beneath.

He wanted to nuzzle his face between her thighs and suckle her hidden flesh until it was marked.

I almost kissed her.

She'd looked so lost, and he'd almost taken advantage of it.

Cypher didn't think she wanted anything to do with him. He couldn't even adequately monitor her scent. Not once in the last several days had she given any indication she liked him.

He wasn't surprised. He was certain he had few redeeming qualities when it came to humans. His jaw ticked.

His systems worked overtime to keep his cock from ripping through his pants and labeling him a perverted creep for all the universe to see. Each time he psyched himself up to check on her, it'd been a whole ordeal.

The rut was growing stronger, and seeing her in his bed, disheveled as if from a long love-making session, messed with his systems.

Decades. It had been decades since he last had a woman, and he was feeling it, sorely.

Cypher cursed under his breath again. *I'm a fucking household name now.* Footage of his scuffle outside Vee's apartment played on all major media channels. *If I want a woman, one will come to me eventually.*

Protestors simultaneously chanted for his destruction and his worship outside the building. He gritted his teeth. Pumping his dick a dozen times the last few days had done nothing but make a huge mess. It hadn't helped him with his knowledge of the female gender. It hadn't rid him of this incessant need. It hadn't helped at all but stoke his desire for her further.

He didn't want another female.

And a creep he was, recording every second—in every angle possible that he could—of Vee in her dress.

She was a sight to behold. Red hair, red dress, pale skin. He had to remind himself that he was a bear, not a wolf, and that Little Red Riding Hood didn't exist.

Dommik had a red-haired mate, but while Katalina's was a naturally curly, soft red from her Irish heritage, Vee was a cute little doll, an odd one with all softness and curves to incite a red-blooded Cyborg to dive willingly into the pits of hell and forget there were systems inside him that could numb him out.

Still, the thought of eating her up made his mouth water. *Candy scented and apple red…*

Something hit the window behind him, driving his lust to the back of his mind. He dove in front of Vee to shield her, pulling out his gun and twisting to shoot. But it was only a man slamming a sign against the glass. The outside security pulled him back, and the man vanished into the crowd.

A hand grabbed his forearm. "Cypher, you okay?"

He glanced down at Vee, worry marring her features.

He lowered his gun but kept his safety off. "I want to fucking kill them all." He wanted to fuck even more, but he kept that to himself. "I'm fine. Let's get this over with."

She dropped her hand, but the feel of her warmth remained.

He strode to the elevator when it zipped open.

A prissy-looking blonde woman peered up at him from a screen she held in her hand. Her eyes darted to Vee, who moved beside him.

"Mia," Vee said.

"Ms. Miles," the blonde responded. "I'm here to collect you."

Cypher grumbled and stepped into the elevator, forcing Mia to move to the side. "Finally," he muttered.

He'd heard of this Mia, but only in passing from some of the other shifter Cyborgs who worked as Retrievers for the EPED. Mia was their contact and managed their file acquisitions. She'd been with them for nearly ten years...and wanted off Earth like most women.

Vee trailed in after him. "I'm sorry I left so suddenly a couple days ago from the interview," she said to Mia as the door closed.

Mia shrugged. "I understand."

"It's been a long few days."

Cypher scowled. *She has no idea.*

"I heard your apartment was ransacked." The elevators opened to a different floor. Mia stepped out first and led them to a conference room across the hall. She stood just outside the threshold as Cypher and Vee entered. "If you need anything, let me know. Nightheart will be here shortly."

The door closed behind them.

Vee sat at the central round table and clasped her hands together. With a low rumble emanating from his throat, he pivoted and made two passes around the room searching for hidden weapons or cameras. Finding none, his attention returned to Vee.

She was staring down at her hands.

"What's wrong?" He went to her side and took the seat next to her.

She stiffened enough for him to notice. She'd been quiet since leaving his ship. No, for the last few days. He hated it. It was like waiting for her to answer his comms when he traveled from Ghost.

He hadn't realized how impatient he was now that he had to wait for things.

"I don't know why I'm here," she said.

"To renegotiate your contract."

"You mean to terminate it so you can be free. To end this."

His lips twisted. "Yes."

"I'm…conflicted, Cypher. I—"

The door opened, cutting Vee off. Nightheart stepped through.

Cypher surged to his feet, knocking over his chair. He stormed to the bastard and grabbed him by the neck, pinning Nightheart against the wall. The other

Cyborg weighed half a ton in metal, but one hand was all Cypher needed.

"Tell me why I shouldn't break your neck right now," he threatened.

"You haven't changed at all."

"You've changed enough for the both of us."

Nightheart smiled coolly down at him. "Do you really want to do this in front of her?"

"I could do it in front of the masses for all I care." The aggression in him amplified. Cypher imagined the satisfaction of bending Nightheart's metalloid frame in two, of ripping the Cyborg's skin off with his teeth.

To finally be rid of the tension built up inside him. To finally unleash the beast.

A primitive part also wanted Vee to see it, to witness his mastery over all others, potential mate or not.

"Yes, but she might care," Nightheart muttered, looking past Cypher at Vee.

Cypher squeezed Nightheart's neck in warning, his nails elongating into claws to pierce him. The scent of Vee's anxiety—possibly fear—drifted to his nose. He paused.

Was she afraid of him? The violence he carried deep inside? *Does she see it?* He wanted her to see…but he didn't want her to be afraid.

Cypher's face hardened.

He released Nightheart with a growl and took a step back. His hands opened and closed several times, fighting the dominance he hungered to demonstrate. He scrubbed his palms over his face and threaded his fingers through his hair, pulling the strands out of the band at his neck. When his body calmed a fraction, he re-tied it and turned to Vee.

She stood staring at him and Nightheart with wide eyes.

"What?" Cypher rasped, moving to her side. She flinched. It wasn't what he meant, but he was too tightly wound to apologize.

Nightheart followed, though he kept his distance and took a seat across from them. *Good.*

Cypher didn't know what would happen if Nightheart got any closer to her. Candy, flowers, and citrus filled his nose, and he pulled Vee's chair back, helping her sit. When she sat, he settled too, but hooked his arm around the back of her seat.

She leaned slightly. The wires in his chest shook.

He and Nightheart glared at each other.

Nightheart shifted his gaze to Vee. "I expected you days ago. So you want to renegotiate your contract."

She winced but nodded. "It's my fault," she muttered. "And yes, if that's possible. I also want clarity. I would have never put Cypher's information out there if I'd known he existed."

"You never asked."

Vee's face tightened. "No… I didn't. I realize that now."

"So, Ms. Miles, you're willing to back out of your dreams for a mistake that's already been made? It's not easy wiping all traces of something like this off the network. Not when there's a universal event involved."

Cypher growled. "What are you getting at?"

Nightheart shifted his eyes back to him. "You know as well as I do, Cypher. Taking your shit off the network will cost more—much more—than what we offered to sponsor Ms. Miles."

"I'm…willing to do everything else," Vee said. "Publicity-wise. Pro-Cyborg politics. Everything."

"Like hell you are!" Cypher barked.

"Unfortunately, none of that will work without Cypher. We can dissolve the contract, and you can repay us the three million and find another way to go to the championship, or you continue what you do now."

"—with me," Cypher said. "That's what you're not saying."

Nightheart shrugged.

"And if I decide to ruin you?"

"Would you really do that to all of our kind, just to get back at me?" Nightheart countered.

Vee shook her head. "I don't understand. What is it that you want?"

Nightheart darted his eyes back to her, and Cypher stiffened. The other Cyborg's gaze sparked yellow—excited—for a split second. It put Cypher on edge.

"Well—"

"Don't bring her into this," Cypher warned.

"I want to know. I have a right to know," Vee said.

"—I want Cypher to join my team," Nightheart finished, drumming his fingers once on the table before him.

"That's it? That's what all of this is about?" Vee muttered. "My life upended, my apartment destroyed, the threats… For him?"

Cypher tensed.

Vee visibly wilted. "Why?"

"He's lost nearly everyone else, and to replace them, he has to be a piece of shit about it," Cypher answered for her.

Nightheart shrugged. "It got you off Ghost, didn't it?"

"Ghost?" Vee asked.

Both he and Nightheart shook their heads.

"It's not going to happen," Cypher warned.

"Ms. Miles…" Nightheart ignored him and turned back to her. "If you can't fulfil your end of the contract, it's also forfeit."

"That's not fair!"

"It's in the terms."

"I'll buy it," Cypher growled.

Vee turned to him. "What?"

"I'll buy out her contract." He stood, offering his hand to Vee. "We're leaving."

"Cypher, you can't," she whispered. "That's too much money…"

He glared at Nightheart. "Take my hand, Vee. We're leaving. Now."

Her hand slipped into his, and he curled his fingers around it, pulling her up. He led her to the door.

"There will be repercussions," Nightheart said.

"For you."

"For her. I can make it all go away."

Cypher tugged the door open but stopped at the threshold. He glanced down at Vee, who chewed on her lip, her brows knitted with worry. She looked up at him, and his heart fell.

"What will you do, Cypher?" Nightheart asked. "Once you buy it out? Leave and go back to your life before? No one wins but you, if you can even call that winning. You'll take away her future, everything she's built all these years, and leave her with nothing while you go back to a small metal room, gatekeeping a ghostly kingdom."

"Wait outside," he said to Vee. "I have something to discuss with Nightheart privately."

"If it has to do with me, I want to stay. I will stay."

There she is, the spitfire.

"It doesn't," he said. Cypher released her hand.

"Promise?"

"Yes."

Vee nodded, straightened out her dress, and moved into the hallway. "Fine. Okay."

He closed the door softly behind her and faced his brethren. Nightheart rubbed his lower lip with his finger, watching him.

The next moment, Cypher was slamming his fist into Nightheart's cocky face and pinning him to the floor. Cold laughter filled Cypher's audio as his body shifted. His head exploded outward with metal, his hair turned to fur down his back, and his nanofiber clothing loosened around him while he grew to twice his normal size.

The rich scent of synthetic blood hit his sensors.

Nightheart continued to laugh. "Doesn't this feel good?"

Cypher sank his claws into Nightheart's chest and threw him against the wall. Before he hit, Nightheart vanished and reappeared on the other side of the room.

A low, threatening rumble tore from Cypher's throat as he straightened to face the other Cyborg, his jaw low, his sharp teeth wet. "Is this what you wanted?" he roared. "For me to unload?" He stalked toward Nightheart.

"It feels good, doesn't it, bear? When's the last time you let him out? The war? You're not meant to be locked in a room, half-asleep for decades at a time."

"That's not for you to decide, you piece of shit."

"No." Nightheart cocked his head to the side. "But you've already made your choice, haven't you? Your humanity may balk, but your animal and your machine are in agreement."

Cypher snarled.

"You're out now, my friend. Do you want to go back to that cage?" Nightheart asked.

The aggression in Cypher wavered, but energy rushed through his systems in sizzling waves. That energy hit every nerve ending and blood vessel before filling his systems, recharging, only to burst back through his body again. Electrical power pulsed, and the excess energy he'd stored away for countless years was finally released… It intoxicated him.

Though twice his normal size, a feeling of weightlessness shuddered through him. He rumbled in delight despite the company and didn't want to pull himself back into the man-shell. Not now, not ever again.

But he dropped his paws to the floor and did so anyway. His body retracted, restored, and shifted to become human once more. When it was done, Cypher stared at his hands as he scraped his nails over the ground, wishing they were claws. His hair fell around him like a veil while he forced the last of the metal connections in his body to lock in place.

When he lifted his head, Nightheart was crouched before him with a contract in his hand. Cypher bared his teeth.

A digital copy was sent to his internal servers, and Cypher accepted it as he sat back on his heels.

"Vee's safety will be continual, whether you're on Earth or not," Nightheart said. "Whether she chooses you or not. She gets what she wants, I get what I want, and you, dear friend, will finally be the Cyborg you're meant to be."

"You're a fucking piece of scum."

Nightheart's lips twisted into a cold smile. "I chose well for you, though, didn't I?"

Cypher signed the contract, sealing his fate. He wasn't going to give Nightheart the satisfaction of answering.

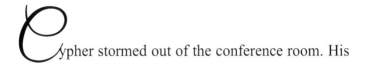ypher stormed out of the conference room. His

eyes were fierce and horrifying, his mouth a sharp line of fury.

He grabbed her arm and pulled her from the building, through the angry protestors who he roared at, making them flee. And when she asked what happened with Nightheart, all he did was snarl as he put her into the hovercraft. She tried to contact Mia, but Cypher snapped his hand over her wristcon and it wouldn't turn back on no matter how many times she tried.

When the airfield appeared in the distance, her frustration built.

"Cypher, tell me what's going on!" she demanded when they landed. She released the seatbelt, fled her seat, and slammed the door before he dared to lock her in and do something else.

She didn't understand what was happening. She had no idea whether her contract had been dissolved or not, whether she had any money or not, and worst of all, what she was going to do now without that knowledge.

She hated it. Hated not knowing, hated how she lost so much control in such a short amount of time. The anger brewing had helped distract her from her worry at first, but it redoubled with a vengeance.

"Nothing," he barked, eyeing her when she stepped back from him. The strain on his face deepened. He headed for his ship. "Nothing that concerns you."

What she hated most was how intimidating he was.

She reluctantly followed. "You keep saying that, but it has everything to do with me." She hurried her steps to catch up. "Do I even still have a contract? And for hecking sake, fix my wristcon!"

The hatch to the ship opened, and Bees greeted them on the other side with a yawn. Cypher scooped the cat up under his arm before Bees attempted to escape, both disappearing into the ship.

She stomped in from behind. "What's going on?"

"We're leaving," he said, setting Bees on the chair in the ship's bridge.

Vee glimpsed around the space, noticing how marked-up and used it was compared to the rest of the ship. Holes in the walls, the chair had crushed armrests, the leather faded and worn thin in parts. There were dents on the floor and marks on the control panels.

She hesitated. "Leaving?"

"Grab your stuff." He stormed past her with a large army bag that he'd hauled up from beside his seat. His heavy footfalls echoed through the ship.

Vee stood there, listening to them, her face scrunching up. How dare he?

She turned on her heel and made her way to his room, where her small duffle awaited. It took her two seconds to zip it up and carry it out. If he wanted to leave, she was on board. She just wasn't going to leave with him.

"Bees!" she called when she checked the bridge and found he wasn't there. Frowning, she made her way down the hallway and toward Cypher, following the grumbling, growly noises he made. She would have preferred to leave without him noticing—to get a head start—but her cat wasn't going to allow that to happen.

Peering into the room he was in, she found Bees exploring the new space.

And guns. There were so many guns, armor and weapons she couldn't even begin to name. Her jaw dropped open as her gaze skidded across the cold chrome closet, which included racks upon racks of the stuff everywhere. It wasn't only weapons and armor, but parts as well. Cyborg parts.

On the back wall was a giant metal bear's head with its mouth hanging open. Long metal teeth were scattered on the table below it. At least she thought they were teeth...

"Is that head yours!?" she gasped. Who has a second head for themselves on display? *Oh, heckfire!*

A shiver of disbelief coursed up her spine.

She'd forgotten how dangerous Cypher truly was. Her throat tightened.

"It's a spare."

Time to get the hell outta dodge.

With his back turned toward her, she crept into the room, picked up her cat, and backed out slowly. She turned and made it several feet toward the open hatch when a blast of warmth spread across her back.

"Where are you going?"

She half-turned to face him. "Leaving..."

"Why?" His voice was deeply gruff.

"Well... I assume you got what you wanted and don't need anything else from me. As per your words, 'it doesn't concern you.'" Vee glanced at the light down the passage before looking back at him. "I figured I'll go get my wristcon fixed."

She hesitated before she continued. "If I leave now, I may be able to before dark. Then I can figure out where I fall within all this mess. It's my mess to clean up, right?" Her voice soured. "I don't even

146

know if my contract still stands. Maybe I'll go stay with my parents for a while." She pursed her lips and made for the exit.

The last thing she wanted to do was stay with her parents. Especially if she had to back out of the championship. They would insist they had been right from the beginning and use it as manipulation to get her to finally go back to school and get a 'normal' job.

But going back to her apartment and seeing her Terraform Zero setup, with all of her things destroyed around it, would be so much more painful.

And staying here… Vee swallowed. She was certain Cypher would go his own way soon regardless, and leaving first before that happened was the better option in her mind. *I gave him his one day. It's time to get back to reality.*

"No," he rasped.

She flinched, unsure if she heard him correctly. "No?"

His hand came down around her shoulder and tugged her back to face him. Vee lost her hold on Bees, and the cat scurried away as Cypher crowded her space. He pushed her gently back against the wall.

Her heart clamored as her eyes focused on his burly chest. "What—"

He bent low and pressed his nose against her cheek. "Why can't I smell you? All I get is sugar and citrus fruits, sometimes strawberries, sometimes oranges. Then honeysuckle."

His face moved from her hair to her ear, where her skin prickled, and down to her throat. Vee shivered again.

"Once the honeysuckle is filtered out, there's only candy again, and bubblegum. It's maddening," he rumbled, his breath fanning her skin.

"I, umm, use shampoo and conditioner, lotion, and perfume spritz... My laundry detergent might be scented too... I buy whatever I think smells good." She pressed more firmly against the wall.

Cypher's eyes pinned her. Arching, scruffy eyebrows and brown lashes framed light hazel-beige eyes that were a little too perfect to be real. Even the hair on his chin and jaw was perfect—like the chaotically messy tresses that fell over his shoulders and down his back.

Vee licked her lips. His eyes darted to them.

She gulped, her fingers twitching at her sides. She was trapped. *By him.* A strange and frightening Cyborg man who she was drawn to. Thoughts of his terrifying bear head flashed in her mind.

He inhaled deeply and shuddered, and a blush rose hot on her cheeks. *I've never been kissed...* Was he going to kiss her this time? Was this really even happening? She clenched.

"God, I need a woman," he muttered and turned his face away.

Vee's brow furrowed. He removed his hands from the wall on either side of her and scrubbed them down his face, groaning.

His words finally registered. Her heart plunged into her stomach, and embarrassment flooded her. She wanted to say something, but nothing came out.

Cypher dropped his hands and looked at her. She averted her gaze.

"Fuck, I'm sorry, Vee. These last two weeks… What's wrong?"

She scrambled from the wall and scurried to find Bees. Damn her cat for making things harder. She found him under a shelf, inside a box. Pulling him out, she held him to her chest and made her way for the exit.

"Nothing," she said quickly as she dodged Cypher at the door.

"You're not leaving," he said, his voice darkening. "It's almost night. It's not safe."

She quickened her steps. A buzzing sounded, and she glimpsed the hatch she was headed for closing.

"Heck!" she cursed, rushing forward. But it sealed shut when she got to it. Vee spun on her heel to face

Cypher. "I want to leave. You can't keep me here against my will. You said we were leaving anyway."

I need to get away. Her thoughts jumbled when she managed to meet his eyes. Embarrassment bubbled up in her again.

He was right there, crowding her space. *Again.* She wanted to curl up into a ball and vanish.

Cypher's face hardened. "Leaving, yes. Together. Not separately. We're not done."

"We are," she whispered. "Please…"

His eyes flashed, and his expression hardened further, but he took a step back. "What the hell is wrong? I won't come onto you again."

Her eyes dropped.

"Oh, for fuck's sake!" he roared.

Vee jumped as Cypher slammed his fist into the metal wall, puncturing it like tissue paper. Bees tore from her hold and dashed deep into the ship.

Cypher ripped his fist out and punched the wall again and again. The sounds carried through the hall like explosions, making her jolt, but they were nothing compared to the Cyborg's aggression.

He grew bigger, more animalistic, and his bear appeared between pummels. In a blink, it was gone, but she knew she would never get the sight of it from her head. Even bigger arms, wider legs, and a snout— a giant metal snout that looked like it could clamp

150

down on her middle and tear her in half without any effort.

But when he twisted back to look at her, he was once again the Cypher she knew.

The hatch opened up behind her.

"Go," he rasped.

"Cypher…"

"You wanted to go. Go!"

"I'm a woman too," she whispered.

For a long moment, they stared at each other.

"What?"

"You said you needed a woman—" gosh, it hurt to say "—and I'm a woman."

His eyes sharpened, and she gulped.

If he refused her this time, she would swear off all men forever and buy more cats.

"Vee, you don't know what you're saying."

"Yes, I do."

"Have you ever even been with a man?"

Her cheeks reddened brilliantly. She didn't even need a mirror to know she looked like a tomato.

"You haven't," he answered for her, clearing his throat. "You haven't been with a man."

"I have toys!"

Cypher turned his back on her. "Oh, devil."

Emboldened, she moved closer. "You were going to kiss me, weren't you?"

"Vee!" he growled and rounded on her. "I don't know if you know anything about bears—"

"I don't."

His hands tightened into fists. "I'm in a rut. A goddamned, shit-eating, rut," he snarled. "If you don't leave now, then you're not leaving at all, understand?"

Vee sucked her lower lip into her mouth. He hadn't refused her after all. The breeze at her back beckoned. She should go, find her own answers, get out of Cypher's control. She knew what rut meant; it meant sex. No, she'd never had sex before, and jumping straight to it wasn't her plan. But even after his show of violence, she couldn't turn around and flee. Not anymore.

She'd always made her own choices and accepted the consequences, even if those choices were wrong. If she couldn't have her dreams, she could at least have this. A man—the first ever to make her want something more than nebulous freedom.

Vee met Cypher's eyes. "I should leave…"

A low, gravelly noise filled her ears. Heat coursed through her at the primitive sound—replacing her embarrassment—making her sex flutter.

"But I—I don't want to," she exhaled.

The hatch zipped closed behind her, and the chance to change her mind was gone.

Her bag fell to the floor as Cypher threw her over his shoulder, sending her ass into the air. He slipped his hand up her skirt to palm her butt.

"Let's see how much of a woman you really are then," he muttered thickly. His fingers slid hard over her panties.

Vee sucked in a sharp breath and whimpered, hoping she hadn't made another mistake.

14

*A*ll Cypher saw was red. Her red hair, her red
dress, her heated flesh. Touching Vee between her
legs, feeling her softness and the growing dampness
between, made the metal plates within his body seize
and jerk. And he saw more red.

Vee fucking wanted him.

He hated Nightheart and what the Cyborg had
forced Cypher to do. He hated he had been so weak as
to fall for Nightheart's bait.

But it was too late now. Nightheart owned him, at
least right now. Perhaps this was a good thing. *Keep
your friends close and your enemies closer.*
Especially if they were other Cyborgs.

I'll get my revenge, one way or another.

Vee's fingers gripped onto the back of his shirt as
he took her to his room.

He'd thought about mating her for the first time in
the bridge, where he'd pumped his cock to her image
a half-dozen times, but he abandoned the idea,
remembering she was unbroken.

Unbroken and over his chair would not be easy
for her, not with how small she was compared to how
big he was.

He considered taking her to his medical lab and removing her hymen, to make the inevitable joining easier for the both of them, but threw out that idea as well. There was no way he'd make it through the procedure without dying from cardiac arrest.

Not while she's in that little red dress.

So he took her to his bed, like a normal man would do.

Entering the room, her candy smell, mixed with his scent, flooded his systems. His mouth watered. Pressing his fingers into her once more, he flipped her over his shoulder and laid her down before him as she began to squirm.

Red hair fluttered out, and her dress caught around her waist. She was a fucking meal. Eyes wide, she pressed her legs together and tried to rise.

He pressed her shoulder to the bed to stop her. "Don't," he warned, not yet finished taking her in.

Cypher lifted his fingers to his nose and inhaled her scent.

Her arousal. His eyes closed in bliss.

There it is.

The smell of her he'd been trying hard to find these last few days. Her most private scent. The one his bear sought desperately. Cypher filled himself completely with her human musk, giving into it.

He shuddered. If she wanted a bear to break her, he was happy to oblige.

He let his fingers fall and stared down at her as she lay before him. Wide eyes gazed back, lips slack and parted. Pouty.

"There's something you should know, human," he rumbled.

"What?"

"Your contract still stands, but not with the EPED. With me," he said.

She jerked under his hand.

"I bought it out. I own you now. Do you still want to fuck?"

Her brows wrinkled. "What?"

Cypher slipped his hand between her legs and cupped her, rubbing the pads of his fingers up and down. "*What* isn't an answer."

Her mouth closed, and she gazed up at him mutely, cheeks bright red. She was beyond stiff so he kept petting her. Her thighs squeezed around his hand as if to stop him. He didn't.

If she said no, or wanted to stop, he didn't know what he'd do. Every second that ticked by without relief drove him closer to madness.

"Y-yes," she murmured at last. He pressed his hand harder against her.

Her hips shunted up. The image made his body seize with lust.

"Thank god." Her heartbeat was intense, thumping, music to his audio. His systems tuned into her. Heat enveloped his hand where he petted her.

Cypher stared. He didn't know where to start. To flip up her dress and tear off her panties with his teeth, to use his claws to free her breasts to his gaze, or release his aching cock to rub against each inch of her creamy flesh.

"Cypher…" Vee whispered his name hesitantly, trying to rise again. He kept her down.

His gaze darkened. "Yes?"

Her breasts, he decided. *I want to see her breasts first.*

"If my contract still stands—" She gasped when he shoved his finger to the very core of her, nearly tearing open her panties.

"Fuck the contract. Think of my finger fighting to get inside you," he said, pushing harder, letting his claw extend to tear the cloth barrier. It retracted and his finger slipped straight into her.

Vee squeaked. Her hips shot into the air, but her tight sheath hugged his digit, and he moved his hand as she shook. "Cypher!"

Saliva pooled in his mouth at the sound of his name on her lips.

"Please!" Vee begged, squirming, her face twisted in shock.

Spinning his finger, he found her secret spot with the pad of his digit. "I'm not stopping you. Say what you need to."

"I..." She dropped her head and clamped her mouth shut, beginning to hum.

Every reaction he coaxed from her vibrated his wires, making his bear purr. Wanting to be deep between her legs, taking complete control of her body, had been the only thing on his mind since arriving on Earth.

But now that he had the chance to dominate her, all he wanted to do was make her go mad. As mad as he was.

I want her screaming and clawing.

Fuck. He wanted the images of it in his head to store for all the years to come. Little Red riding her motherfucking bear. Precum shot out from his shaft at the thought.

I'm a bad Cyborg, after all. His lips pulled back into a grin he couldn't hide. "What are you trying to say, little human?" he goaded, circling the tip of his finger over her g-spot continuously.

"I—"

He slid his thumb over her clit.

Vee's head thrashed. "I wanted to know if you're still my partner for the event—oh, heck!" she cried out as he rolled her clit.

A swell of anger returned at her question, and he ripped his hand out from between her legs. She fell to the bed like a ragdoll, her legs partially open now and shaking.

Cypher grabbed the lapel of his jacket and jerked it off. "Yes."

Her eyes opened. "Thank you," she whispered.

His hands stopped midway from tugging off his nano armor. "Why?"

A small, almost indiscernible smile lifted her lips. His chest tightened, and his anger died abruptly.

"I don't know," she said softly. "For being kind…"

"Kind? I'm not kind." He pulled off his shirt with a grunt. Flashes of images of all the beings he'd gored during the war slid through his mind.

"Yeah, you kind of are."

He snarled and unbuckled his pants, and then removed his gun. "Fine. You owe me three million and *my time*, which is a lot more than most people can afford. Since I know you'll never be able to repay me with cash, you can satisfy my goddamned rut for as long as we're working together. Do you find me fucking kind now?"

Kind? It made him want to laugh. He reached down and tugged off his boots.

She pursed her lips, sitting up. "Actions speak louder than words. Louder than grumbles, too." Her gaze darted over him, and he knew what she saw.

A wall of muscle, built and honed by countless hours lifting weights, maintained beyond his body's set parameters. And scars. Deep scars that never fully healed from his time at war. Kind men didn't have scars.

He grabbed her hand and pressed it to his abdomen, where a particularly deep one carved a small dent in him. "This is from shrapnel, from an explosion I helped coordinate at a human sympathizer base for the other side. No one survived."

Sliding her hand lower, he stopped it over a groove along his pelvis. "This was from a poisoned Trentian scythe held by a Knight guarding fields of grain. We set them ablaze, starving out the locals."

Vee's fingers clenched under his hand. He led her palm farther down, where his pants fell open, until he wrapped her fingers around his cock. She stilled under his perusal.

"And this is because of you," he told her, his voice deepening at her touch. He released his hold and his pants slid down his hips to hang.

For a moment, she didn't move. It was agony.

But when she did, he could've fallen at her feet and licked her soles, and professed dangerous and obsessive love.

---

*H*is words about war saddened her but fell from her mind when Cypher placed her hand on his cock. Huge and steely hot, her fingers wrapped around him and squeezed slightly as his hand fell away.

This was the first cock she'd seen in person, the first she'd ever touched.

And she was touching it before she'd even had her first kiss.

Vee sat up straighter as the tip of it angled down. She hefted it up in her hand until it was upright. *So heavy.* She brought her other hand forth to hold him while she explored with the first. Heavy and big, like the rest of him.

And smooth, she mused, cupping Cypher's perfect shaft to rub her palms up and down it. He wasn't overly long but he was girthy. Like a fist. It made her nervous.

Butterflies filled her belly.

A low, guttural sounded her ears. She glanced up to see him with his eyes shut tight, his hands clenched at his sides, and his hair a veil around his face. He was huge and towering over her. Vee moved her hands up and down his cock faster.

His lips twisted, and his breathing grew labored.

Power returned to her all at once. Heady, erotic, much-needed power.

She pressed her lips softly to the broad head of Cypher's cock and gave it her first kiss. He groaned her name.

She dabbed her tongue to where buttery precum released and licked the slit.

"Vee," he rasped again.

Emboldened, she slid her tongue across his cock's head.

"Vee!" Cypher grabbed her hair and forced her mouth off him.

She gasped. "What?"

"I'm going to burst in your mouth."

"Is that…wrong?"

Narrowed eyes looked down at her. "No," he grunted.

She moved to take his cock back into her mouth. "Then I'd like to continue."

Right before her mouth enveloped him, Cypher tugged her head back, eyes flashing. "How about you listen to me instead?" He forced her down onto her back and leaned over her.

"But—"

The words never came out. He pressed his fingers into her open mouth and against her tongue. "I want my cock elsewhere."

The warning was evident. She bit down on him lightly.

Darkening hazel eyes flashed again, and it was the last thing she saw before she was on her front with her ass in the air. Vee gripped the bedding as Cypher's smell flooded her, and he ripped off her underwear.

She squirmed in shock. "Wait!"

"Shut up, Ms. Miles," he barked. His hands came around her face and forced something into her mouth. Her underwear, she realized. She wanted to say she wanted to be kissed first, a real kiss, before…

His hand came down on her ass and she jerked into the air.

"Fuck," he said.

Fuck was right. Vee's eyes widened with shock.

His hand came down again, and her whole body jumped off the bed. Her legs gave out and lay flat.

"Fuck!"

163

Vee held onto the bedding tighter, readying for another slap.

Even then, when it came, she wasn't ready. Cypher's palm came down on the other side, startling her anew. She sank her teeth into her underwear.

"I'm not a good man," he said. His mouth on her ear. "Nor am I kind."

Shivering, ass burning, she didn't know why his threats made her want him so much more.

His hand groped her butt, squeezing and spreading each cheek in turn. "I found pictures of you while traveling across the universe. Pictures of *this*," he squeezed her ass cheek again. "Nothing has made me salivate more."

Vee moaned around her gag.

He pulled away from her, and she missed his mechanical heat immediately. Stiffening, she waited for more slaps, but none came. Instead, his hands curled around her hips, lifted her ass back into the air, and opened her wide from behind. Exposing her in every way possible.

Shifting her hips a little, his fingers returned to her inner flesh, spreading her there as well. Vee buried her face into the bedding.

A string of muttered curses spewed from him.

Then his breath was there and she just about died.

She whimpered as the tip of his tongue jabbed into her. Holding her open, his fingers expanded and touched every part. Each second, his tongue moved farther inside. She cried out when he pressed his thumb into her ass. He chuckled.

Cypher didn't leave one place between her legs untouched, unlicked, or unprodded. With his tongue buried deep, he thrummed her clit and ass simultaneously. Essence dripped from her.

Vee gripped the bedding for dear life. This wasn't what she'd expect from her first time.

"Cypher," she moaned around her gag.

His tongue slid out, and she moaned again with loss, but then his fingers left her clit and penetrated the tight space—two *big* fingers.

"Cypher!" she gasped again. His name came out muffled.

His fingers spread in response, stretching her out. And right as another wave of embarrassment rushed through her, his hand left her ass and slapped her butt. Once again, she fell flat onto the bed.

Shaking, Vee clamped hard around his fingers and cried out. She spit out her gag and rubbed her brow on the bedding. "I can't," she whined, reaching behind her to grab his wrist. He took her hand and spread it on the bed next to her face.

"It's going to hurt, Vee," he said.

"I know."

"I'm preparing you."

She squeezed her eyes closed.

"I'm going to break you," he continued.

She exhaled slowly.

He pulled her legs back open, sliding them out and over the bed. "Ready?"

Was she ready? She barely knew Cypher, and that lack of familiarity made her throat tight and her toes curl. He'd done more to her—with her—than anyone else had, and it made her reel.

But I like it.

"Vee! Answer!"

"I'm ready," she answered.

A roaring grumble filled the air. He pressed atop her, his muscled body lining with hers, trapping her. It moved strangely, sliding and contracting, and through her haze, she realized that it was the metal plates inside him shifting. The hand covering hers beside her face formed metal claws.

Oh my god.

Hot, blunt metal probed her opening. She stared at Cypher's claws and bit down on her tongue.

It pushed into her. Vee squeaked.

His cock's head stretched her wide. His claws dug into the bedding, and they ripped holes into the cloth.

"Vee," he whispered, pressing his lips to her shoulder. With his shaft's head pumping in and out, he shifted her hair to the side and caught her chin, turning her face toward him. "I'll take care of you." His mouth found hers.

A sigh escaped her. Cypher breathed it in greedily and thrust into her.

She yelped at the pain. He swallowed her noises, plunging his tongue into her mouth. Her body went rigid, and tears sprang to her eyes. He pulled out with a groan. She was given only a moment's relief before he slid back into her, slower this time. There was another aching stab as he pushed deeper. He kept her mouth locked with his, stealing her discomfort.

Vee realized she never had control or power, not once. Not since she pretended to be him online and caught the Cyborg's attention.

Cypher pulled out and pushed back in.

And he broke her as he warned her he would, spreading her wide, even claiming the last murmurs of her innocence with his mouth. His hair fell around her, covering her neck and hands.

Vee rested under him as he grew and changed. His lips left hers to caress her cheek and then her ear. With each new thrust, his cock went farther. She tried to relax but his pace was relentless, his mouth on her flesh becoming ever more demanding.

167

And then growls tore from his throat. Primal, animalistic, deep growls. Like a rabid beast. Completely inhuman…

The need to see him overcame her. Was he still Cypher, or a machine? Was he taking her as a bear? She shivered.

She tried to glance behind, but he threaded his fingers into her hair and stopped her. Instead, he reared away and pulled up, slamming hard back into her.

She cried out as her hips shunted forward and into the air. A long moan followed as he pulled out and did it again. Tears beaded her lashes and the hand covering hers vanished to wrap around her front, finding her clit.

She tensed in anticipation of his metal claws but they never came.

Pinching, pushing it, he surged into her again, this time stopping halfway and circling his hips. His tip hit that perfect inner spot, and Vee's hitched moans stopped, replaced by soft gasps. Pleasure rushed her veins.

He continued until she was a quivering mess, barely able to hold herself up. And when she melted—moans growing louder—Cypher plucked her clit and pushed his cock back in.

Bliss hit hard and suddenly. Vee shrieked, surging back to impale herself upon him. Rippling shocks vibrated her nerves, and she wrenched the bedding in her grip.

"Yes…" A deep grunt met her cries as warm waves sent her spiraling. Cypher's fingers strummed her clit so fast it nearly hurt.

Her body jerked back and forth, and her sheath clamped down around him. He pumped, harder and faster than before. Her cries built each time his thick cock stretched and rubbed that sweet inner spot.

Vee clenched her eyes shut and bit down on the blanket beneath her. His hips pummeled hers, and he moved back over her, his knees on either side. She reached back and pushed against his thighs for leverage and was met with unrelenting metal.

And when she didn't think she could take the attack anymore, he got bigger, more savage. Cypher's body fell around her like a cage, holding her in place and hard into the mattress. His face fell next to hers, his cheek pressed to hers, and his primal noises filled every last space of her mind.

He slid his heated tongue across her flesh. Pushing his hands beneath her, he cupped her breasts.

"Vee," he groaned, dark and desperate. "Vee, fuuuck."

He thrust wild and hard and then stopped.

There was a moment of nothing right before he came. Heat spilled inside her. Cypher stilled. Vee didn't move as his hands left her breasts and slid down to her bare hips. He rose back up above her.

Gasping, his hands pushed her thighs apart as the wet heat between them built.

He's watching himself fill me. The thought blurred in her head. A heady glowing feeling swept through her.

When he pulled out, his seed gushed. Vee whimpered. She moved to rise but Cypher's hand came down on her back, stopping her.

"Stay," he commanded.

She slumped forward and closed her legs as she heard him move to the bathroom and turn on the water. When he came back out, she managed to catch a glimpse of him.

Tawny skin, tapered hips, blocks of muscles met her eyes—and the big fist of his cock that was still hard and hanging between his legs. He was gorgeous. She curled her legs under her and pushed down her skirt to meet him.

She was still dressed.

Did that matter?

Niggling thoughts ran through her head.

He stopped in front of her, pinning her with his mechanical eyes.

"Was I… good?" she whispered.

"Yes," he said.

He picked her up and carried her to the bathroom, where he stripped her naked and washed her body from head to toe.

He didn't say another word as he lathered an ointment between her legs that took away her ache, nor when he led her back to the bed—somehow now completely clean—and tucked her in. Nor did he say anything as he curled himself around her and fell asleep.

Vee settled against him and found rest in his arms.

$\mathcal{T}$he next day, Vee woke up to snores with an arm draped around her, holding her body tight against what she thought could only be a giant or a golem. Possibly a rock.

Part rock, she decided, feeling something hot and big pushing between the groove of her butt. Her heart thumped at the alien feel of Cypher's cock. Hard and surreal, it dawned on her that she was no longer a virgin.

And it was this Cyborg, one who was probably three or four times her age with his arm hooked around her, who'd taken it. A Cyborg who, right now, she was being attacked for even associating with. One who had helped save humanity from enslavement and utter destruction not several generations past.

She scrunched her face, thinking of the hurtful messages painted on her apartment wall and her media page. Disgust for her kind grew. She'd always been a loner before, but now...

Now I want to scream and fight back.

Still aching as she listened to Cypher's snores, Vee shuffled slowly out from his arm and, to her surprise, managed to climb out from the bed without waking him. She nearly tripped from soreness. Raw between her legs, she scurried bow-legged to the bathroom.

Inside, she found her wristcon that Cypher had removed from her last night and placed it back on. She swiped it and discovered it working, greeting her with a slew of messages. Her disgust grew even more. But the messages from Mia caught her attention.

Vee read them quickly. They reiterated what Cypher had already told her—a transfer of contract.

He paid for me.

He paid three million freaking credits.

Vee sagged a little. *How am I ever going to repay him?*

The ache between her thighs almost made her feel dirty.

She closed down her wristcon and scrubbed her face, emerging from the lavatory—and was met with Cypher, naked and godlike, sitting upright on the bed with his legs over the side, staring at her. His tousled hair draped around him like a chaotic halo.

"I don't like you leaving my side without me knowing," he murmured.

"I didn't want to wake you…"

"Bears sleep deeply, more deeply than they should. I fall into hibernation too easily. From here on out, while we're together, you are to wake me if I fall asleep and you rise first."

"About that—"

"Come here," he ordered.

Vee started and almost stepped forward, almost listening to him without thinking. She fisted her hands and remained still. "I want to repay you for what you did, buying my contract and freeing me, but I don't want to repay you with my body," she said.

"You tell me this when your breasts are out?"

She jerked her arms over her chest, glimpsing his hard cock between his open thighs. "It makes me feel dirty."

"Come here."

"No. You don't own me."

"You had no problem with me owning you last night."

Her cheeks heated. "That was different…"

"How so?" He cocked a brow.

"I went in before knowing what you did—with the contract."

"And you stayed even when I told you," he countered. "Come here, Vee."

Each time he told her to come, her belly fluttered.

"If you feel dirty," he continued, "let me help with that. Don't think about what this is between us as a contract… Think of it as mutually beneficial.

174

You got access to your dreams, and the EPED got me. You get to keep pursuing your dreams—with freedom, but I get you."

She swallowed. "That's practically a contract."

"Except you want me, too. Mutually beneficial, see? Are you an adult or not?"

Vee flushed with anger. "Fuck you!"

Cypher's lips lifted into a wicked smile. "Exactly."

She grabbed her dress off the floor in the bathroom and made her way to the door. *How dare he...* He couldn't keep her here against her will, contract or no. But before she could reach the doorway, Cypher's arms came around her and tugged her back against him. She felt everything—his shaft on her back, his muscles pressed to her skin, his overwhelming heat.

His warm scent surrounded her.

He settled his chin on the top of her head. "See?" he whispered. "You want me too."

Vee's face fell because he was right. She did want him. She wanted him unlike she'd ever wanted anyone before in her life. He made her want to do stupid things. Was it a Cyborg thing? Did they release chemicals into the air that drove people mad?

Or was it because they were so handsomely heroic and dangerous, and pretty much a bright utopian fantasy like the made-up worlds in her game?

She hmphed.

She didn't fight him when he guided her back toward the bed. He pulled her onto his lap, turning her to face him like she weighed nothing, and forced her to straddle his hips.

He settled her over his cock. She clenched as the tip of his bulky shaft pressed to her opening.

"Do you see how wet you are? Your body already prepares itself for me. Would you prefer to be in debt to me forever, or enjoy this transaction instead? And just so you know, Vee, I'm still furious about everything that's happened. Your body has been the only relief I've gotten from all of this."

A twinge of guilt returned. Heat rose to her cheeks when he vibrated his thumb over her clit.

"You like feeling a little dirty. We all do." He pushed her chin up with his finger and pinned her with his eyes. "You didn't really have a choice? If you didn't want to bear my rut, then you should've fucking left last night when you had the chance."

Vee shivered at his words, pressed her brow to his shoulder, and moaned. It didn't matter how much she ached; she wanted him, and he knew it.

"You're my partner?" she whispered, asking him without really knowing why or why she needed him to answer the same question again. She needed to hear it, even while he stroked her body to fire, needed some reassurance for this choice.

"Yes," he growled.

She sucked her lips into her mouth and nodded. His tip pushed into her, and she braced for it.

But it went no further as he held her above him. They stared at each other. She rocked back and forth as his finger continued to pulsate over her clit.

"Cypher," she whimpered.

He slammed her down on top of him, and she shrieked. Stretched beyond belief, Vee squirmed and gasped.

"You okay?" he rasped. His hands came up to grasp her hips.

She shook. Despite the ache, she was okay. "Y-yes," she whispered, her forehead falling against his chest. He tugged her hips up and slammed her back down on him. Vee cried out and gripped his shoulders hard.

He used her, moving her on him savagely. Up and down, thrusting deep, then sliding her back up his shaft only to do it again and again. She rocked and squirmed to gain leverage but it was to no avail. His hold only tightened, his pounding increased.

And the more savage he was, the more mechanical he became. Cypher's speed was inhuman. Moans tore from her, and she bucked. Electricity sparked every nerve ending as sweat beaded her brow and her skin warmed. Her muscles quaked. She had no choice but to ride this machine, his grip belting her in place.

Stars spotted her vision.

When her flesh prickled and every part of her vibrated with him, he slammed her down hard and roared. Hot cum shot up into her. Gasping out, she sagged, nearly destroyed. He pumped in spurts, and she was raised off the bed as his hips shot into the air. Cypher caught her up against him as he stood and rocked, grinding their pelvis together.

Vee tried to hook her legs around him but her muscles refused to cooperate. She hung limply in his hold instead. He lifted her off him and laid her on her bed. She moaned weakly when his mouth and hands came down to play with her breasts.

Like an animal, he squeezed and suckled them, shaking above her like his body wasn't in control. Her legs fell open, and his seed gushed out.

Snarling sounds filled her ears. And when she was sure they were going mad, Cypher thrust his fingers into her and pressed her inner spot.

Vee screamed as she came, and for one blissful moment, she wondered if she'd died and gone to heaven.

16

*H*e had control. Full control of Vee, and it shook him. Something dark and primitive emerged to strangle him, and try as Cypher might, he couldn't get it to let go. He frowned, rubbing his hand across his face. *Fucking control of her but not of myself.*

It made the logical part of him wild. The man, excited. The bear, ferocious and needy. A needy, sexually starved Cyborg. Not a good combination.

He barely stopped himself from punching the wall of his ship as he waited for the hatch to finish opening. Vee stood beside him carrying her cat, and it took everything inside him not to snatch her up and press her against the wall and have his way with her instead. He had meant for the two of them to leave the ship behind two days ago, but after yesterday morning, she could barely move from his bed. Guilt and satisfaction plagued him seeing her there.

He had experienced the same emotions when he'd lost himself on the battlefield long ago.

It didn't take much to convince him to keep her sequestered for a little while longer. *Like a goddamned, long overdue war prize.*

The morning light blasted his eyes. With their bags over his shoulder, he led Vee back to his stolen hovercraft.

Luckily for him, she didn't wear a dress today. He made her put on her jeans and one of his shirts, which he tied at her back to keep it from hanging to her knees. It did little to shake the strain in him, but it was better than a dress he could flip up at a second's notice.

Stuffing their bags into the hovercraft, he scanned the old airfield, gazing back at his ship in the distance. It was locked up tight so he'd be able to collect the rest of his arsenal and supplies when he returned, but he paused anyway. The cruiser was the only vessel he ever owned.

Now he was the captain of Stryker's old EPED ship.

"You okay?" Vee asked, looking at him from over the top of the vehicle.

"Yeah."

She canted her head in that suspicious way of hers, and her red hair blew like flames to the side.

Cypher cleared his throat. "Let's go."

A few minutes later, they were soaring through the airways toward the city's spaceport.

"So you haven't told me where we're going," she said.

From the corner of his eye, he saw Vee clasp her hands in her lap. "My new ship."

"You have a new ship?"

"Yeah, an EPED-issued one, with all the state-of-the-art bells and whistles to do my new job."

"I'm…"

He glanced her way when she went silent. "You're what?"

"I'm sorry you had to do that—take a job with them, that is—and the part I played in it all."

Cypher grumped. *She should be sorry.* But hearing her apology and the obvious guilt in her voice wasn't what he wanted. "Don't be. No one could force me to do something I didn't want to."

Stunned, he considered what he just said.

"I suppose you're right. I still am sorry, though."

"Then we're even because I'm sorry I threatened you," he rumbled, still reeling from what he said. Had he been forced to sign? Or had he wanted the job after all? Cypher pushed the troubling thoughts from his mind when the cityscape opened up to reveal the giant spaceport. Hundreds of ships, big and small, came into view before the airways forced him to lower his vehicle to stay out of take-off space.

Above, flashes of light and long streams of smoke rose in the air like spears where ships had recently taken off or landed. Higher than that, dark dots littered the skies where the leviathan ships hovered. They were ships that couldn't land on Earth because of their size, or those that could only land on designated space fields far from any city.

He parked the hovercraft in the private EPED lot and ushered Vee toward the port. The entryway loomed ahead with a glitzy chrome and glass sign that said: *Welcome to Space*.

"I've…never been here before, or space," Vee said with awe beside him. Bees meowed, trapped, struggling to be free from her arms. Vee didn't even seem to notice. She just held her cat tighter.

"It's not all that interesting," he muttered, heading under the archway.

"I think it's probably the most interesting. I can't even imagine what it truly looks like. I bet my game doesn't do it justice."

"It's a whole lot of emptiness, a whole lot of black, with the occasional splash of color. The stars look the same here as they do up there."

"Maybe you should look at them more closely next time." She laughed. "I know if I ever get the chance, I will."

"I'll take you up later."

He stopped. Did he just say that?

"We'll see." Vee chuckled, not even noticing his mishap.

To take her up would mean a lot. Bureaucratic bylaws aside, no one got the chance to leave unless they paid a significant amount to a vacation company, owned their own ship, or worked a job that required or allowed it.

Before they made it to the doors, a woman stepped in front of him, mouth agape.

"Are you Cypher?" she asked.

He glared at her.

"Oh my god, it is you! Can I get a picture, an autograph?"

The woman turned on her wristcon and crowded up next to him before he could respond. Several flashes went off, and she stuck a holoscreen in his face. He scribbled some gibberish, and she skipped away happily.

There was a tug on his jacket lapel. Expecting to see Vee, he was surprised to find a young boy. "Can I get a picture too?"

Stunned, he sought Vee's eyes. She smiled at him.

"Sure, kid." Cypher kneeled, helped the boy with his band, and got the picture. This time when he wrote his name, he made it clear. When he stood, the boy's mother was beside him, eyes wide.

"You're the Cyborg on the news," she said, grabbing her son to her. "The one who beat up those men on the street. Get away from him, Mika!" She dragged her son away, glancing back at Cypher with horror.

"It's a Cyborg!" someone shouted.

Vee flinched next to him, and he moved to her side.

"Let's go," he said, pressing his hand to her back and moving her toward the doors. But it was already too late—a crowd was gathering around them. Drones littered the sky above, and cameras came out. Cypher frowned and pushed through but more people closed the gap.

"Vee, stay close," he ordered.

Bees yowled in response, and she nodded.

Questions screamed at them, hands came out to grasp at their bodies. Every excited sentiment and word of hate filled the space. He stopped short of tugging out his gun.

"Get out of our way!" he bellowed, eyes narrowing.

"Cypher…" Vee whispered.

Someone jerked her out of his grip, and she cried out. Bees fell at Cypher's feet as he saw her get pulled into the fray.

Snatching the cat up under his arm before Bees ran off, Cypher thrust the closest people away. "Fuck off!" Red clouded his vision.

Some stumbled back as others spit and threw things at him.

"Cypher!" Vee screamed.

Fuck it. He swiped his arm out, not caring about his strength or who he hurt. Being pulled away from the crowd, he found Vee being carried off by several men.

One saw him.

"Go, go, go! He's coming!" the man yelled.

Cypher was on them in a second, breaking the arms of the two men holding her. His head burst open with metal. With bear teeth and claws, he bellowed in rage. Screams filled his ears.

Vee was on the ground at his feet, and the men were fleeing by the time his roar ended. Furious, he handed the cat to her, dropped their bags beside her, and surged after them.

Drones dropped down into his path, and he swiped them away. "Halt!" one ordered before it exploded upon the pavement next to him.

He grasped the back of the shirt of one of the men holding his now-broken arm, throwing him onto the ground. Climbing over the man, Cypher wrenched his jaw open and roared into his face. Urine flooded his nostrils. He pressed his claws to the man's throat as his victim sobbed.

"Don't kill me, don't kill me," the man begged. "I don't want to die!"

Cypher's mouth shifted back inside him. "Why were you taking her from me?"

"I—I don't know! It was a job. We were given a job!"

"By who?"

"They didn't give us a name!"

"What did they fucking look like?" he asked, lifting him only to slam him back down onto the ground.

The man burst into tears and blubbered for his life, repeating *'I don't know.'* Disgusted, Cypher removed his hand and rose.

"Human scum," he spat. He looked for the other two, but they were long gone. Instead, there was a huge area of space around him and dozens of onlookers staring at him. He leveled his gaze on each of them, and they turned away and fled.

Wiping the dust off his clothes, he cracked his jaw and his neck, righting his internal plates. He pivoted toward Vee.

She was on her feet, horror struck, Bees squeezed to her chest. Security flanked her on either side. They lifted their guns as he neared.

"Stand down, Cyborg. We'll shoot!"

Cypher growled. "You have nothing to fear from me." He stopped in front of Vee and gazed down at her. "I only hurt those who hurt what's mine."

Vee swallowed and looked down.

"You need to come with us." They didn't back down.

Cypher flicked out his badge and showed it to the nearest officer. "This should settle it."

The officer scanned the badge and dropped his gun. "Back off, guys. He's with the EPED." The other guns dropped, and they moved away.

Cypher didn't take his eyes off Vee; she was tense. "Are you okay?" *Afraid?*

Of him?

She nodded once. "I think so." Bees hissed loudly. "I don't think Bees is, though." Vee gasped as the cat dug its claws into her shoulder.

"Let me." He took the cat from her arms and stuffed the feline in his jacket, zipping it up. Scanning the vicinity, dozens of people still watched them. "Let's go," he muttered. Hauling their bags over his back, he wrapped his free arm around Vee and ushered her into the port.

No one stopped them this time.

No one dared.

Security checkpoints waved them through, and within minutes they were back on the airfield—a private one owned by the EPED. With the image of his new ship downloaded into his head, and all the codes that ran it, he powered it on from a distance and followed the thread of electricity that now bound them.

All the while, he scanned the databases with the faces of the men that tried to abduct Vee.

She was quiet and shaking under his arm. Cypher was ready to taste blood. If she was now afraid of him, he would fix that. Everything else, he would fix too. It just might take a little more time.

Who's after her? Cypher's lips twisted.

Vengeance returned to his mind. He pressed Vee to hasten her steps as they neared his new vessel.

When it came into view, the hatch lowered and a ramp came down to meet them.

"Here we are," he said.

"That's…that's your new ship?" Vee whispered in awe, finally breaking her silence.

He gazed up at it. "Yeah."

The *Repossessed.* A fitting name for a remodeled ship that once belonged to his brethren. Long and sleek, it was nearly ten times the size of his cruiser. With better speed, better arsenal, several floors, and a state-of-the-art medical and scientific lab, the *Repossessed* was a thousand times more expensive than his cruiser. It was better in every way.

189

He was certain Nightheart had his bugs hidden throughout to spy on him.

Not one for sentimentality, he helped Vee up the ramp.

If she thought her contract was expensive, she was going to be in for a rude awakening for how much Nightheart paid for *him*. How much a Cyborg really cost.

As the hatch lifted, he set Bees down and scanned the area. New ship or not, money or not, freedom or not, what Cypher wanted most was someone else's death.

He flushed the smell of the man's urine from his senses and twisted back around right as the hatch closed   tight.

17

*S*taring at the ship around her, Vee didn't

know how to feel. Adrenaline made her breathless and strained her body. And she hurt. It was like the few days of escape Cypher had given her hadn't happened at all.

She watched Bees run down a glistening corridor before stopping to hiss at a vent, and all she could focus on was the terror of being manhandled by strangers. She rubbed the feel of their hands from her arms.

For the first time, she really considered quitting—everything.

Cypher pulled her into his side, and she melted against him. "Come, there's a medical lab situated farther in. Let's check you out."

"I'm fine." She tried to push away.

He picked her up in his arms instead and carried her forward. "I'm sure you are, but do it for me anyway. Your cat clawed you pretty good."

Vee sighed and rested her head against his chest.

If Cypher hadn't been there... She wrenched her eyes shut. She didn't want to finish the thought.

He pulled her even closer. Nuzzling him once, she inhaled his scent and opened her eyes to look at him. His face was stony and cold, strangely focused, like he was on a mission, but she didn't think it had to do with finding the lab.

When they reached the lab shortly after, Vee couldn't help looking around the large space, which was crisscrossed by walkways above. Huge glass enclosures stood on all sides with doors between them, each hooked up with screens and lights. Smaller enclosures sat in the central space. Some had plants within—exotic vibrant green plants. A clean chemical smell tickled her nostrils, threatening to replace Cypher's scent.

She swore she saw an enclosure with a giant multi-storied cat tree in it that surrounded the interior on every wall, including the glass.

For Bees?

Couldn't be. Vee shook her head.

He didn't stop as he walked them through double doors at the end that zipped open when they neared. It led to another hallway, even cleaner and more glistening, newer than the one they entered from the hatch.

Cypher led her through a side door filled with medical equipment. There was a medical pod in the middle, and behind it and between privacy glass, several beds. There was another opening farther back, but she couldn't see through it.

Cypher set her down on a table beside the pod.

"I'm fine," she mumbled again when he loaded up a screen beside her. Swabs and bottles appeared from the wall like magic.

He grumbled in response and ignored her.

She sighed and gave up. It was the least she could do—listening to him—since he saved her, she realized.

He gently pulled out her arms and cleaned up her scratches, applying an ointment on them that took away the sting.

She flinched and leaned back. He was taking care of her. *Again.* His fingers caressed a bruise on her forearm that was beginning to bloom. A low growl sounded from his throat.

This surly half-man was taking care of her.

In the short time they'd known each other, he'd done more for her than anyone else she'd ever met. Vee reached up and swiped away tears. He caught her wrist and licked the tears from her knuckles.

It was such a strange thing to do, but when it came to Cypher, it didn't seem odd at all.

"I don't know how I'll ever repay you," she said, shivering as his tongue delicately slid over the back of her fingers.

Cypher lifted his head. "I don't need payment."

"But you've done so much for me, more than you ever had to, or should have, considering the circumstances." She lowered her voice. "I...I should probably quit." But as soon as those words left her mouth, she felt sick. They felt wrong. She didn't quit things. She didn't give up. She never gave up.

"Are you afraid of me?" Cypher asked.

Her brow furrowed. "What?"

"Are you afraid...of me?"

"No."

"Not even after what you saw outside the space port?"

Vee stared at him, confused, before it occurred to her what he meant. He'd transformed, partially, into a beast. Maybe it was because she'd already known what he was underneath that it hadn't bothered her. Maybe she was desensitized due to her lifestyle.

Maybe it was because those bastards were trying to abduct me.

"No," she told him again. "You don't scare me. Everything else scares me right now. I don't like it. I don't like being scared. Anxious, sure. Excited, nervous, overwhelmed, fine. But scared? I've never felt like this. But despite all that, you're not the cause of it." Vee sagged.

"I'm going to make them pay."

"Who?"

"The people who destroyed your home, those who tried to take you away from me today," he growled.

"Don't," she quickly said. "Please."

"You don't want them to go away?"

"I want them to go away, but it's not your problem to deal with. It's mine. I'll call the authorities. If the funds are still in my account, I can afford an android for security. At least until things calm down."

Cypher laughed, startling her. "I *am* the authority, and androids can't do shit. They can't investigate—at least not the government-issued ones—and they can't immediately differentiate friend from foe. Every second counts."

He reached up and tugged a strand of her hair, his face softening. "I told you you're under my protection now. Let me do what I'm good at." He stepped back and helped her off the table. "I'm good at this. And besides, I'm feeling particularly violent right now."

Vee inhaled sharply. "I already can't repay you for what you've done so far. Are you after my first and second born child?" She let out a soft, self-deprecatory chuckle.

His gaze heated, and his body tensed. A blast of warm air rushed over her. She wanted to look away but couldn't. Numbers coursed across his pupils.

Cypher visibly grew, looming over her, an impenetrable mountain of muscle and metal.

Her pulse quickened.

He reached up and cupped her nape.

The feel of the men who'd grabbed her vanished with his solid presence, wiped clean from her mind.

Nothing could get to her with Cypher in the way. He was a wall. A hero who clawed at her thoughts, screaming he was unbeatable in every way. There was so much violence around him, it was easy to get caught up in it and forget everything else.

Her skin warmed.

He makes me forget, makes me face reality. And not the reality that demanded she focus on her dreams.

Vee licked her lips. *He's making me lose myself.*

"We should check out the rest of your ship," she said hurriedly.

If she didn't get space between them now, he was going to rut her again. She was certain of it. She liked his attention, but there was violence emanating from him.

Vee swallowed, her sex clenching, still partially raw from being used so hard the morning before. Everything was moving so fast that her mind hadn't quite caught up to it all yet.

Cypher dropped his hand and stepped away.

The fiery heat went with him, and she immediately regretted all of her choices.

"You're right," he said, turning for the door, striding away from her, taking his comforting presence with him. "Let's see how much I'm worth to Nightheart."

Vee curled her arms over her chest and followed him.

The ship was beautiful. Out of this world. As they went from room to room, her heart fell into her belly. It made her envious. She didn't feel like she fit in amongst all the twinkling and high-tech machinery. And the longer their tour took, the further Vee lagged behind. She wanted to fit amongst it all—she wouldn't have entered the championship if she hadn't longed to be more than a gutter rat. But she didn't feel comfortable here… Cypher's life would always be far beyond anything she could ever reach.

I pushed him away.

The need to find a space—her own space—to digest the day and make a plan became overpoweringly urgent.

She was about to tell him she was tired and would like to lie down when the next room opened, and Cypher went still at the threshold. Vee moved to his side and peeked in.

Her lips parted in awe. She pushed past Cypher and went in.

"Oh my goodness," she gasped.

What lay before her was a gym of sorts, except for a bench and weights over to one side, the entire room was set up with the most beautiful Terraform Zero equipment she had ever seen. And not only was there one rig within, but two, the second with a larger and more solid chair in the middle.

A chair for a Cyborg.

She went for the smaller one and skimmed her fingers over the back. Embedded in her seat was her name tag and her neon red and black colors. The smell of leather tickled her nose. Hooked behind it were a visor and headset, both also having her logo.

Shaking, she picked the visor up and placed it over her head. The screen and the colors of the game materialized all around her in a beautiful array. An AI welcomed her back, loading up the login page.

Heart thundering, she typed her passwords in and verified her account. And as if her real life hadn't been broken apart at all, all of her virtual life's work popped up in front of her. Untouched. Ready and waiting for her. Her fingers trembled.

Vee pulled off her visor and turned to Cypher. He'd moved to check out his rig set up beside her.

"Did you…" She could barely form the words. "Did you do this?"

He placed his hands on the back of his chair. "No."

"Nightheart?"

"Most likely."

"How? Why?"

He shook his head. "I don't know." He didn't look at her, scanning the room instead. Something was up, and she could only wonder what.

She was setting her visor down when her gaze caught on the virtual reality suits hanging on the wall. As if possessed, she walked to them, stopping before the one that was hers. She reached up but stopped short of touching it. Cypher stepped up beside her.

"Can I?" she asked.

"It's yours," his raspy voice tickled her ear.

She didn't need to be told twice. Her fingers fell on the Kevlar material, feeling hints of the wires and sensors within it, and tears sprang to her eyes. She pulled the suit down, hugged it to her chest, and looked at Cypher imploringly.

The space she so desperately needed was right here. In her game. A buzzing excitement shot through her, raising her spirits.

He grumbled. "Don't let me stop you."

Her lips spread into a grin. Vee rushed from the room to find a place to change.

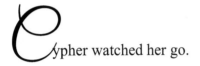

Cypher watched her go.

In minutes, Vee had gone from weary to exuberant, and it wasn't because of him.

Cypher looked around the room with envy. It hadn't been him who'd installed or ordered the machines in his ship—he hadn't thought about it. This wasn't his gift, and that infuriated him.

No, it had been Nightheart.

Bastard.

His asshole boss was going to plague him continuously, he knew it. His asshole boss was killing him.

Cypher recalled Vee's wide-eyed fascination, her breathlessness, her happiness in its purest form—and it was all because of Nightheart.

Not me.

His hands clenched into fists. Vee's crazy candy scent filled his nose, and his body hardened. Pressing his closed fist to the wall, he stopped himself short from punching through the metal.

I can still give her vengeance. The heads of her enemies.

The thought settled him.

I can still give her victory.

That would be the best gift of all.

Cypher cooled his systems and stormed from the room, heading for his new bridge. Before he joined Vee in the fake worlds she thrived in, several fuckers needed to be rooted out and disposed of.

Hunting and killing was more fun to him, anyway.

18

*D*ays coalesced together, and the storm calmed in Vee's head. She established a new normal, feeling more like her old self again. She lost time in Terraform Zero, testing and backtracking, fighting new physical and non-physical opponents. There were heatwaves, droughts, and in one case, on Yria, the water planet with sentient life, some settlers mating with the primitive aliens.

Resulting in a whole new predicament she'd never encountered before.

On the other hand, Juntao, her prime mineral planet, now had two corporate factions vying for materials, each settled in separate locations planetside. She had to tackle the hardships of both at the same time as they experienced different seasons, different species, and entirely different geography. It was less about colonization, but she had to prepare for everything for the championship.

As she stared at Yria's beautiful blue orb, an alien STD formed, badly hurting one of the male humans. A dozen pop-ups arose about the implications. Vee sighed, tugged off her visor, and stood, stretching her limbs. She couldn't deal with a viral outbreak right now.

The championship would mostly be broad strokes, with only a dozen or so nitty-gritty details based on actions taken. But seeing the webs created by cause and effect had a way of tilting one's reality dangerously close to paranoia. Vee rubbed her eyes and glanced at Cypher's rig.

Bees slept on his chair.

He hadn't joined her once, and that bothered her knowing they would have to make decisions as a team on the fly.

Will we be able to?

If she learned anything from the Cyborg she now shared space with, he liked to have control in all things—including her.

I miss him. She walked over to his chair and scratched Bees behind his ears. In the days since their arrival, he hadn't allowed her to leave, not once, but he'd also avoided her. He'd gone out several times to procure things from his other ship, but did it when she was busy—only leaving a virtual note for her to find later.

Being on a ship was interesting, but the days melted together after a while. Especially with the portholes closed. *Had it been days? Or weeks?* She'd explored everything Cypher allowed her to already.

And she was lonely.

Vee chewed on her lip and stared at his chair. She hadn't known how much she craved his attention until it was gone. She closed her eyes. *Get used to it. You're getting attached, and he's not going to be around forever. This is temporary, only temporary.*

Our lives lead different paths. He's not boyfriend material.

He's a dang Cyborg!

It's not like he was a guy who lived down the hall from her apartment or someone she met at an event. *And the way we met...*

She still felt guilty about it.

Vee pulled her hand away from Bees' fur and went for the door. A mewling meow followed her as she made her way to the bridge.

I only want to see him. Maybe smell him... She didn't plan to disturb him—he'd been disconnected and grumbly each time she peeped in. The panels were open ahead of her, and she quieted her steps. Large screens displayed numbers, maps, even people.

She frowned and stopped at the threshold. Cypher faced away from her, standing before the screens, still as stone. He was out of his head; she was sure of it. She leaned against the doorframe and watched him.

The buzz of electricity tickled her ears, the airflow of a vent somewhere behind her, but Cypher didn't make a noise. It was as if he were part of the ship itself. The only things that gave him away were his clenched fists and the scowl she was sure would be on his face.

He wore a tight black suit, a loose jacket, and had his long hair pulled back into a low ponytail—*god, he was handsome*. He was all muscle and toned curves. Her fingers twitched, remembering the velvet feel of him.

He belonged in this ship—in this bridge—but he also belonged shirtless and in a loincloth holding a spear, hunting prey in the wild. She pictured him as one of the alien primitives generated in her game, living in a hut, flourishing under the suns and moons.

And where was her place in all that? Behind a virtual world right now, gazing on.

"Vee," he said, startling her.

No matter how quiet she was, he always knew when she was there. Heck, he always knew where she was *anywhere*.

"Come here," he ordered.

She moved to his side, and several images flew up on the screens before him.

"Do you recognize them?" he asked, indicating one image that was larger than the rest.

Her brow furrowed. Of course she recognized them. "They're Deadly Dearest, and that woman in the front is Diatrix Greer. The others are her teammates. They're one of the teams we're competing against in the championship."

"Right."

She turned to look at him. "Why?"

"They're loosely connected with one of the men who grabbed you the other day."

She stilled. "What?"

"They have ties with several groups—"

"They're female forward."

"Not only female forward, they're female dominant. They believe the alien war was only won because of the superiority of women. Human women, not even Trent women. And they see it's time to rise and take down mankind."

Vee hmphed. "That's crazy. They're an all-female team, but they don't strike me as anything more than dedicated players seeking to better humanity."

"They want to start an all-female colony."

"So? A haven for women I presume? There are places like that here."

"They don't like you, Vee."

She already knew that, based on her limited interaction with them, but targeting her outside the game seemed insane. "If they targeted anyone, it would be one of the male teams. One of the more established male groups that always win. Not me."

206

"Or they don't give a crap about them because they're a dime a dozen. You, on the other hand, are a lone female, a rising star—someone I'm sure they may have even considered an ally, or someone they saw as direct competition for their message—who fell onto their radar when you accepted sponsorship from one of the most male-dominated agencies in the universe, outside the military. The addition of me probably didn't help."

Vee chewed on her lip. "So you're saying I'm being harassed because of them?"

"I'm not one hundred percent certain but I will be very soon." He snatched up his gun and put it within his jacket.

"Wait. What are you going to do?"

He moved for the exit. "I'm going to question them."

"Are you going to harm them?"

"Not unless they give me a reason to."

She scurried to keep up with his stride, worry filling her. "You can't just go after them without evidence! What if they're innocent?"

She didn't care if Deadly Dearest was innocent or not; she only cared about him.

"Then I'll find out."

Vee grabbed his arm. "Cypher, stop, please!"

He turned to face her, face hard, eyes distant.

"I don't... I don't want you to do this. Please," she begged.

His lips twisted. "Are you trying to stop me?"

"Yes! What if you go and confront them and something goes wrong? What if you get hurt?"

He chuckled almost like he *expected* something to go wrong.

"What if they're waiting for you, and you're playing right into their hands?" she asked.

"So now you think they're smarter than they probably are?" he asked in return, amused.

Vee let go of his arm and shook her head. "I'm just saying we're safe here, right? They can't get to us if we're in your ship? It's impossible, I take it."

He cocked his head.

She threaded her fingers together in front of her. "How about we stay under the radar, away from them? Maybe if they're involved, they'll decide it's too much effort to try and go after us if they can't even get to us?"

Why did she care so much about him leaving?

"Vee, you're overreacting—"

She swallowed hard looking away.

"—but you don't know how terrible people can be," Cypher continued. "Think about what's happened in the last few weeks to achieve your dreams, even if most of what's happened wasn't your fault… Now imagine if you were someone else who knew full well what the repercussions are, and with a steadfast ambition, would do to achieve their dreams?"

"Don't go," she pleaded anyway, despite what he was telling her.

His face softened. "And when we do have to leave?"

"Then we'll play it safe, take extra precautions, and make it to the championship in one piece. If you do go out there and something does happen, it could be all over the network within minutes. It's not worth it, not this. You've been after restoring your anonymity this whole time…"

"You're worth it."

Her lips snapped closed.

"I won't leave," he grumbled.

Her mouth parted in relief. "Thank you."

"But you have to distract me."

"I—"

He reached up and rubbed a strand of her hair between his fingers. "Are you up for it?" His voice lowered, heated. "Rutting, if you're confused at all. Letting me have at your body the way my bear needs it? The way a man needs it?"

"I thought since I pushed you away…" She found it hard to continue.

In a niggling, remote part of her mind, she still couldn't believe Cypher wanted her. Maybe it wasn't Cypher that wanted her; maybe it was the mindless bear inside him. She shook her head before the thoughts could take root and worry her further.

"That I would leave you alone?" he growled. "The only thing I'm leaving alone is your raw pussy. There's no amount of healing ointment that'll heal you up after taking me as you have. You can push me away all you want—my cock will find its way back between your legs. Until our time has come to an end, that won't change, I assure you. Not unless you walk away. And a warning, Vee, if you do that, it'll be very, very hard for me to not try and stop you."

Her mouth fell open. One minute she was begging him to not leave and possibly commit murder, now his ferocity was aimed back at her. It was like whiplash after days of returning to a degree of normalcy. He removed it all from her in a hot minute.

"Like that Cyborg Zeph and the woman he abducted?" she whispered.

Cypher's body tensed. His big hands grasped her shoulders. "Exactly like that."

Blood raced through her veins. She believed him. He stared hard, pinning her with his strange eyes, and Vee gulped.

Did the protesters and anti-cyborg groups actually have a legitimate reason to be afraid?

Everything in her screamed at her to run. To leave now before things went any further between them. If she had learned one thing about Cypher in their time together, it was that he didn't lie.

He has all the power in the universe to take everything away from me.

Her heart thrummed, her body heating.

"Well, Vee, do you want to find out what lengths I'll go to to convince you to let me take you to bed?"

"No," she whispered.

A hungry expression crossed his face. "Good."

He flipped her around and pushed her to the wall, falling to his knees behind her. Vee caught herself and pressed her palms to the cool metal as Cypher reached around and unbuttoned her jeans, tugging them down her thighs in one swift movement. Her panties followed soon after.

His fingers pulled apart her cheeks, exposing her entirely from behind, and Vee jumped when his face fell upon her.

Cypher groaned thickly as her mind caught up to the onslaught.

Holding her open, he pulled her hips toward him, and his fingers surged inward to tease her sex. She jerked again. This time, he kept her still.

"Missed this," he rasped, his hot breath fanning her sex.

Then his fingers were inside her, scissoring and touching, his tongue licking her dewy skin. Her brow fell to the wall as a moan tore from her throat.

She ached for him, and she was certain he knew it because he laughed with her every twitch, her every plea.

"By the time our partnership comes to an end, you'll be taking me like a bear and not a man," he warned, plunging one finger in and out sharply. "Practice makes perfect, little spitfire."

She didn't want to think about their partnership coming to an end, but *oh*.

Oh.

Vee's nails scraped along the wall.

He rose and pressed his body up behind her, his fingers slowing between her legs to spread her out. With one arm wrapping around her front to play with her clit, the thick head of Cypher's cock nudged her opening. He dropped his fingers to her labia to caress it as his tip pushed inside her.

She braced—imagining him as a bear, churning with need from such an animalistic picture—as his cock spread her wider. A long-winded sound slipped from between her lips. His legs pressed to either side of hers, his body arched to spoon her smaller one from behind while his mouth rubbed across the back of her head.

He drove into her, taking her in one thrust, and Vee cried out as her feet lifted off the ground. Her pants and underwear dropped, forgotten to the floor.

Drawing back his hips, he viciously surged into her again, pinning her body fully to the wall. Fast and hard, he pumped into her. Vee lost herself to the primal noises the Cyborg made. He held her tight as she slipped up the wall.

Her feet hooked back around his calves to vie for a modicum of control when his body straightened to its full height and his tip pushed right into her sensitive inner flesh.

"Fucking come," he demanded, hitting that spot several more times more in quick succession. "Strangle me." Cypher pinched her clit with his fingers.

She tensed and screamed, her body helpless but to follow his orders. Palms sliding across the wall, she buckled, trapped, clamping, searching desperately for purchase.

"Yes!" Cypher wrapped both of his arms around her and pulled her back, pumping up into her violently.

His grunting turned to roars as he fucked her midair until his cock expanded and his seed gushed deep within. Her core pulsated, her orgasm unending.

Minutes passed as he came. Vee held onto the arms banded over her chest as he slowly spun them in a circle. Exhausted, she dropped her legs and closed her eyes.

When she opened them, she was back in the Terraform rig room, being carried to her chair.

With a grunt, and a gasp on her end, Cypher pulled out of her. Seed gushed out everywhere.

"Lovely," he rumbled, and an embarrassed, exhausted blush rose to her cheeks.

She watched weakly as he pulled up his pants and buckled them. Legs shaking, Vee grasped the back of her chair to hold herself up.

Cypher left and returned a moment later with a damp towel. And as if she were incapable, he cleaned her up, leaving no spot between her legs untouched. When he was done, she leaned forward and rested her head on the chair.

Sated, she relaxed as he massaged her backside and thighs. She couldn't even bring herself to care about how exposed she was anymore, feeling an ever-constant trickle of his seed drip out from her.

A small smile lifted her lips. *He still wants me.*

His warm hands deftly took away her tension.

"I like you," she whispered.

His hands paused before continuing. "I know. I like you, too."

Vee settled into the warm glow coursing through her and chose to, for once, live in the moment.

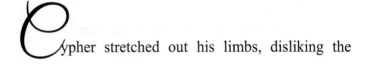

ypher stretched out his limbs, disliking the tight mesh that covered his body from head to toe. Vee insisted he join her in Terraform Zero, and he finally relented, especially when she changed into her skin-tight suit in front of him.

He hadn't initially wanted to—what he wanted most was to go after those who were after Vee—but seeing her excitement at the request and the hope in her eyes changed his mind.

The same excitement she had when she first saw the rig room. It continued to anger him that Nightheart had a leg up on him when it came to Vee's happiness.

He tensed at the possibility that if Nightheart wanted her, would he be able to take her away from him? Would she go with the other Cyborg if she had a choice?

If Nightheart tried…

Cypher would make do on his promise and kill the bastard. Fuck, he'd kill a lot more than just Nightheart if anything got in his way now. He'd tear the motherfucker limb from limb and scatter Nightheart's metal frame from one end of the universe to the other. Anything leftover, Cypher would ship to the aliens to do with what they pleased. Total annihilation.

She's in my fucking cave. His bear rumbled internally as he eyed her repositioning her chair outside her rig. It would take an army to get her away from him now.

I'm not a good man.

He wanted to rip a hole in her suit and take her again. He wanted to spread her legs and fill her with his seed. He wanted to claim her like the dozens of times he already had. It was never enough, and he was afraid it would never be enough.

The plates inside readied to shift.

I should've stayed within Ghost. If he had, none of this aggression would be plaguing him right now. *But then...if I had, Vee wouldn't have someone to look out for her.*

He also didn't want her to know that hundreds of people had gathered outside the spaceport to demand his arrest, or that the media had spun her sponsorship contract as being dropped by the EPED for *'insubordination'* and *'bad publicity.'* She'd barely logged into her media account since he turned it back on, and keeping her distracted—keeping *both* of them distracted—was in their best interest.

He turned away and moved his chair outside his rig setup as well. Every day he prayed—*prayed!*—for his rut to end. Perhaps once it did, he'd have full control over his mind again and could get back to business.

A bear's rut was supposed to produce offspring, but he had no intention of impregnating Vee. Not right now, at least. Perhaps that's why his rut continued and grew worse with each passing day.

But fucking her to oblivion wouldn't help either one of them.

"You'll need to log into your personal IP and network and make an account. Afterward, I'll send you an invite to join my team," Vee chirped, having no idea about the chaos going on a short distance away from her. She began to attach the straps of the rig to her suit.

The smell of sex still lingered in the room. He'd lathered her with ointment and healed her each time after he took her—and he'd taken her as often as he could, hoping it would be the last he'd need to do so. But the need remained unending. The swell of her butt and the curves of her petite body made his hands twitch to play.

Even during wartime, amid battle rage, he'd been able to numb himself out to a point. He couldn't now.

Something inside him was against it to the core of his being.

"All right," he said, barely keeping the want from his voice. He tied back his hair and shoved on his visor. He completed the account process in less than a minute and found her tag, Vee_Miles. He shot her a request. "Cypher_Cyborg," he muttered.

Creativity wasn't part of his makeup.

Vee's invite came immediately, and within moments, her profile, her life's work flooded the virtual space all around him.

Planets swirled, bright and beautiful, all different. When he focused on one, lists of stats came up belonging to them. This virtual space was nothing like seeding into the network's systems that he and his brethren could do. No, this was beautiful, another dimension entirely.

Vee popped up beside him, and her avatar, which looked nearly the same as how she looked in person except for one change, stunned him. Her vibrant red hair had burning embers along her strands. It was how he imagined it in his fantasies—truly on fire. He reached out and touched it, surprised there was sensation—silk and heat—coming from the glove of his suit.

Undeterred, Vee slipped away. He tried to catch her, but she fell through his grip this time.

A surge of anxiety tore through him.

"These are my planets," she said, once again not noticing his turmoil. "Some I've completed with success, some are from competitions that I've retired, and the few dozen in the back are ones I've failed, and sometimes failed again in trying to colonize without mass death." She chuckled.

His hand slipped through her again. "Why can't I touch you now?"

"I told my suit to dematerialize. It scans and senses what you're thinking—if it knows you well enough. And these suits"—she spun around—"are amazing! I've never worn something so accurate and sensitive."

Cypher dropped his hand. "Right. Can I fuck you in them?"

She stopped spinning. "I…"

He chuckled. "Perhaps we'll find out later."

Wide-eyed and blushing, she nodded. A coy smile tilted her lips for a second.

Hell, she's so easy to toy with. He'd had her many times now, but had also not allowed her to explore him back. When he took her, he took her completely. He couldn't do it any other way.

If anyone tries to take her away from me again...

His mood darkened.

Vee swallowed thickly. "Well…let me introduce you to my greatest passion."

She turned away from him, always unaware of this predatory nature. It only emphasized how innocent she was and how bad of a Cyborg he was for taking advantage of her and not finding a better substitute for his fever.

Greatest passion… He knew what his greatest passion was currently.

For the next several hours, Vee went through the basics of the game, which he knew instinctively but enjoyed her excitement in explaining. The happiness in her voice calmed him.

And as the hours passed by, he was surprised how much she took his mind off of everything when it was he who wanted to shield her.

When the basics were finished, and what was considered a 'game' ended, the real tactical draw began. From weather patterns to agriculture, to bodies of water, to accessibility, the game had everything. His mind took it all in and stored it away, but it was Vee's fascination and depth of knowledge about every aspect that floored him.

The eagerness in her voice, and the passion she showed for it all enlivened him. It wasn't even a job to her, but she took it as seriously as one. Like how he took his job seriously on Ghost.

It was beautiful.

Cypher silently listened as Vee brought up her planets and explained their draws and drawbacks. After lingering in a login hub for hours, they spiraled 'planetside,' and he could've sworn he felt the give of grass beneath his boots.

Grass. Real fucking grass. When was the last time he'd been on grass? Had he ever? He checked his databases and couldn't come to a firm conclusion.

Fucking grass.

"Yria is one of my favorites," she said as he kneeled to run his hand over the ground in awe. The sound of waves was somewhere off in the distance. "It's been a challenge, though, what with the lack of landmass and the sentient lifeform already here. And several human colonists have STDs from laying with the aliens."

He rubbed a blade between his fingers. "Can you give them medicine? Have you run any tests?"

"Not yet. It's hard to land here, and I currently only have a finite amount of supplies. The aliens are far more primitive than we are. They fear the tech. They don't fully trust me yet."

"Have they gotten sick, or just the humans?"

"Not that I know of, and if they have, they probably won't let me near them with a needle without me risking death. If I die—which does happen—that puts me back quite a bit."

Cypher stood, looking around. A breeze lifted his hair and ruffled the leaves of the trees nearby. There was chirping coming from among their branches. It was all so real. "Then why bother?"

"If we all die, then it's a failure. My death is the only one I can reconfigure." Vee laughed. "The point of the game is to reach the goals set out from the beginning, and how to solve the problems on the way—in the best way possible."

"Then all you can do is make your colonists aware of the situation and give them what medical treatment you can. If they choose to continue to sleep with the aliens, that's up to them. If the aliens refuse help, don't press it, unless your people begin to die. Diseases aren't easy. Species relations less so."

Vee sighed. "I know. It's just sucked since getting here in the first place was hard. Relations with the aliens residing here was hard in the beginning, and now this… They have the numbers to wipe us out if they want to."

"And then there'd be war. Look at what happened with us and the Trentians." Cypher waved his hand. "We killed each other indiscriminately for nearly a hundred years, even though we could communicate and understand each other's customs. Unless the beings of Yria are inherently peaceful, crossbreeding may be the only way to ensure future relations. Get the data you can from those humans who are infected, and hope you can make a cure. Otherwise…" He shrugged. "Why bother? Move to a different area on the planet."

Vee stared at him pointedly. "You're right. But we bother because it's important. Yria, if we can establish ourselves on it, will provide food, resources, knowledge, and of course water, for our people who dwell in space. And a much-needed station and haven in this galaxy for people and aliens in distress. There's no other stop within galaxies from Yria. But it's the water that's most important. There's an abundance here."

"It's fake."

"It doesn't have to be. Yeah, Yria is an AI-generated planet in Terraform, but there are water worlds out there like this one. Someday we may not have a choice but to land on one, and having data like this"—Vee flicked her finger and dozens of screens came up around her—"would be invaluable. It's only a matter of successfully establishing a colony now, and an infrastructure."

"And if the Yria aliens want to keep their home to themselves?"

She slumped a little at his question, like she'd been worried about that for a while. "Then we go back to diplomacy, and if that doesn't work…a different, less viable location on the planet. I refuse to take what isn't mine. I refuse to kill or war unless it's in self-defense."

"Hmm." Cypher glanced around, enjoying the simulated wind on his skin and the wildness around him a little too much. "It's beautiful."

"It is. I love this world. I've been to many, from frigid planets to rocky asteroids with nebula views, but this one… This one makes me desperate."

"Desperate?"

"To win. To go out into the universe and see it for real. To experience, for the first time in my entire life, a place like this, untouched by man and industry— pollution. Something pure and untamed and unlike what I've always been around." She smiled. "Being here virtually is one thing, but I can't imagine what it'd be like for real."

Cypher's lips did the unthinkable and smiled to match hers. He couldn't help it. Listening to her talk about the wilds his bear loved made him happy. More than anything, he wanted to make sure she saw places like this in real life and experience them.

He missed the wilds. He missed the open air, the breeze across his skin, and the freedom. He'd denied himself so much for so many years.

It had been his choice to sequester within Ghost City for years, but he never really thought about the freedom he had behind that choice. Especially when there were probably hundreds of millions of people who were as desperate as Vee was to have an inkling of choice. If you were born off Earth, it was easy, and if you managed to leave it, as long as you didn't come back, nothing much could stop you from staying away.

And women... Ever since the war, they've had it worse. A lot worse.

Trentians were after them. The Earth government sought to hoard them and keep them far away from the aliens, and because of that, their rights were stripped. They had pretenses of equality, could still get jobs in the military, and jobs on other worlds, but it was always through the government itself or a corporation that worked through the government like the EPED—or a rare, special license.

"You'll see it," he said, moving to Vee's side and taking her hand. He vowed he would give her this gift.

She looked up at him, hope in her eyes. "You really think so?"

"Fuck yeah, because we're going to win." He pulled her virtual body into his chest, banding his arms around her. And he felt her, all of her, even though he knew she was strapped in a rig a half-dozen paces away from him. He'd missed so much, he realized.

A dark, possessive, and strange sensation spiraled through his body and clamped around his heart. A feeling that surged when Vee softened in his embrace. And with it, the bloodthirsty fury he'd also held for those who tried to take her away from him.

Cypher rested his mouth upon Vee's fiery hair.

But this…

This moment with her I'm not going to miss out on.

His vengeance could wait.

20

*T*he next couple of weeks passed by without incident. She and Cypher fell into a routine of practicing for the championship and spending time together—whether it was sex or otherwise. Even Bees fell into a routine. Each morning, Vee would find him sleeping on Cypher's chair on the bridge. Next, he'd follow her into the lounge where she fed him. Afterward, she'd take him to the menagerie enclosure of cat trees and walkways and watched him play and explore.

A kitty paradise.

Cypher put a sensory band on Bees' collar to allow her cat to wander the ship without incident. There were few places he couldn't go. That, and the premium cat food in the replicator, made Bees a very happy feline.

For a time, Vee relished the privacy they had. Their little makeshift bubble. The ship made her feel safe. And when she woke up at night, frightened that someone was dragging her away, Cypher was always there to calm her down, petting her body, and assuring her she was safe—safer than anyone in all the universe.

He'd been a lifeline, one she unwittingly grown accustomed to.

It made her nervous. It made her toes curl. It made her hug him close at night with the threat that she may never let go.

Time was running out. *Their* time was running out.

The championship was a little over two weeks away, and the semi-final was in three days.

Vee scraped her fork across her plate, pushing her scrambled eggs back and forth.

Cypher walked into the lounge with Bees under his arm and programmed a coffee in the replicator. The smell flooded her nostrils—the scent was amped up by the boosters he added so his body could *feel* a buzz.

She glimpsed his expression, and once again, it was unreadable. She frowned but hid it by taking a bite of egg. He sat across from her and sipped his drink.

He watched her, staring hard like he often did, and it always made her self-conscious. Vee took another bite of egg as her palms slickened under his scrutiny.

One would think that after weeks of sharing a bed with the Cyborg, she'd be used to his perusal.

But she wasn't.

The intimidation he made her feel persisted.

I don't belong with him. It was that thought alone that kept her unsettled. She couldn't quite convince herself that this wasn't all an elaborate dream, and that she was going to wake up at any second.

I don't want to wake up.

Vee looked down at her plate.

"We've been called to NeoElite's headquarters," Cypher said. NeoElite was the gaming company that owned Terraform Zero and funded the championship each year.

"We have?" She frowned, swiping on her wristcon. Lo and behold, there was a message waiting for her from NeoElite. She skimmed the material. She and Cypher, and all competitors and teams participating in the event, were required to officially sign in and meet with the managers tomorrow.

They were to be given the scenario for the semi-final event for the following day. A lead-up that would directly relate to what was given for the championship.

It's happening. Vee shut off her network access. She looked up to find Cypher still staring at her.

She crossed her legs.

"So we leave tomorrow," she said. A shadow of something darkened his expression for a split-second, but it was gone before she could read into it.

"Seems so," he rumbled.

"In two weeks, this will all be over," she whispered.

He didn't respond. He only looked at her.

Vee licked her lips. "Thank you for everything."

"Stop thanking me."

"I can't. I won't stop thanking you."

Cypher gulped down his coffee and got up. At the door, he glanced back at her, as if he hadn't heard her. "Are you coming?"

She nodded and stood, following behind him as he strode toward the rig room.

They spent the day in her game. But unlike all the others, the disquiet between them continued.

One of the Yria aliens gave birth today, and though they didn't need to be present for it, they were. Despite everything that had happened on the planet, even the potential of a disease outbreak, Yria was nearly finished and deemed a success.

She should be happy, excited, pleased, but she wasn't. All she could think about was her time with Cypher would soon be over.

Her favorite planet had become *their* planet. And like everything else, it was coming to an end.

When evening came around, she was exhausted. Not even an alien baby, her first one ever, had lifted her mood. Not even seeing Cypher holding it in his arms and checking its health with a delicacy that didn't belong to him lightened her heart. Instead, her mood had grown heavier.

Then it hit her, when she stripped from her suit and put it away to be sanitized overnight, that she was going to miss him.

She picked up her jeans and shirt and clutched them to her chest. Her gaze followed the powerful muscles rippling across Cypher's back as he pulled off his shirt.

I'm in trouble.

She was going to miss this, and him, and there was nothing she could do now to stop it from happening. He would be leaving Earth to be Nightheart's errand boy. Their paths would diverge, and there was no way to stop it. Vee rushed from the room, escaping into the bathroom, and dove under the shower before her tears had a chance to fall.

He'd know if she was crying. He knew everything.

Who am I kidding? I'm going to more than miss him. Vee wiped her face even as the water fell upon her. She didn't want any evidence of her tears to show.

The door to the bathroom opened. "Vee?"

"Yeah?" *Please go away.*

"You okay?"

"I'm fine! Just needed a shower."

The stall door opened, and Cypher stepped in. Naked and powerful, he filled the space, and she willed her heart to numb. His eyes met hers as the water drenched them both, and he cupped her face with his hands, forcing her to look at him. Warmth rushed through her, alongside a terrible aching yearning.

"You can't hide from me," he said.

"I wasn't hiding."

His lips twitched. "Tomorrow will be fine. I promise. We'll be fine."

She blinked. *He thinks I'm worried about tomorrow?* In a way, she was, but her worry was overshadowed by the thoughts of losing him.

He's my first. He'd ruined her for all other men. No one could possibly compare to the hero who stood before her, who blocked the water from landing on her face from above.

"Yeah." Vee forced a smile. "We'll be fine."

Cypher's eyes flashed, numbers coursed across his pupils, uncannily beautiful, and her heart wrenched a little further. She lifted her hands to grab his wrists. He leaned down and kissed her, and she rose on her toes to meet him even though her heart was breaking.

Long and slow, and full of adoration, she relayed her feelings into the kiss. *Love.* She tried to tell him she loved him. She couldn't say it. She didn't have the courage, at least not yet. But she did everything she could to show it.

Her lips softened beneath his, and their tongues met as they took turns teasing and playing, discovering each other under the cloak of steam. Fresh and thirsty, she drank all she could from him, and she was so very thirsty.

When he pulled away, she was weak with dehydration.

That night he didn't make love to her despite her efforts. She opened herself up to him, curled around his large body, and he did nothing more than kiss her. Vee had no idea how to take it—she just kept her tears welled up inside. She needed him inside her, but he wouldn't have it.

She lay awake in his arms until Bees cried for breakfast and the following day began.

He's   already   gone.

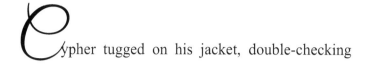

ypher tugged on his jacket, double-checking the firearms secured to the vest—two guns small enough to be hidden but powerful enough to get the job done lay beneath it.

Whether it was to warn, to maim, or to kill.

The assault rifles, snipers, and even his star magnum remained behind. If his beast couldn't do what a gun couldn't, then he didn't deserve to be a Cyborg.

In the back of his mind was his first acquisition from the EPED.

It was his first job from Nightheart, sent to him from Mia, who had become Cypher's contact instead of Vee's. Mia was the contact for all the Monster Hunting Retrievers who worked for the EPED.

He escorted Vee from the *Repossessed* for the first time since they arrived weeks ago. His back tingled as she stepped off the ship, his hands clenched at his sides. She was leaving his den, and his bear didn't like it. *He* didn't like it.

Cypher went on full alert, scanning the airfield.

Having Vee all to himself had healed parts of him he didn't know were broken. He'd never looked forward to being near someone until her, and now that she was always around, he'd grown used to it. The more time he spent in her company, the less he wanted to return to his isolation.

And that shocked him. Nearly sixty years of enjoying solitude were erased in a few short months. He found comfort in her presence and had a new outlook on life.

It burned him knowing that Nightheart might've been right. Not that Cypher would ever admit it to him or anyone else, but the Cyborg fucker who was now his boss might know a thing or two about the real world that Cypher didn't.

On another docket Mia had sent him was his option to hire a crew for his ship. At first, he had ignored the suggestion but now... Now he wasn't sure.

He pulled Vee against his side and leaned down to sniff her hair. *Do I want others, or do I only want you?* She leaned into him, and the wires in his chest vibrated and blazed. *I only want you.*

His first acquisition, which would send him to Kepler of all places, was due to start the day after the championship. Less than twenty-four hours after the game. He only had two weeks left of this to deal with, and he could be away from Earth, enjoying a sense of freedom once more.

But there was one small hitch.

Her.

The EPED's private airfield was empty except for a few engineers who left them alone. Instead of heading back up to the spaceport above, he had an EPED hover vehicle delivered down to them for safety. The other stolen one had been reclaimed by its owner, and he'd transferred funds to the man to apologize for its theft.

Vee settled into her seat, and Cypher closed her door. Was it sorrow he saw on her face? His lips twisted. He couldn't be sure. But fuck was she beautiful. *Two more weeks.*

His need to dominate and control her every move hadn't faded, and he believed it was because of how innocent she was. His hands shook to grab her against him again, to ruffle her up, to watch her eyes widen, and then rut her into a gasping, sweaty mess against the side of the vehicle in view of everyone who might be around.

Yet she'd still be cute after all that. He wanted to ruin her cuteness, to make her look like she'd been well loved so everyone would know she belonged to him. His chest tightened each time the urge came on.

She'd wanted to sleep with him last night, and he'd denied her. Cypher scrubbed a hand down his face. It'd been a hard night. How could he take advantage of her when he was planning on leaving?

I'll steal her. The thought burned in his mind. *I'll take her with me.* Darkness rose within him. *She'll have no place to run once we're in space. She'll be all mine, all the time, and I'll never be alone again.*

Thoughts like these plagued him. Hourly.

When did I become so fucking obsessed?

Moving to the driver's side, Cypher groaned, adjusted his dick, and ducked in. Earth vehicles barely fit him, but he managed.

He inhaled deeply, needing Vee's scent to calm him, but it wasn't there. Instead, he smelled himself—on her—and it overpowered her wild candy sweetness. Cypher rumbled. The loss of her scent was bittersweet.

But damn, did he like that she smelled of him.

Two weeks.

Two weeks to devour her and get her out of my systems before I do something dangerous.

He was on the path to becoming Zeph. Cypher anticipated speaking to the other Cyborg now that there was a connection between him and the crocodile.

Vee twisted her hands in her lap, pulling Cypher from his thoughts, and he shot the hovercraft into the sky. The stifling silence continued between them.

He knew she was worried, but he didn't know the best way to comfort her. He was beginning to believe there was something else on her mind other than her safety.

Bypassing the crowds, he sped to join the nearest airway and headed it toward NeoElite's headquarters in the city.

"You okay?" he asked, the silence getting on his nerves.

"Yeah."

"Why are you quiet then?"

"I'm thinking."

"About what?"

"About the semi-finals tomorrow."

He waited for her to say more, but she didn't. Before he could question her further, their destination came into view. His brow furrowed.

They were ushered into an indoor lot lower on the high-rise, and the second he powered off the vehicle, Vee was already out of the hovercraft and approaching the nearby attendant. Cypher growled and moved to her side, taking her arm.

She stiffened but didn't pull away.

They were led inside and through a bright, colorful building. On the walls were posters of past championships and players everywhere. Screens played back the latest footage of the Terraform game, including trailers for future updates. There were plaques and trophies, and every person they encountered thrummed with excitement.

Some gave them side-eye looks, and some scurried away as they passed by, but no one said anything and no one engaged either him or Vee.

Put in a lounge laid out with food and alcohol, others stood around eating and drinking. He recognized some of the other Terraform Zero teams. He'd studied them all.

Cypher surveyed the small gathering for Diatrix and found her talking to another participant in the back. He'd taken a step forward when Vee planted her feet and refused to come with him.

"Don't," she said. "Let's just focus on the game, not on her."

Cypher tore his gaze from Diatrix, fighting a snarl. "I can't do that."

Vee reached up and cupped his cheek. "Yes, you can."

He grumbled.

"Do this for me," Vee pleaded.

"If she tries anything, she's dead."

Vee gulped but smiled. It was her smile that stopped him from needing to feel his gun in his hand, from extending his claws.

"Fine, but do it after the championship, okay? You're such a bear."

Cypher flexed his fingers and released Vee's arm. "There won't be time—" His lips flattened when he realized what he was about to say.

Vee's eyes narrowed. "What?"

"Never mind. Want a drink?" Cypher stormed away before she could question him further.

There wouldn't be time because after the championship, he was leaving.

She won't be safe if I'm not around.

His jaw ticked as he grabbed two beers and bit off the caps with his teeth. *I'll make sure she's protected.* He handed one to Vee, who studied him with obvious worry in her eyes. *Goddamn it!*

A well-dressed man entered the room, saving him.

"Hello everyone! Thank you for coming today. As you know, not everyone can make it in person. Some are still traveling to get here or have prior engagements, but they will be here later today."

Everyone stopped chatting and turned to face the speaker.

The man continued, "My name is Derek Johansburg, and I'm the lead designer for Terraform Zero 19, which will hopefully be on the market sometime in the next twelve years."

Vee gasped. Cheers and claps filled the room.

Cypher slid his gaze to Vee to see the excitement on her face. Envy flooded him.

Derek waved his hand. "But none of that matters because the yearly championship is right around the corner, and we're expecting record viewership for the semi-finals leading up to it."

"When will we receive the planet's summary?" someone interjected.

"In a few minutes. But first, I'd like to go over the rules." Derek's eyes landed on Cypher but darted away. "Not only is this our first year with an all-female team, but we also have a renowned Cyborg in our gaming ranks. One we had no idea even played our dear Terraform Zero. The staff and I are abuzz with excitement! The viewership is going crazy. Unprecedentedly so... So I must reiterate what is expected from all of you talented people—and machines—while representing our prestigious community tomorrow and the championship following..."

Derek's features turned stony. "There will be no fighting between teams inside the stadium or outside. Keep your shit to yourself and your hands off each other." Derek glared at Cypher again while he said the last part.

Cypher's jaw ticked.

"There will be no changes or leniency on the rules. If you hurt your leg and can't get into the rig, too bad. There will be no sharing the planet design once it's been given to you. The planet has a slight change in model for each team and will be easily traced back to whoever it's been leaked from. That team, or person, will be disqualified immediately and will be ineligible to participate in any future Terraform events, local, national, or otherwise. If you cheat, we'll know. Don't fucking cheat. If you're caught cheating, not only will you be disqualified but we'll ruin your chances of ever finding a job in the colonization field. This may be a game to you, but whoever wins will potentially have hundreds of thousands of lives put in their hands."

Derek straightened. "And lastly, have fun, give it your all, and be animated. If you're boring to watch, then our cameras won't give you any media time, which could destroy your chances of future opportunities. Our sponsors like a good show. They fund the system and keep this ball rolling so we can all enjoy its outcome. If our sponsors are unhappy, we're unhappy. Are we all clear?"

Several people mumbled and agreed. Others laughed. Cypher glanced down at Vee beside him and frowned. She was smiling again, despite Derek's shit, and he wanted to shake her.

She's too good for this.

Derek's fake excitement returned. "Everyone, check your NeoElite login!"

There was a rush of movement and murmurings, followed by intense silence. Vee held her wrist in front of her as her screens popped up.

An image of a planet appeared. Audio was suggested so Vee turned hers on when others in the room did.

"Welcome to Laprencia, a planet discovered outside the Andromeda Galaxy. With its unique location and high volume of water, the Earth government has greenlit it for colonization efforts. With one ocean and an abundant landmass, Laprencia is ideal for not only colonization efforts, but also ideal for a military base, an intergalactic port, and has the potential for mining resources.

"Upon initial readings, the environment is safe for humans, and gravity is similar to that of Earth. Clear weather patterns can be viewed from space, with a cycle around its nearby sun to be approximately forty-two hours.

"The one immediate drawback, and what must be achieved for the semi-finals of this year's Terraform Zero games, which will either give you an advantage or disadvantage for the finals, is that Trentian aliens have already begun to colonize this same planet. The

Andromeda Galaxy is owned by humans, but Laprencia is on the edge and could be argued that it is out of human jurisdiction. It would make a great diplomatic port for the aliens. The choices you make as a team will either ensure progression to colonize, or could start a war.

"Good luck.

"We wish you the best from the staff of Terraform Zero 18 and 19."

The audio ended and was replaced with silence. Cypher frowned. *Trentians.* The idea of encountering one, even a fake one, made his systems surge. Though there'd been hard-won peace between the species for several generations, he and all Cyborgs couldn't alter the deep codes of animosity they held for them.

He had been programmed to eradicate Trentians, been programmed to win a war that humans were threatened with losing. Logically, he had moved on from that time, but his coding hadn't. And no amount of updates could suppress them enough to numb him completely.

Diplomacy with Trentians? He sneered. *I'd rather destroy them.*

A different, darkening hunger bloomed within him at the prospect. One he couldn't control, try as he might. Cypher's hands fisted.

Vee stood mutely, staring at the slowly spinning planet in the hologram before her.

Did she know this might happen? The way she gazed at the planet made him think she didn't.

He glimpsed the others, and it seemed many shared the same concerned expressions.

"Now that all of you have received your quest, on behalf of myself and the Terraform Zero organizers, we suggest you get a good night's sleep tonight in preparation for the event tomorrow. We wish you well, and oodles of luck. The universe will be watching. That includes potential future employers and our Trentian fans." Derek turned to leave, and a clamor of people moved to stop him and ask questions.

Cypher put his hand over Vee's wristcon. "Let's get out of here."

"Yes," she whispered.

As he was leading her out of the room, they were stopped by Diatrix.

"What do you want?" Vee asked, narrowing her eyes at the woman.

Diatrix smiled. "Oh, Vee Miles, you're so cute! I'd never forgive myself if I missed you—"

"Did you hire the cretin who nearly kidnapped Vee?" Cypher interjected.

"I have no idea what you're talking about. I only came to wish you two good luck tomorrow."

"You do know. I know everything there is about you," Cypher warned. "I know who you're affiliated with."

Diatrix's smile wavered. "Is that a threat?"

"Yes."

"What a shame. I was hoping that all this anti-cyborg sentiment was only spewed from idiots. Perhaps they're right." She shrugged, tossing her ponytail back. She pressed her finger to Cypher's chest. "I would think a machine who'd been subjugated by men would have different views, but it seems you're just like they are. Terrible. I can't wait to see how you handle the Trentians. Oh, the bloodbath. I couldn't have asked for a more exciting challenge. Guess this means we won't have to worry that you'll cheat." She grinned.

He slapped her finger away. "Come near Vee again and you're dead, understand? I don't give a crap about you or your views, or this charade for all that matters—"

"Cypher!" Vee tried to stop him but he continued.

"Life and death are all that matters. Get the fuck away from us before I do something only you'll regret."

Diatrix stepped back. Her eyes sharpened, and she shivered with rage despite her forced smile. Cypher led Vee down the hall.

"We could've been allies," Diatrix called.

He stopped, turned back around, and flashed his gun. "Cyborgs don't have allies. Take a history class, human. It might do you some good."

He had Vee stashed away back in the hovercraft within minutes and took to the air. Gritting his teeth, his seething only grew worse. She was tense beside him, but he couldn't calm his systems down.

By the time they made it back to his ship, he was enraged. The second the hatch closed, he tore his jacket off and stormed to his arsenal. Pulling a gun from his vest, he shot rounds into the wall at the back. Each weapon he emptied, he grabbed another, until holes littered the metal.

It wasn't enough.

He threw his weapon aside and slammed his fist into the wall, again and again, until the metal panels gave way, and nothing but smoke filled his nostrils. Sparks came from the exposed wires behind.

"Cypher," Vee whispered behind him.

He twisted around, baring his fangs at her. She stumbled back.

"Leave me!" he roared.

She backed up, turned, and ran away.

He   transformed.

he next morning, Vee fed Bees, who she'd kept locked in her cabin all night against Bees's will. Crashes, booms, and guttural roars came from outside her door throughout the night. She didn't dare intervene, hoping Cypher would calm down eventually and come to her.

He hadn't.

Even when the noises stopped, he didn't join her. And when she snuck out to find him, all she found was the panel doors to the ship's bridge closed, and no way for her to get in.

For the second night in a row, he hadn't lain with her.

She stared at herself in the mirror and combed her hair, studying her body. She looked tired, a little haggard, and even the gleam of her red hair seemed dull. Sleep? What sleep? She spent most of last night fidgeting in bed.

Vee sagged forward.

Is there something wrong with me?

Is Cypher's rut over? Had he only lain with her because of it? He had grown distant and increasingly angry, and she was at a loss as to what to do to help him.

Despite the semi-finals starting in a few short hours, it barely mattered at all anymore. Not even with the added stress of Trentian involvement. Vee worried that she'd grown to care far more for Cypher than he ever would for her.

God, I'm fucked.

She pressed her hands to her chest, certain she'd feel cracks beneath her palms. She stood there for a time, wishing her emotions were tangible and that she could trap them away deep within.

Damn him. She chewed on her lip.

With a long, shuddering breath, Vee straightened, rubbed color into her cheeks, and left the room—with Bees following at her heels. It didn't take long before she found Cypher waiting for her in the back of the ship in front of the open hatch. He was gazing out over the docked vessels in the field. Folded over his left arm was both of their gamer suits.

Her heartbeat increased. Her toes curled.

"Good morning," she whispered. Though she wanted nothing more than to bombard him with questions, to ask about the noises last night, and most of all, to ask why he was pulling away, she kept her words locked inside.

"Morning. You ready?" he asked.

"I think so."

"Good. Let's go." He stepped off the ship.

Vee licked her lips and followed him. Tension radiated off of him.

A few minutes later, they were sailing through the airways at breakneck speeds and requesting docking permits at the virtual world stadium. Her heart thrummed when it came into view.

This was happening. *It's really happening.*

When they landed, they were greeted by a rep who ushered them into a private waiting room that overlooked the stadium.

Vee moved to the window and shivered. It hit her like a truck. Today was the semi-finals. It was here. Despite everything, time had continued throughout it all.

People filtered into the seating spaces on every side, carrying signs and wearing the colors of their favorite teams. She pressed her hands to the glass when she saw people in *her* colors, with images of her and Cypher on their chests.

"Oh, God…" she muttered.

Cypher stepped up next to her and joined her looking out. "Looks like it's going to be packed."

"We're ready, right?"

"Yes, and even if we weren't, it's too late now."

Vee curled her fingers. *Oh, God! I'm not ready. I'm not ready!* Cypher had been too much of a distraction.

His hand came down on her head. "You'll be fine."

She twisted away with a terrified squeak. "We haven't even discussed what we're going to do about the Trentians!"

Cypher's face hardened. "Whatever is necessary."

"Oh my God, we're going to lose." She was going to hyperventilate.

"They've never added a stipulation like that in any of the past games," Cypher muttered, following her back into the room. "I uploaded and studied them all into my head last night."

"I know," she said on an exhale. "The game's never gone there before…" It didn't make her feel any better; it only made everything worse. "Are you going to be okay?" she asked, glancing up at him.

"We'll see."

Oh, God.

The next hour went by in a blur, she and Cypher changed into the gear and waited in silence. His mood progressively darkened, and his eyes faded. She knew he was somewhere off in his head, doing whatever Cyborgs did, and she couldn't bring herself to disturb him. Nerves seized her.

When the intercom went off, and distant cheers filled her ears, she jumped from her seat in a panic. An attendant came and fetched them, and they were led down to the stadium floor where thirteen rigs were set up, some bigger than others to accommodate larger teams.

Adrenaline surged through every cell in her body. *This is it.*

I can do this.

I can't do this!

Straight across from her was Deadly Dearest and Diatrix. The other woman gave her a chilling smile and waved to her, but then the cheers boomed and the teams began to be introduced to the crowd.

Her and Cypher's name were called third, and *boos* mingled with the cheers. Cypher grabbed her hand and held it up between them. The *boos* grew louder but so did the cheers. Anxiety threatened to drown out any courage she had left.

Cypher helped her into her rig, and she let him. An electric numbness took over. After he grabbed her visor and set it on her head, he leaned down, startling her further. His face blocked out everything else.

"Remember, you're not alone. I'm here with you all the way. No matter what happens, I'm here." His lips brushed her brow.

"I'm glad you're here," she whispered.

He smiled, and her heart melted. She leaned into him. It was a stolen moment of reprieve.

"We're a team," he said.

"Yes. The greatest team."

"Let's land on Laprencia and show the world what we're made of. What *you're* made of."

His words calmed her some. Vee nodded. "Yes!"

Cypher pulled away, tucked a strand of hair behind her ear, and turned and strode to his rig. He attached the straps around his muscled frame. When he was finished, he winked at her and pulled his visor down.

A huge hologram surged up above them, showing their championship virtual login and the planet spinning in the background. Similar screens emerged atop the other teams' rigs. Inhaling, Vee tugged her own visor over her face. The technology scanned her pupils, and she appeared next to Cypher.

Unlike her change of hair, he looked the same as he did in real life. A fantastical space warrior.

She could hear Derek's voice as she approached Cypher's digital side. "Today we begin the 317th Annual Terraform Zero Semi-Finals!"

Cheers erupted. Cypher took her hand. Derek went on introducing Laprencia to the crowd, ending on the Trentian involvement. Cypher's grip on her hand tightened at the mention of them.

When Derek was done, the turquoise and green planet before her unlocked, and another wave of cheers sounded. This was it.

Adrenaline zinged through her body.

She had no idea what to expect, but she was prepared. She knew she was prepared. The beginning of a new game was the best part.

The most exciting.

"Here we go…" she said, moving forward.

The screen flickered before she could jump to the planet's orbit. She frowned. That was different. Sometimes she started on space stations in the past, but never this.

Within the next moment, she and Cypher were on a strange ship with battle-clad Trents surrounding them, poising laser spears and aiming guns at their persons. Vee froze as Cypher jerked out his weapon.

Confused, Vee looked around. *This isn't right.*

A silver-clad alien wearing a horned helmet stepped between the guards surrounding them with pale eyes that looked flamed with white fire. From head to toe, his armor gleamed white-silver, covering every inch of his body.

She inhaled, annoyed, but kept her emotions in check. *People are watching us.*

"I am Commander Lotrin, a Knight of Xanteaus, and you have trespassed in airspace claimed by my people. Who are you, and what business do you have here, humans…?" Lotrin hissed the last word. His eyes pinned her.

She'd never been this close to a real Trentian before, not even a half-breed. Until yesterday's announcement, the Trentians had never been in any Terraform Zero game. Near-mesmerized by the sight, she swallowed.

Cypher inserted himself in front of her as Lotrin took a step toward her. "Back off," he warned. Cypher's nails vanished, and metal claws appeared.

Vee put her hand on his arm to calm him. "It's not real, remember?"

"I can smell him."

She frowned. "And you can feel my hand. Doesn't make it real. He's only code backed up by game AI."

Lotrin looked at them curiously, and though she was unnerved by all the weapons pointed at her and the alien's strange expressions, she kept her cool.

Slowly, Cypher eased, and Vee moved next to him.

"Commander Lotrin," she began, keeping her voice level, "we don't believe we are trespassing. This planet is not under either human or Trentian jurisdiction. And if it were, it could arguably be under human law."

"Is that so?" Lotrin said. "I never understood how a people could claim an entire galaxy. It matters not. We have arrived to settle."

Vee's face scrunched. "Under space law—"

"Created by your kind. Not mine."

"That *your* diplomats and ours have created together after the war, these worlds between our galaxies are open to all if they are not under either government's domain. We are not trespassing. Please lower your weapons. We can work together."

Lotrin scowled, and the heat of his hatred singed her soul. Her stomach sank.

This is a game. This isn't real.

Why does it feel real?

Vee's heart raced as she waited for the Trentian's next move—with their creepy, almost ghostly presence—knowing they could kill her at any moment. If that happened…

Minutes ago, she was nervous about going in front of a crowd. That all seemed like dust in her mind when compared to Lotrin and his men.

This isn't Terraform Zero. Not once, ever, had she started colonizing a world with the threat of death. The game wasn't about that. Vee slid her hand back into Cypher's.

Is this a set-up? Derek's words came back to her—sponsors, money, entertainment—even the political climate and Cypher being a player. She frowned.

Lotrin's men lowered their weapons. She sighed with relief.

Maybe I'm overreacting...

"Tell me why you're here," Commander Lotrin spat. "Or I will arrest you and you can await trial back on Xanteaus Trent."

Vee licked her lips and released Cypher's hand. He hadn't said a word since she'd moved forward, but she knew he was on the brink of lashing out. "We're here for the same reason you are, to see if Laprencia is a world that can sustain human life—"

Lotrin's pale eyes flared. Both men tensed.

Vee added, "We're not here to fight or to stop your efforts. Our people live and work together on many planets now. The first generation of half-breed children are adults now, and they need a home. Why not work together?"

Commander Lotrin's eyes moved back to her. "Do you think I would trust you so easily? When you have someone like *him* standing next to you?"

Vee stiffened. "You know what he is?"

"Cyborg," the commander sneered.

"Alien scum," Cypher threatened back.

"How is that possible?" she asked. *The game shouldn't have biocode on any player...*

"Possible? Any Knight of Xanteaus would be able to tell a Cyborg from a human with a glance," Commander Lotrin said. "They are the scourge of the universe, nothing more than a manmade blight, a cheat of Xanteaus' life's organics. Every Cyborg should be eradicated and split asunder." He took a step forward.

"You dare threaten me, ghost?" Cypher growled, his body expanding.

Several of the alien guards raised their weapons again.

"I would never, in a million Xanteaus-granted lifetimes, ever work with a Cyborg."

Everything that she'd worked so hard for was vanishing right before her eyes. It'd only taken minutes for the situation to escalate. Cypher pulled his arm back, and she flew between the two men.

"Stop!" She threw out her arms to hold them back. One of her palms landed on Commander Lotrin's chest, the other on Cypher's. *Cold and hot.* They both stopped.

"Please," she begged. "We want the same thing. We want a better future without war. We can't afford to fight. We've all lost so much already. This isn't worth a fight."

She looked at Cypher, who glared at the commander, before turning her face toward Lotrin.

Curiously, he gazed at her hand and lifted his free one toward it. Vee tried to snatch it back, but his gloved hand caught her wrist.

Cypher roared. He tore her away from the commander, wrenching her arm, and she slammed into Cypher's chest.

All hell broke loose.

The alien guards attacked in unison, and she was pulled from Cypher's arms. In a flash, he transformed—ripping his virtual suit to shreds—into a monstrous mecha bear. Every humanoid part of him disappeared under a frenzy of metal and laser sparks. Vee screamed as spearheads stabbed at him from all sides.

Someone pulled her back, and she fought for release. She shouted *stop* at the top of her lungs, but no one paid attention. "Cypher!"

Vee tried to swipe her hand out to stop the game and pull them out, but whoever held her grabbed her arm. When she closed her eyes to source out her intentions through the rig, nothing happened.

Her eyes shot open, looking for another method to power down or rewind, when Commander Lotrin stepped forward, holding a silver lightning rod above his head. Dread coursed through her. As if it all happened in slow motion, Cypher turned his face toward her as Lotrin slammed the tip of the rod down into Cypher's back.

Their eyes met. His flashed once. It was the only part of him she recognized. And then the light in them faded. He seized as if electrocuted, and fell to the floor with a *boom.*

"Get us out of here, get us out of here, get us out of here!" Vee cried.

Commander Lotrin thrust his spear farther into Cypher's back, and Vee sobbed.

"Please no more. Please!" She couldn't take it. Pain ripped through her. "Please! I'll do anything, anything, just spare him."

Lotrin paused without looking at her and tugged his weapon from Cypher's back. Sparks and blood erupted from the hole. Tears flooded her eyes as Cypher's body shook and vibrated, and tried to transform back into a man.

"It's not worth it," she whimpered. "This isn't worth it." Vee wrenched her eyes shut and prayed to be pulled out. Could no one hear her?

Was this a rule for the championship? She couldn't remember ever being told it was, or if it had been in the past. The smell of copper blood and heated metal filled her nose, and she gagged.

Then something floral replaced it. Her eyes snapped open to find Commander Lotrin kneeling in front of her.

"Release her," he said to whoever held her from behind.

Vee swiped her hand across the air to pull up the files, but nothing appeared. She was either not in her game, or she was in someone else's.

"You'll do anything to spare him?" Lotrin asked. "A Cyborg?"

"Yes!"

"One who has killed many, thousands, a mass slaughterer. You'd do anything for that?"

"Yes…"

His fiery eyes hooded. "Then I feel sorry for you." He straightened and stood. Just as it seemed he was going to leave, he reached out his hand to her. "You have much to learn when it comes to the value of life."

She stared at his hand mutely.

"Take it. If you want to join us in colonizing Laprencia, take it," he said.

"I want Cypher."

Lotrin's face darkened. "It's a game, Vee Miles."

She shook her head and sniffled. "Not anymore. Not to me. This isn't the Terraform Zero I know or have ever played."

"You'll give up everything for him?"

It wasn't even a question anymore to her. "Everything," she whispered. Even though somewhere far off, she could hear the crowd of the stadium, it didn't change her answer. Cypher had given up everything for her. She hadn't realized that until now, and she would easily do the same for him.

"What a shame." Commander Lotrin turned his back on her and threw out his hand. The very screens she'd been desperate to make appear materialized for *him*.

Then the alien guards vanished, and the surroundings changed. Cypher was still out on the floor, but his body was fully intact again, and the sparks and blood had vanished. He lay there unconscious, and she wondered if he'd been thrust into another instance in the game, or held somewhere else…

Vee licked her lips. *If this isn't my virtual world, was he even there at all?*

She glanced away. It was only her and Commander Lotrin now, overlooking Laprencia and its beautiful alien landscapes. Still, the Trentian commander's presence unnerved her.

Shaking, she slowly climbed to her feet and went to his side.

"Are you really here?" she asked. "Or are you part of the simulation?"

The Commander turned to her and smiled coldly.

23

*C*ypher glared at the Commander Lotrin with contempt. Every code and well-crafted fiber of his being urged him to kill the alien. It didn't matter that the war had ended nearly a half-century ago. Those parts of him hadn't changed.

The need to thrust Vee behind him and protect her body and soul coursed through his wires like hellfire.

But time had given him reason, knowledge, and a tiny bit of wisdom. He held back. There was something else happening around him that put him on edge. He gritted his teeth, looking at the alien ship in disgust.

Something's wrong.

He forced his instincts down and focused on the strangeness. Within seconds, the culprit was known. *The game's codes.* They flickered and crashed around him.

The moment he entered Terraform Zero with Vee, nothing felt right. Even as he gazed at the alien soldiers around him while Vee talked to the commander, Cypher knew something was off.

He reached out and touched Vee's arm, and although she glanced at him and there was warmth under his fingers, the feel of her wasn't the same as when they played together at his ship.

Frowning, he shuttered his systems and surged his digital consciousness into the codes of the game. Immediately, he came across codes written over codes, three times over.

I'm in a different simulation than Vee.

Within seconds, he hacked and unraveled the mess before him. It was sophisticated, but nowhere near the level of Ghost City. Vee's fake persona was tugging on his arm and asking him where he was when he had the worst of the simulation's codes suppressed. Even though he knew she wasn't really there, he pulled her under his arm and pressed her to his side.

"I'm finding my way back to you," he muttered.

"But you're right here?" Her voice was a dream.

"Cyborg scum," the commander snarled. Cypher numbed his own codes out to not fall for the Trentian's bait.

Fucking cheaters.

He found his and Vee's simulation, partially overlapped but in different instances. Working fast, he untangled the rest of the web.

An array of colors saturated his vision, a feeling of vertigo.

"Cypher!" Vee screamed when his simulation finally crumbled around him. Blood-curdling, her cry thrust him back into virtual reality.

"What the hell—" Cypher gasped. He looked around, disoriented. Blood and sweat filled his nose. They'd definitely been in different simulations.

Vee, no longer under his arm, was being held back by a Trentian soldier as she fought to reach Cypher. Pain erupted through his body, his senses seized, and he temporarily blacked out. Shock and electricity suffused him.

Something had gone disastrously wrong on her end. Lying on the floor, he tried to rip him and Vee out of the game entirely, but nothing worked. His body struggled to cope with the sudden change. Gritting his teeth, he realized he wasn't even human anymore—but bear.

While he crawled his way out of the darkness and heated miasma, Vee's cries for him abruptly stopped. His claws tore the ground, and the pain keeping him immobilized faded.

"Vee," he muttered, but the words never sounded.

Forcing his eyes open, he found her standing next to the alien commander overlooking the planet Laprencia.

Hatred erupted.

All the aggression built up inside him surged to the surface to lash out and murder the Trentian, but his body remained paralyzed. The smell of Vee's fear replaced all other scents in his nose.

Get to her.

Get to her before he touches her.

If she touches a Knight of Xanteaus, she's bonded to him forever.

Even in a simulation, Cypher couldn't let that happen. The thought alone drove his systems wild with pain.

Lotrin's hands twitched at his sides.

Vee, move away, he urged.

"I'm as real as the game is, Vee Miles," the Trentian said. "Part of Terraform Zero's updated AI when edition 19 comes out. Does that settle your question?"

Vee's voice wavered. "I don't like this. I don't like what you're doing. Is every team going through the same scenario?"

"It's against the rules to ask about the other teams. You may see their data afterward."

"But you and I are talking about something that shouldn't even be made aware of by you, as a simulated being. You shouldn't even know about what's happening, only reacting to my choices. That's the point of the whole thing. And Cypher…" Vee turned back to look at him.

Cypher tried to speak, but she didn't react. *Does she see that I'm here? I'M HERE!* He wanted to shout.

"If you killed him, he should've reloaded." Her voice was filled with pain.

"He was never killed," Lotrin said.

"Let us go then. I'm done. We're done. It's obvious that Cypher and I are being used for ratings or for something else, I don't know. But doing this to us is wrong, and not what I signed up for. I've been used a lot since this all started, and I'm so freaking sick of it."

"So be it," Commander Lotrin said. "But not a few minutes ago, you said you'd do anything for the wretched malformation behind us."

"I meant it," Vee snapped. "Now end this! *Please.*"

"All you have to do is take my hand."

Cypher's eyes widened.

"Why? That's not how this works?"

He heard the slide of leather and armor being removed. Cypher groaned. *Don't.* The words wouldn't come. *Don't touch him.*

So far in the distance that it almost seemed like a dream, the crowds in the stadium roared.

"Consider it a new addition to the game, like the simulation you're experiencing now," the Trentian said. "Unless you'd like to join me on Laprencia and help me colonize a world both our species could benefit from? The choice is still there."

Vee shook her head, staring at the commander's outstretched hand.

The commander continued, "You pressed your hand to my chest. You did it without fear of what that could do to you."

"I stopped you from attacking Cypher."

"And he from attacking *me*. Still, you willingly touched me. There is nothing to fear. You'll soon be gone, failing this world. It's done."

The game world flickered, sparked.

Cypher watched as Vee stared at the alien's pale hand, and it nearly broke his mind.

Vee reached out to take it.

Cypher choked, horrified and enraged.

Lotrin smiled.

Their hands touched, and Cypher exploded through the system, ravaging its codes completely. Electrical currents shot through his body, and he was able to move again.

The moment he jumped up, the game vanished, and the stadium came back into view.

He tore off his visor, sickened, and twisted to face Vee. She stood staring at him a rig away, tears coursing down her cheeks, her arms hugging her middle.

Throughout the stadium, a silence fell, and other teams tugged off their helmets.

Derek's voice surged, cheerful and deceptive as ever. "Looks like we have a glitch, folks, but seeing as we're so close to time, we're tallying the results for team placement."

Without taking his eyes off Vee, Cypher ripped the cords of the rig off his body. He rushed to her side and tugged her into his arms. She burrowed her face into his chest, and his bear groaned in satisfaction.

"It's over," he murmured. "It's over."

"I watched you die," she whimpered.

"No, you didn't. I was never there at all, not until the end." He didn't tell her about the pain. It didn't matter.

Vee lifted her head and met his gaze. "What do you mean?"

"They put us into two separate simulations. What you saw wasn't real."

Her face paled and a horrible numbness settled into her eyes.

"It was real," she whispered.

He pulled her back against him and hauled her out of the rig. Without waiting, he headed for the stadium gate, but stopped when he heard Diatrix laugh. He turned to face her.

Her laughter abruptly ceased. When he took a step toward her, she balked, but she held her ground as he closed the distance.

"What do you want, Cyborg?" Diatrix spat.

"I know you're behind the attempted kidnapping. Just because you haven't faced the music yet doesn't mean I'll forget," he warned, scowling. "Keep an eye out, Diatrix. I'm coming for you." Cypher turned and walked away.

"You shouldn't threaten her," Vee mumbled. Her grip on his arm gave him a small amount of calm. "They'll use it against you…"

"Like I fucking care."

Cypher had a plan, and it was a bloody one. He was done playing games.

He and Vee left the stadium as Derek announced the placements.

24

*T*hey made it back to his ship in record time despite the efforts of the championship's producers. When the producer's tried to stop them, Cypher showed his gun, and they backed off.

Bees greeted them when the hatch rose, nuzzling his legs. Vee picked the cat up and went to feed him in the lounge. Cypher watched her go, deciding not to follow her.

She touched the Xanteaus Knight. He hadn't the courage yet to bring it up. Cypher's hands fisted, and his knuckles cracked.

It wasn't real. He told Vee that several times over. Why couldn't he fully believe it himself? Especially when it came to that dreaded connection between Vee and the alien. He had the logic, the rationale, he had his mechanical side… But none of it helped when he replayed that scene in his head.

He made his way toward the bridge, shooting a comm to Nightheart.

The Cyborg answered immediately. "Let me guess—"

"I need a favor," Cypher interrupted.

Nightheart chuckled.

"Did you watch the semi-finals?" Cypher asked.

"I had it streamed into my systems."

"Then you saw what happened to me and Vee."

"That you blanked out and crashed their systems? That won't help you win."

"No," Cypher growled. "What happened wasn't that…" They must've not aired Vee's simulation to the crowd, only his. His anger grew. Did they hope he'd provide more entertainment than her? Not only had the producers used them, Cypher now knew they didn't give a shit about Vee's merits. "There were two simulations. They separated the two of us, and I had to break down the codes to join hers."

"Hmm? Interesting."

Cypher narrowed his eyes. "Did you know?"

"No. I have no business with Terraform Zero. Any connection I had ended when you bought Vee's contract. What really happened?"

"I'll send you my feed, what I was able to view." Cypher pulled the stream from his systems, encrypted it, and fed it to Nightheart and his connection. When he finished, he dispersed the trails.

Nightheart went silent in Cypher's head.

"Fuckers," Nightheart finally said, his voice cold. "I want them destroyed."

"You also want your name and face off of the entire network. You ask for a lot of hard to deliver things," Nightheart growled. "Is Vee okay?"

"She's as okay as can be. She's done..." He trailed off.

Cypher agreed wholeheartedly with her decision, but a twinge of guilt still stabbed at him anyway.

"Looking further," Nightheart said, "it seems that the two of you still placed. Not well, but placed in a recoverable position."

Cypher frowned. "What?"

"Your simulation—at least the simulation that was aired to the media and crowd. The one that doesn't show you being speared by a Knight. You and Vee placed eighth. It seems some teams failed even worse with their relations to the Trentians."

"Fuck," Cypher muttered under his breath, collapsing into his captain's seat. "It doesn't matter. I want them wiped."

"That's not possible."

"It isn't?" Oh, it was possible. It just wouldn't be pretty. Cypher knew what he was asking for.

"I'm trying to restore our names throughout the galaxy. I haven't even begun to rebuild a reputation with the people after Zeph's stunt last year. You were supposed to fucking help with that, but look where we're at now! I can't get the swine to disperse outside my building. Humans commit egregious crimes every day. One Cyborg loses control, and we're crucified."

Cypher had never heard so many words come from Nightheart at one time before.

"Now you want me to deal with this?" Nightheart sighed. "I'm beginning to think you weren't worth the trouble."

"I'm not the asshole who poked a sleeping bear," Cypher snapped. "You deserve all of this and more, you piece of shit. Are you going to help me or not?"

Nightheart's voice lowered. "On one condition."

Cypher scowled. "What?"

"Your contract with the EPED is extended fifty years, and we take them down on my terms."

He didn't care about the terms, only that NeoElite games would be ruined. "Ten years."

"Forty."

"Ten." He wouldn't cave.

"Thirty-five."

"Over my dead mechanical body," Cypher warned.

"Thirty-five, or you're in this alone."

Cypher palmed his face. "Twenty." He caved.

"Deal."

Cypher sat back. *Twenty* more years of dealing with Nightheart, twenty more years of servitude to get his vengeance. *For Vee.*

It's all for Vee.

Realizing what he'd just done—what he'd just signed up for—hit him like a truck.

An encrypted file popped up in his systems, and he opened it to find a new contract. It was the same one as before but with the extended time frame. He accepted the terms and shot it back to Nightheart.

All for her.

He did it for her, without a thought.

What have I become?

Is this what happened to his other Cyborg brethren when they met the women they were with? Katalina worked for Dommik and they'd bonded in close proximity, Stryker had answered Norah's distress call and fell for her during a world-ending storm... And then there was Gunner, who actually got close enough to a woman during his exile because they had been jailed together while she'd pretended to be a man. No one woman would've gone near Gunner otherwise—willingly at least.

Human women were becoming dangerous creatures to Cyborgs. And it wasn't only shifter Cyborgs taking mates, it was the other models as well. Jack and Atlas came to mind.

As if his thoughts summoned her, Cypher heard Vee's soft footsteps behind him. He always knew when she was checking in on him, even though sometimes he pretended he didn't.

But I'm Nightheart's man now, and almost for an entire duration of a human lifetime. A human lifetime… Cypher looked at Vee.

"When do you want NeoElite gone?" Nightheart's voice came through.

"As soon as possible," he answered, still gazing at Vee. "But I have several things to take care of first."

"Of course."

"I'll reach out to you later."

He was about to shut the line when Nightheart stopped him.

"Cypher, I don't want to have to keep reiterating this, but for all our sakes and especially mine, don't get caught by the media again. You owe me your soul already."

Cypher growled and cut him off. He stood and went to Vee. Her neck strained up to keep their eyes locked as he neared.

"We're in eighth place," she whispered.

He pushed back a strand of her hair. "You checked?"

"I needed to know what happened…on the outside. What everyone saw, if they saw what I did… If it really happened. They didn't."

"I know."

She nodded. "I'm glad."

"You are?"

Vee wiped the back of her hand across her mouth. "What happened… It hurt seeing you like that—*dead*. I know you said you weren't. I don't know. It feels personal what happened, and I'm glad it wasn't seen by everyone, played back on every channel, made into something that it wasn't—or *isn't*—to make me hurt any worse. D-does that make sense?"

His mouth twitched. "Yeah."

"Good. Can we go to bed now?"

Cypher dropped his hand from her hair. "Sure."

Vee lowered her head like his response made her sad.

He took her hand, raised it to his mouth, and kissed the back of it. "Let's go to bed."

He pulled her after him as he led them to the captain's quarters. Afterward, she went to the bathroom, and he heard the water turn on. She left the door open. Cypher stalked to the threshold, stopping before he entered.

Steam filled the room, and he eyed the outline of Vee's body within the cleaning stall. It'd been days since he'd last rutted her, and his cock jerked to life. Days of torture. Days of guilt and confusion and endless wanting.

Days of knowing that this would all soon come to an end.

It would be easier to break the ties of their relationship, he'd thought. Easier when she won the championship and pursued the life she'd always sought, easier for him to leave and never return. It wasn't in him to follow her even if he could, and he'd considered it. *Really* considered it. He wanted her that badly. Sex or no, she was the first true companion he ever had.

But Cyborgs were meant to lead, not follow. His codes quaked at the idea of pursuing a life that wasn't his, even if it was Vee's. As a man, he didn't mind...but as a machine, even an animal, the idea made him restless—made his systems shy away.

On the other hand, the championship was dead in the water, and her life was now in flux. Though his was staked down in cement and unchangeable at this point.

The water stopped, and the blowers blasted on a second later.

Vee opened the stall. She stopped short and stared at him.

Clean and perfect, smelling like him and his ship, her hair windblown around her face, his mouth watered. His body heated.

His eyes flashed with emotion as he took her in, small, delicate, and perfect in her sweet nakedness. *And mine, all mine.* His hands clenched at his sides. He wished—he wished she was his.

A dangerous thought took over his head.

She can be.

Vee curled an arm around her chest and reached for a towel to cover herself. His eyes darkened at the movement.

"Don't," he ordered.

She stopped.

"Come here."

She cocked her head, swallowed, and came to him. His bear shook with delight, the metal in his cock vibrating. It bulged and strained against his gamer suit.

If I can't seek my vengeance tonight, I can have her.

A blush heated her cheeks. *She has sad eyes*, he realized. They glistened.

"Do you still want me?" she asked.

Cypher bared his teeth. "How can you ask that?"

She looked away. He cupped her chin and turned her face back to him.

"You haven't joined me the last few nights... Is your bear's rut over?"

"For you, never."

Her lips parted. In that instant, he jerked her against him, pulling her soft, naked curves hard upon him, and lifted her to take to bed. Laying her down, he rose over her and stripped off his clothes. They tore in his haste as he roved his eyes over her from head to toe. Every inch he memorized, placing it in his mind to keep him company always.

Seeing her calmed him.

She spread her legs and raised her hips from the bed, opening for him.

"No," he rasped, placing a hand on her belly and pushing her down. "I'm taking my time tonight."

Her eyes widened, and she slumped but nodded. Her arousal bloomed the air between them. With saliva filling his mouth, he leaned down, shifted his cock to press against her skin, and sucked one soft nipple into his mouth.

It peaked under his tongue. Pulling it between his teeth, he plucked and pinched the other one with his fingers. Vee's moans filled his ears.

After lavishing, he pulled up to blow on them. "I'm here," he reminded her.

A whimper escaped.

"I'm here."

"I think I love you, Cypher."

He stopped. His eyes tore from her breasts to her face. Tears appeared on her lashes. His heart quickened, excited and terrified all at once.

Vee blinked the tears away.

He moved to kiss them. "Don't cry, little spitfire."

He tried to find the words to say something endearing back to her, but he couldn't. They didn't come. Electricity blazed through him, quaking him to his core. Darkness and possession surged, and it unnerved him—more than the blood he would soon seek from his enemies.

I could easily do what Zeph did. I could steal her away and flee across the universe. He realized he could do worse than that…

He *would* do worse than that.

He chose to say nothing, pressing his mouth to hers instead.

Cypher took her slow, enjoying every inch of her body, learning every marking, freckle, and imperfection. He devoured her curves with his hands and mouth, moved his tongue to wet her everywhere, from toe to earlobe and each place in-between. He buried his face between her legs and drank her down, fucking her with his tongue, nibbling with his teeth.

There wasn't a place left on her body that he didn't touch. That he didn't mark and return to his possession.

He took the tips of her fingers, where Vee touched the Knight of Xanteaus, and sucked them into his mouth. Cypher would do so every day for however long they remained together to satisfy the agony growing within him.

After he'd thoroughly marked her flesh, he spread her legs on the bed and drove them both over the edge. Tight and ready, she was the softness to his hard shell, opening for him and him alone. Each moan and caress of her hands on his flesh drove him a little madder, a little more hurried, and his lovemaking turned frenetic.

He wanted to fuck her hard enough to entwine their souls together. Did he even have a soul?

Cypher roared when he came, rocking his body, trapping her between him and the bed. Vee wrapped herself around him and joined him in devilish bliss.

Breathing her in, his madness only grew.

She loves me.

Savagery returned.

He rose from the bed when she was sleeping soundly and tucked within the covers.

Cypher walked out of the room, to his arsenal, and dressed. Strapping weapons to his vest, he readied to find his bliss once more tonight.

And with his jaw half-shifted, his teeth pointed to fangs, he walked into the night, eyes aglow with rage.

25

*C*ypher left the spaceport behind, taking his hovercraft to a high-rise on the other side of the New America metropolis.

It wasn't NeoElite he was after, but those who tried to take Vee from him weeks prior. Though time had passed, it was still fresh in his mind. That was one of the bittersweet perks of being a mechanical creature—memories never truly faded.

He parked his vehicle several blocks away from the high-rise. Once he'd checked his weapons, he left the hovercraft behind, sticking to the midnight shadows. Smog flooded his nose, and with it, disgust. During his short time on Earth, he hadn't found much he enjoyed about it. He didn't understand why his brethren, like Nightheart and Stryker, wanted to stick close by the human hub.

My ancestors, the bears that made up my unusual DNA, roamed these lands once. He couldn't imagine that this city may have once been the home of a lush wilderness filled to the brink with animal predators. Thousands of years had passed since then.

He was the predator now. The last remnant of his ancient ursine kin, the great bears of Earth. Did he deserve to be the last one?

When he reached the high-rise, he seeded into the IP he traced—Diatrix's. It wasn't hard. Even if it was, it was common knowledge on the network where Deadly Dearest trained.

Moving toward the door, he disrupted their security system and let himself inside. Unlike Vee's dismal building, this place was clean and maintained—near glitzy with moderate wealth. The smog of the city didn't penetrate its walls, and what he saw were clean floors, freshly painted walls, and artwork on the walls of the entryway.

The office was closed. He blanked out the security cameras as he headed for the elevator.

Minutes later, he stood before a door with a sign on the front. Deadly Dearest's brand. Bright pink, bright yellow, gray and black.

Vee's was simpler, better.

It brought to mind the virtual bunnies that infiltrated his room on Ghost City. His lips tugged into a slight smile. In the time he'd spent with Vee, he only saw her playful, quirky side on a few occasions. He was determined to see it more.

If I can convince her…

Cypher stamped the thought from his mind and punched through the door. It flew into the back wall with a crash, breaking furniture in its path.

Noises of people waking filled his ears. He stepped into the large partial studio apartment as several women fled from side rooms to investigate the noise.

He smelled Diatrix before he saw her.

A yell sounded, but it didn't faze him. He made his way to Diatrix right as she appeared from behind a curtain.

Her eyes went wide with fear as he pulled out his gun. One of her team members screamed.

"C-Cypher," Diatrix gasped, stumbling backward.

"You hired men to kidnap Vee."

"I didn't!"

"There's no sense in lying. I found the correspondence between you two weeks ago."

She shook her head.

"Why?" he demanded.

"I didn't!"

He stepped toward her. "I can make you talk."

With her back against the wall, she shook.

He heard the cock of a gun.

"Back off," someone snapped.

Without looking, he heard several other guns have their safety guards clicked off.

"Shoot me all you want," he said without taking his eyes off of Diatrix. "Nothing you own will pierce my metal."

"Back off! We called the authorities!"

He laughed. "No, you didn't. You can't, not with the people you're affiliated with. Not with what I'm sure you have hidden behind your Terraform Zero team front." His eyes flashed. Diatrix's lips sharpened into a hard line.

He saw her nod once.

And the sound of gunfire blasted his ears.

Cypher grasped Diatrix by the neck as eight bullets hit his back, his neck, his head. Most fell from his bulletproof vest but the others... they stung and implanted into his body, where they caught his mainframe.

Pain ripped through him. He pushed it from his mind as his body sought to numb it out.

"Why!?" he roared in Diatrix's face as more bullets hit him. He felt her swallow beneath his hand around her neck. His grip tightened as gun smoke filled the space. "What was the fucking point?"

The fear left her eyes as she stared at him. Anger and disgust flooded them instead.

After everything that'd happened, he was done playing games.

Taking one of his guns out from under his jacket, Cypher twisted back and shot each of the shooters. They seized and fell, shocked and stunned but not dead. When he turned back around, he and Diatrix were the only two left standing. He slid his stunner back into his vest.

Furious now, she glared at him. "Do it. Kill me! You'll only prove my point. Men know nothing but violence."

"I didn't kill them," he growled. *Though I should have.* "They're the ones using real bullets. Although I have some waiting for deployment. Not to mention you hired them to do what you say you detest so much."

"So you're a coward?"

Cypher snapped his teeth at her face, making her flinch. "You don't know the meaning of that word, woman."

"You know nothing about me!"

He released her neck, and she sagged back against the wall, reaching up to rub it.

"I know you're using Terraform as a front," Cypher said. "That you're part of an organization that undermines law and order, and that you fucking hired men to take Vee from me."

"Is she that important to you? I should've tried harder," she hissed.

Cypher snapped his hand out and grabbed Diatrix by the neck again. "You really want to die."

"You killing me would prove everything I've ever stood for. Are you really going to walk out of here and let me live? Why come in the middle of the night with guns otherwise? Just get on with it!"

He pushed her back against the wall. "Not before I get my answers."

"Answers? Look at me, Cyborg. Really fucking look at me. You'll kill me when you get them."

Tightening his hand around her throat, his eyes flashed upon Diatrix's face, analyzing her image. Her features rose behind his eyes as all the information he'd gathered about her pooled around it in racing feeds of text.

He knew most of it already. Diatrix Greer, born offworld aboard a cargo ship to Anne Greer, a worker on the vessel. Cypher frowned. The cargo ship made deliveries back and forth from Earth to Elyria. As an Elyrian citizen, Anne Greer wasn't subject to as many travel restrictions as an Earth-born woman was. But Diatrix, born in space and on the way to Earth, was.

Information about Anne stopped when the woman died of a strange flu ten years after Diatrix was born. Mother and daughter remained on the cargo vessel during that time.

There was no information about Diatrix's father.

Nor was there any real information about Anne Greer's job.

"Your mother was a ship whore," he muttered. Anne had been a woman, hired by ship crew, to live onboard and keep the men company during long periods in space. It wasn't wholly legal, but it didn't matter. Everyone looked the other way.

A surge of hatred suffused Diatrix's eyes, and he got his answer.

"Yes," she said.

"Were you?"

Her lips twisted.

Whatever age Diatrix was, alone in space with what her mother's profession was, things could've happened. Disgust filled him.

But it made no sense why Diatrix sought to take Vee.

"I would never give myself to one of those men," Diatrix spat. "Or any man."

Cypher released her neck again, and this time, she remained standing. "I don't give a shit about you, what your past shaped you to be. Were you sabotaging us so you'd be the only female-led team?"

The pettiness of humans never ceased to shock him.

"Sabotaging, sure, but she wasn't the real target, Cyborg. You were."

Cypher snarled. "Why?"

"You're so damned blind. How can you even call yourself a Cyborg?"

A low rumble rose from his chest as the plates in his torso expanded. Moans sounded behind him, and he knew the women he'd stunned would rise soon. He couldn't shoot them again without killing them, and he'd rather not kill them for Vee's sake.

What am I missing?

His mind surged, scanning everything. His eyes took in and analyzed every bit of information he had about Diatrix.

The one thing he couldn't get an answer to was her father.

Her father.

Stiffening, he reached back into his jacket and pulled out his gun.

She smiled. "I told you that you would kill me once you realized."

Diatrix Greer was a Trentian—a half-breed with Trentian blood coursing through her veins. Cypher's systems went red. The image of Vee touching the virtual Trentian commander shot to the forefront of his mind, and all his rage came crashing down.

"Your kind has killed mine for so long, so hatefully, it was in my blood to risk Deadly Dearest and hurt you. Vee? I have nothing against Vee, only that she betrayed all womankind when teaming up with you."

Cypher stumbled back as his hand shook, resisting the urge to aim and press the trigger.

Diatrix continued, unconcerned, "My mom may have been a ship whore, but it was my father she loved. They met on Elyria. He was killed before I was born, and she hid my identity. Like most of my kind, we hide amongst you. I don't just hate men. I hate mankind. I may look like a human woman, but I'm Trentian to my bones. And you, Cyborg, are the antithesis of why my species is all but devastated."

His kill codes raged. This wasn't like how he felt in Terraform Zero facing the commander. This was all too real. *I'm being taunted, goaded by what I was designed to kill.* Sirens went off in his systems, his codes creating a stranglehold on his control.

He'd been created for one purpose, and one purpose only: the destruction of all Trentian life.

Numbing out, he raised his gun to press it to Diatrix's brow.

"Do it," she whispered. "Kill me. Let the universe be reminded of what you truly are. An abomination."

I should've listened to Vee, he thought as his finger twitched. *I should've stayed away.*

He had come to get answers, not kill. And now he was about to leave behind a slaughter the whole universe would know of.

"Do it!"

Cypher dropped his gun. "No."

Diatrix growled and slammed her fists into his chest. "Do it!" she screamed. "Coward! Kill me!"

It was his turn to stumble back. "No." He palmed his head and turned away. Fists pummeled him from behind, stinging his gunshot wounds.

"You *are* a coward!" she yelled. "Kill me. Kill me like you killed my ancestors!"

Cypher wrenched his eyes shut and fled for the exit. He forced his body forward as several of Diatrix's women tried to stop him. Pushing through them, he roared, fleeing.

"Coward!" he heard Diatrix bellow as he ran.

26

*V*ee woke the next morning alone. She reached out for Cypher, already knowing he wasn't there but hoping otherwise. Instead, she found Bees and curled herself around her cat.

Languishing, her body was relaxed, and her mind was devoid of stress. At least for the moment. A smile tilted her lips as she nuzzled her Bees's fur, thinking about the night before.

I told him I loved him. A huge weight she hadn't even realized she was carrying had been lifted. It didn't matter that he hadn't said it back. She hadn't expected it either way. It was just nice to know that whatever happened now, she wouldn't have any regrets.

She sucked her lower lip into her mouth. Still, she didn't know what her confession would mean for her and Cypher. It wasn't in her to beg him to stay, or to take her with him into space, but her heart thudded at the idea.

She pulled out her wristcon and turned it on, shaking her head. *I have to find my own way.*

Checking her media site, she found it filled with congratulations and encouraging words despite her placement. Some of the trolls still lingered, but with the effort she'd put in over the last month—and Cypher's—less hate plagued her comments section.

It proved that no one saw what happened to her and Cypher in her simulation.

Now I need to announce I'm dropping out...

Vee sat up, curled her toes, and pulled her legs under her. Wistfulness edged her emotions about giving up, about she and Cypher being a team, but she was okay with it. If anything, she'd come to realize that being in the spotlight wasn't for her. The championship wasn't for her. And that from here on out—with the money she'd made—she was going to invest in another means to help those like herself stuck on Earth. The only good thing that came out of it was *him.*

And I thought I watched him die. A stab of pain churned her gut.

She pulled up the contact information for NeoElite to notify them first when she heard a loud crash. She glanced up toward the door. Bees jumped off the bed.

"Cypher?" she called out.

No answer.

She tugged on a pair of socks and went to investigate. Not finding him on the bridge, she headed for the lounge, the empty laboratory, expecting him to be on the move. He was in neither area. Her chest squeezed as she made her way to his arsenal.

She sighed with relief when she found it empty.

A groan pricked her ears, and she turned toward the sound. "Cypher?" she called again. It was coming from the medical lab. The door zipped open as she neared.

Her face fell. Cypher stood with his naked back turned toward her with a dozen or more bloody, reddened wounds. His whole body strained, and something fell out of one of the holes to hit the floor with a ping.

Her reverie from minutes before faded to dust.

"Oh my God." Vee rushed to him. "What happened?"

Cypher grabbed her hand before she touched the reddened skin on his upper arm. He caught her eyes. "A mistake."

"What do you mean a mistake? These are bullet wounds!" The terror of losing him crashed back into her.

"I know."

She yanked her hand from his. "What did you do?"

He shook his head.

Like she'd take that as an answer. "What did you do? Tell me!"

"I confronted Diatrix."

Vee sagged. Her stomach churned. Of course he did. He'd been planning on it. She knew he had been. "Not for me. You were hurt because of me."

Cypher grabbed her shoulders and pushed her against the wall. "Of course for you. I wouldn't do it for anyone else."

Her guilt grew when he winced. "I can't stand you being hurt."

"This? This is barely a scratch."

"Not to me. After what I saw yesterday…" Her voice hitched.

"Vee…"

She wiped her eyes. "Don't. Not while you're hurt and bleeding. I can't think straight seeing you bloody. You know what you mean to me." She clenched her hands closed and moved to the counter where a bunch of hypodermic wet healing cloths had been pulled out. "Sit," she ordered.

He glowered, stepping back. "You don't need to take care of me. My body will heal itself once the bullets fall out."

She snatched a cloth. "Then I'll clean the blood off you."

"Vee..."

Her eyes narrowed to slits.

After a temporary standoff, he sighed, pulled out a stool, and sat down. Vee moved to the back of him as another bullet popped out. She caught it in her hand before it fell, hating the heaviness of it between her fingers. Setting it aside, she lightly pressed the cloth to the red areas around the wound.

She gathered his hair and pushed it over his shoulder.

Her throat closed at the sight before her.

He'd be dead a dozen times over if he were a human man.

Her fingertips hovered between his wounds, little more than a ghost of a touch. His skin was warm, but it did little to make her feel better. She jerked her fingers back when his muscles flexed. "Sorry," she said.

He grumbled softly. "I liked it."

Vee bit down on her lip, uncertain how to respond. She kissed the top of his head and got to work.

Time passed as she cleaned his skin, caressing the healed areas as she went. Most of the holes were free of bullets before she started, but whenever he strained or his plates moved under her hand, another would emerge for her to catch.

Each hole that no longer had a bullet was in a different stage of healing. Watching his skin thread itself back together didn't make her feel better. She leaned down again and gently kissed the wounds that had closed.

Cypher stiffened. She pressed her brow against him and breathed.

"What happened?" she asked.

"It doesn't matter."

"It does to me."

Silence was his response.

"Did you kill her?" Vee needed to know.

"No. She's alive and well. Maybe bruised."

"You didn't kill her?"

"No."

Her heart thrummed. "Thank you."

"Don't thank me, female. She's only alive to prove a point. I'm eager to go back and finish the job."

Vee lifted her brow from him. "What do you mean?"

He didn't answer.

"Cypher? What do you mean?" She moved to stand in front of him and stopped when she saw the rage in his eyes. His eyes had gone a bright yellow, and even still, there was darkness in them. "What happened?"

"She was never after you, Vee. She was after me. Diatrix is a half-breed. She's Trentian. Her hatred for men goes beyond their sex, and she hates my kind most of all. Like I do hers."

"You can't be serious? Half-breeds aren't allowed on Earth. She doesn't look alien at all." She thought back to the few encounters she had with the woman. Not in a million years would she have ever thought Diatrix was half-alien.

"Apparently there's a lot more residing here than we know of. If they can hide from my kind, they can easily hide from humans." His gaze moved to the wall behind her. "At least she has a reason to hate me…"

"What are you going to do?" After what she saw in Laprencia's simulation, she couldn't believe Diatrix still lived.

"Nothing."

"Nothing?"

"Yes." Cypher tore his eyes from the wall behind her and stood. "I'm going to shower." He stormed from the room before she could say anything more.

Stunned, Vee watched him go, listening to his heavy steps recede into the distance. Minutes passed as she stared at the exit. Part of her wanted to chase him down, but something stopped her.

He doesn't want me to follow him.

Why would he?

Ever since she pretended *to be* Cypher, his life had gone up in flames. Though she only knew a little about his past and what he was doing before he sought her out, she knew his life had been altered completely because of her.

And the EPED.

But still because of *her*.

Now that everything has come to an end—Vee wrung her hands together—maybe his feelings toward her had dulled as well.

Where mine has grown, have his staled? She looked around the medical lab, the bloody bullets on the floor catching her eye. *I'm not worth this. Maybe he's come to the same conclusion.* Her chest squeezed, her heart sinking.

She made her way back to the captain's quarters knowing what she needed to do. Pack up, get out, and move on. Move on somewhere far from here so she could keep a modicum of pride. As she neared the room, the sound of running water sounded. She chewed on her lip and walked in anyway. *I'll be quick, then I'll wait in the lounge.*

Vee made the bed, picked up her clothes and threw them in her duffle, and rounded up any other items she'd been using since her stay. She heard the water turn off right when she finished typing in a code on the panel next to the room's door to clean the space with cleaning bots.

Cypher stepped out of the lavatory, steam rushing around his large frame, right when she tried to scurry out the door. His eyes landed on her, and she stopped.

"I didn't mean to interrupt you—follow you," she said.

"What are you doing?"

Her eyes settled on his muscles slicked with moisture. He was naked on the threshold, his long, wet hair plastered to his godlike frame, and his thick cock semi-erect.

Her lips parted, and her gaze slid appreciatively over him. Everywhere. She clenched.

God, there goes my pride.

"Packing up," she gulped. She couldn't see his wounds, but the way his face sharpened at her words convinced her that Cypher wasn't bothered by them anymore. "I'm going to officially forfeit from the championship. I figured since—"

"No, you're not."

Vee's lips pursed. "What?"

"You're not going to forfeit. And you're not going anywhere."

She sighed when he grabbed a towel and wrapped it around his waist.

Guess he's not going to use the dryer...

She swallowed. "I thought you were with me on this."

304

"I was, but I changed my mind."

"Cypher, after all that's happened, I don't think—"

He held up his hand. "We're doing this Vee, whether you like it or not."

"And the Trentians?" she asked.

"I can deal with them." Cypher turned away from her and grabbed a fresh bodysuit and jacket from a panel that opened up from the wall. "Drop your bag, Vee. I won't let you leave even if you try."

She sighed again, but a blaze of excitement zipped through her. She watched him dress, the material sliding over his tawny skin, hiding the dew of water he hadn't bothered to wipe off. Even with his wounds still showing, red but no longer open, she wanted him.

She dropped her bag. "Are you sure?" Her excitement built.

Maybe he did want her to stay. Even if it was for a little longer, she'd take it.

He eyed the duffle at her feet. "Yes."

"We're really going to do this?"

His eyes moved to hers. "We're really going to do this."

"We're in eighth place. We may be thrown in separate simulations again… There could be more curveballs."

His lips twisted into a smile. One of his rare broody bear smiles. "Then we'll just have to prepare for the worst."

"Why? Why do you want to do this? After everything, after coming here to get out of it, after Nightheart and the EPED and the protestors and Diatrix?"

He moved to stand before her, towering, looking down as she strained her neck to look up at him. She swallowed again as heat surrounded her.

"Because I realized something, little human. You and I have been hiding for far too long. *I* have been hiding for far longer. A lifetime's worth. The universe has changed around me, and I let it happen, ignoring it all the while. Life isn't war anymore, and hiding doesn't help anyone. My long hibernation ends today." He cupped her chin and leaned down. "And you, Vee, have woken me up. Now it's time to finish what we started." He placed a small kiss on her cheek.

Her heart thumped. With his other hand, he closed his fingers over her wristcon.

"Yes," she whispered, feeling more hope in her then she had since she first met Nightheart in his office nearly two months ago. "Let's finish this."

27

*T*he next week went by in a blur. From dawn to dusk, she and Cypher remained in Terraform Zero, working through Laprencia and what was given to them from NeoElite. They spoke of little else, only the game, only the world. It became real in her mind, like Yria had, a place that existed and would immensely further mankind. It became real because Cypher made it that way for her.

He had a knack for taking everything seriously. Even when she wanted to try out a strange challenge, like basing their colony and sharing information with the Trentians and Commander Lotrin, he stopped her. Their governments were separate, though they now worked together, and in real life, any Trentian collaboration wouldn't be done by colonists. Not at an official, world-building level.

She didn't like the lack of trust or cooperation, but she understood. The war hadn't been all that long ago… Though it was before she was born, there were still people who remembered it, were devastated by it, and Cypher assured her that not enough time had passed for relations between the species to be depended upon.

Trust, after the loss of hundreds of millions of lives over a century, would take much longer to cultivate.

The goal was to have human settlers live on Laprencia.

Cypher made it clear that it would be the same for the Trentians. Hatred ran deep to their souls when it came to humankind. That, and in many places of the universe, secret wars continued. Places like Elyria, where half-breeds made up a portion of the population, were an anomaly.

And the commander in her game was different from the commander she'd encountered during the semi-finals. He no longer had knowledge of the 'world' outside the simulation and seemed less real. Whether it was a difference between Terraform Zero 18 and Terraform Zero 19 that was still in development, she didn't know. But she was thankful for it.

The day of the championship came.

She gazed out over the stadium packed with fans, wringing her hands. She'd washed them several times, but they were clammy again within minutes. Vee had thought the stadium was packed before, but now—now it was endless. Every seat was filled, people hanging over every rafter. And it had grown, towering an additional four floors to accommodate the masses.

The stadium had become a partial dome, and people were everywhere.

It was frightening and exciting.

Each team who competed in the semi-finals was back, and she was sure they all had something to prove. A blast of heat licked her spine, and she saw Cypher's reflection appear in the window behind her.

"The day's finally here," she said. She almost couldn't believe it.

"It won't be long now."

She shook her head, meeting his in the glass. Over the last week, they'd barely spoken of anything but the game. Both avoided the inevitable that was going to happen once it was done. He hadn't acknowledged that she loved him, and she was still okay with that during these final days.

He also hadn't taken her to bed again, not for sex at least. He'd kiss, wash her, curl around her under the covers, but sex…there'd been none of that. And it wasn't because he didn't want it; she knew he did. She'd felt his heavy shaft press against her all night long.

He never went further. And when she'd tried, he'd capture her under him and suffocate her with kisses until she stopped. Deep, dark, hungering, lingering kisses that seduced her as much as they confused her, and she longed for more.

He was stealing and breaking her heart at the same time, leaving nothing but a jumbled mess of emotions she was terrified to sort through.

Everything will be over this time tomorrow…

"Cypher." She turned to face him. "We need to talk."

His eyes flashed, and he nodded, glancing behind him. "Yes. But first, I have a surprise."

Her brow creased. "A what?"

He turned from her, walked to the door, and opened it. Her parents jumped and laughed excitedly, rushing into the private room.

Vee gasped as they enveloped her in their arms.

"Oh my. Look at you!" her mother cried. "So sleek and pro in that suit of yours."

"Mom," Vee said, still stunned.

Her mom squeezed her hard and pulled back, a grin across her face. "Look at you, Vee. You're such a beautiful young woman."

"Hey, let me get a hug in." Her dad said, pulling Vee from her mom's grip.

"Dad…" Vee mumbled as she was crushed against his chest.

"We're so proud of you, honey."

Tears beaded Vee's eyes. Her mom's arms came around the both of them. She relaxed.

"You're here," Vee whimpered.

"Of course we're here! We wouldn't miss this for the world," Mom chastised. "We're only upset you didn't tell us sooner. We haven't heard from you in weeks! We've been trying to get a hold of you for so long now. We decided the only thing to do would be to come out here."

Vee squeezed her eyes shut and burrowed her face into her dad's chest. "I'm sorry," she cried. "I'm really sorry!"

She hadn't known how much she needed to see them.

"It's okay, honey," her dad mumbled, pulling back to look at her. Vee wiped her face. "We were real worried after all the media coverage. Good thing you've had someone nearby to protect you. He assured us you were safe."

Vee glanced at Cypher as her dad turned to him. For once, her space warrior appeared utterly uncomfortable.

"Thank you for keeping our baby safe," her dad said.

"Yes! Thank you, thank you, thank you!" her mother agreed.

Vee smiled as Cypher shifted his eyes back and forth between her parents and her.

"Of course," he grumbled.

Dad reached out his hand. "You're a good man."

Cypher's expression turned pained. He stared at her dad's hand for a moment before taking it.

"We owe you a lot," Dad continued.

Straightening, Cypher pulled his hand back. "A good man? You owe me nothing. It's my duty to protect human life—innocent human life—and I'll protect Vee always."

Vee's heart squeezed, and she moved to Cypher's side, reaching up to tug on his low ponytail. The muscles strained in his arms, and he pulled her into his side, trapping her hard against him. A blush rushed her cheeks knowing her parents were watching.

It was completely out of the ordinary of her Cyborg.

A blazing heat rushed through her, and with it, a smidgen of hope.

Her mother studied them curiously. "We can't thank you enough."

Vee extinguished her hope and pulled out from under Cypher's arm. *I can't hope for this.* If she let herself hope for more from him, she was setting herself up for a lifetime of hurt. Vee wiped her hands on her suit pants and forced a smile back to her lips.

"I'm glad you're here, Mom," she said.

Her mom cupped Vee's cheeks, her perusal continuing. "Me too, baby. Are you doing okay?"

Vee nodded. Was she? "Yeah." It was an honest answer. "More than okay."

Mom's smile returned. All the while, Vee sensed Cypher's looming presence at her back.

A loudspeaker turned on. *"Contestants, please make your way down to the stadium entrances."*

The breath left her. She rubbed her palms on her pants again. "I guess it's time."

Beaming, her parents hugged her once again.

"You're gonna do great," her dad said.

"I hope!"

"And if you don't there's always school…"

Vee groaned.

Cypher wrapped his fingers around her arm and pulled her from her parents. "Time to go," he said, saving her.

Thank God—*thank God*—he was there.

Mom kissed her cheek. "Colonize the crap out of that planet!"

Chuckles filled the room.

"We'll try." Vee let Cypher lead her to the exit.

"We'll be right here watching!"

The door shut behind them as Vee pivoted to wave. When her parents vanished, her hand dropped, and she turned to Cypher. "I can't believe you got them here."

"They were already here, bothering Nightheart for information. It wasn't hard once my boss told me to take care of it."

"Right." Vee's smile was genuine this time. "Dad's right too, you know. You are a good man."

His face hardened. "If only you knew my thoughts, little human."

Her lips fell, and she cupped his cheek. Her chest blazed with emotion. "Everyone has bad thoughts, Cypher. Doesn't change who we are. I can't say all my thoughts have been good, especially lately. A lot has happened—to both of us—and if someone told me two months ago the guy in my EPED contract was real and that I would care for him like this, I'd have brushed them off. It's been a rollercoaster, but regardless of all that's happened, you, Cypher, are a good man. A good Cyborg, if you prefer."

His hand came over hers, and his sharp eyes pinned her.

There was a flash of emotion, but it was gone too soon. Vee licked her lips.

"Contestants, please make your way to the stadium gates. Introductions start in five minutes."

Their hands dropped. She had so much more she wanted to say, so much she wanted to convey, but there was no time for that now. There was also so much she wanted him to say, even if it wasn't what she wanted to hear.

Everything lately seemed like one long goodbye. And the more that goodbye was pushed out, and the longer it expanded, the more she felt she was drowning.

Vee took Cypher's hand, threaded her fingers through his, and together they made their way down to the stadium.

When they arrived, the other teams were already being announced. Each brought on a roar of the crowd, far louder and far longer than last week.

She shifted from foot to foot, waiting for her and Cypher to be called. He remained quiet beside her. She looked his way. "You're not going to say you'll be there with me?" she asked, half-kidding but mostly desperate for him to speak.

"I made that promise last time and broke it. I will try."

"We have our signal." They'd come up with a response tactic if they thought NeoElite separated them into two simulations again. She would whisper *murder bunnies*, and if Cypher didn't whisper it back, then they'd know.

"We do," he responded.

Halo Grail was called.

She cocked her head. His quietness was killing her. "Why are you distant?"

"I'm focused."

"You're lying."

The Brandons were called. Only three teams left.

"It doesn't matter," he said.

"It does to me." What was he not telling her? Her brow furrowed. *Drowning. I'm drowning.* "I won't be able to focus today if I'm worried about you."

"I'm monitoring the security, everything. Making sure nothing like last time happens—or worse. Nightheart is nearby."

"He is?"

"Yes."

"Is there something wrong?" *Is that why he feels so far away?*

Deadly Dearest was called.

He turned toward her. "Nothing is out of the ordinary. We only have to win."

"You sure?"

"Yeah, little spitfire."

"Vee Miles and Cypher."

Vee squeezed Cypher's hand. "You got this."

He chuckled softly. Some of the strain left his shoulders, but that strain transferred into her.

"We got this," she amended.

"We do."

They stepped onto the stadium grounds together as the crowd roared.

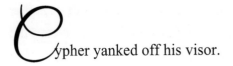

ypher yanked off his visor.

Eighteen hours. It had gone on for eighteen fucking hours, much longer than he and Vee ever put in at one time. There'd been one mandatory break in the middle, but most of the players never left their rigs. Vee didn't want to either—being so far behind in scoring—that he'd had to force water down her throat and demand she eat an extra booster energy bar.

He tore off his rig straps and stormed to Vee's side right as she took her own visor off. Pulling her into his arms, the crowds grew wild again now that the game had come to an end. Cypher scanned the arena; there were fewer people here than when they'd first started.

Vee smiled up at him.

"You okay?" he asked.

"Yeah."

"Let's get you some food."

He took her hand and led her from the stadium. In the distance, he saw the sun rising in the sky.

Fuck.

Leading her back above to their private lounge, they found her parents asleep on the couches within.

An attendant quietly came in, congratulated them, and placed down several plates of food.

"It won't be long now until they announce the winners," Vee said, sitting at a table overlooking the stadium. "We'll have to go back down when they do."

"Hmm." He hadn't known the game would go on for so long.

I'm due to leave Earth… Today. He hoped he'd be able to remain long enough for the announcement. It was ultimately up to Nightheart and the spaceport's schedule for departure.

But that wasn't solely what bothered him…

He hadn't yet told Vee he was leaving. That he wanted her to come with him.

Cypher watched as she ate her food. There was exhaustion etched upon her face, but her skin still bore a vivid radiance. *So beautiful.* It pained him. It pained him to know he was certain if she didn't choose to come with him willingly, he might force her to join him anyway—steal her away, or worse, blackmail or bribe her.

His jaw tightened at the thought.

Nothing for the entire event had gone amiss. He almost didn't believe it was possible. Not even Diatrix spared him and Vee a glance as they walked by her earlier. Their simulation remained the same as well.

And the Trentian Commander, Lotrin, Cypher's real test, hated Cypher as much as he did last time, but the aspect that he was a Cyborg hadn't come up again. Though his conversation with Diatrix did. Over and over again in his mind. Cypher was certain that night with her would haunt him for as long as he lived.

Diatrix had a reason for her hatred, and he…he did not.

All he had was old codes in his systems, put there by the very men Diatrix hated, that determined his behavior and reactions.

For his life, Cypher had lived under someone else's shadow. Some stranger or military organization had manipulated him since he was created. And he'd let them. While other Cyborgs had adjusted and adapted since the war, he'd hidden away on Ghost City, remaining the same.

Hibernating.

I'm not a good man. He sat back.

But I can be.

A buzz sounded in his head. Nightheart was trying to link with him. Cypher sighed.

Vee looked up at him and smiled as she chewed.

I want to be better for her. If not for himself, then for her. *Vee deserves a hero.* Not some messed up mecha bear without a system's update in several generations. A bear that was barely clinging to humanity deep inside.

"Nightheart's trying to get a hold of me," he told her.

Her smile wavered. "Oh?"

"Yeah, I'll be right back." He stood and left the room, sensing her questioning eyes on his back. When the door to the lounge shut behind him, he linked his IP.

Nightheart's voice filled his head. "I'm heading up to where you are," he said.

"Why?"

"I have news to discuss with you and with Vee."

Cypher frowned. "What news?" Had something gone wrong after all? Every time he seeded into the stadium's security, he saw nothing amiss. Not even the anti-Cyborg protestors outside were a cause of concern.

"You asked me to take care of NeoElite and Terraform Zero. I did. Now it's time to end all this crap and move onto what matters—your job."

Cypher ran a hand over his face. "I haven't told her."

"Told her what?"

321

"That I'm leaving today."

There was silence on the line for a moment.

"You've been fucking her for over a month. You should've told her the fucks are coming to an end. If it's more than that, I'm certain she knows by now you're leaving."

"I want her to join me," Cypher scowled.

"And what qualifications does she have to help run an interstellar top-secret ship?"

"She's brilliant. Did you even watch the championship?"

"The championship she didn't even place in?"

Cypher stilled, his jaw tightening. *Fuck.* They didn't place. If Nightheart said it, it was true. Cypher didn't know what his boss had done with 'taking care of NeoElite' for him, but even so, there was no reason for him to lie.

Cypher palmed his face again when a shadow skirted the corner of his eye. He looked up to see Nightheart strolling down the hallway toward him, brown hair perfectly slicked back, filling out an expensive black suit that only emphasized the Cyborg's domineering aura.

Somehow Nightheart's new getup suited him better than the nano-shifting battle suits they wore during the war. Nightheart was scarier in a suit.

Cypher dropped his hand and scowled. "Vee's more than a fuck for me," he snapped.

Nightheart shrugged. "I don't care anymore. She stays or she joins you. If it's the latter, it had better be by choice. She has less than six hours until take-off. Your chosen crewmates are already on standby to board at the spaceport, and Mia has you scheduled to arrive at several interstellar ports between your first acquisitions. You'll be making a short stop in Elyria."

"What for?"

"Need you to pick up Hysterian. He's joining the team."

Hysterian, another Cyborg shifter, one who had little use on the battlefield so Nightheart and Cypher rarely encountered him. The other Cyborg was more useful up close and personal, positioned to oversee the operations that involved traitors and deserters of war. Hysterian was tasked to get whatever information was needed out of them—using his unusual DNA.

The man was a manipulative torturer, even if he'd never raised a weapon toward someone or drawn blood.

Toxic. The motherfucker was *toxic*.

"You're running out of options, it seems," Cypher said.

"Never." Nightheart pushed past him and opened the door.

Vee hadn't moved from the table, but she was joined by her parents now. Cypher scowled at Nightheart's back as he followed him into the room.

Vee's eyes widened at Nightheart's approach. "I didn't know you were going to be here!"

She moved to stand, but Nightheart waved her down. He took a seat away from the group. Cypher, fuming, dropped down beside Vee.

"Nightheart?" Vee's mother eyed the new Cyborg apprehensively.

"The president of the EPED," Vee tells her.

Her mother's eyes widened as well. "Oh…"

Before she could genuflect, Nightheart interrupted, turning to Vee. Cypher curled his arm around the back of her chair.

"First of all," Nightheart said, "I want to congratulate you on completing the championship and achieving what you sought out to do." His eyes shifted to Cypher's. "Despite the unfortunate challenges they put into this year's game. Which will not go unpunished… I'm certain."

The Trentians.

"T-thank you," Vee said.

"On that note, as of yesterday, I bought out all available NeoElite stocks and have made myself part owner of the gaming and colonization company."

Vee's mouth dropped. "What?"

Nightheart continued, "I made assurances that the championship would not have any other *curveballs* to incite ratings and manipulate its players. You should thank me." He crossed his arms. "Despite some opinions, we take care of our own."

"Right. That's how you take care of them?" Cypher snapped. "By giving them tons of money?"

"I have a corporation to run, Cypher, and a PR nightmare to deal with, no thanks to your 'help.' What would you have me do? Declare war on them for no reason and shoot down their staff? Don't be worse than Zeph. I can be vindictive."

"Wait..." Vee sat forward. "What are you two talking about?" She looked questioningly between Nightheart and Cypher. "Cypher what's going on?"

"He asked me to take care of NeoElite after what happened during the semi-finals," Nightheart answered.

"You what?"

Cypher growled. "No one hurts me or those under my protection and gets away with it."

"They're going to think we cheated! If we place or win, they'll speculate we bought it."

Nightheart waved his hand. "No one knows of the change in leadership yet, and cheating won't be an issue."

Vee ran her hands through her hair. "I can't believe you guys." She stared wide-eyed at the table in front of her. "Why didn't you tell me?" She looked at Cypher. "Is this what you've been hiding?"

Cypher frowned. "I—"

The intercom sounded. *"Contestants, please come down to the stadium floors for the final ceremony!"*

"Oh, it's time!" Vee's mother quipped, ignoring the tension. She scurried to Vee's side as her daughter slowly stood, eyes ablaze.

Cypher and Nightheart rose as well.

"You're going to be great," Vee's mother said. "Whatever happens, you were perfect out there yesterday. You'll always be a winner in my eyes."

"Mom…" Vee groaned. She fell into her mother's embrace. "I'm glad you and Dad came. It's been so long." Her gaze slanted to meet Cypher's, the frustration there loud and clear.

"We wouldn't have missed it for the universe," her dad said.

Cypher watched the exchange despite Vee's annoyance at him. Vee's parents made him uncomfortable. Her mom smiled up at him, and his brow furrowed. Familial relations were something

Cyborgs didn't have, at least not at creation. Seeing the affection between individuals that only have a shared connection through biology was strange to him.

If he thought about it, perhaps his Cyborg brethren could be considered family, at least the shifter class. But still, none of them shared DNA, only creators.

He'd never shown affection toward anyone besides Vee.

Nightheart cleared his throat, scattering everyone. He turned to Cypher. It was clear his boss was as uncomfortable as he was. "Finish this and head straight back to the spaceport. You leave this evening." He nodded at Vee and turned on his heel, fleeing.

Cypher's lips twisted.

Fucking hell.

As if things couldn't get worse.

Silence fell across the room.

"You're leaving?" Vee whispered.

Fucking Nightheart.

Vee's parents moved away, not wanting to be a part of the conversation. He didn't blame them. He didn't want to be part of it either. He sure as hell wasn't going to have it in front of anyone, especially not Vee's parents.

Cypher took Vee's hand and gripped it tightly. "Like you said, we need to talk," he growled. He pulled her from the room and led her down to the stadium floor.

29

*V*ee's stomach churned as she and Cypher waited in line with the other teams.

He's leaving tonight?

Pain laced through her. Her heart beated erratically, and there was sweat under her arms. Cypher had ushered her to the stadium, scowling the whole way. He still scowled, his face hard and taut. She couldn't look away from him, afraid that if she did, he would vanish. And that would be it.

She would be left here heartbroken, in front of the universe, to put the shattered pieces of her heart and her life back together.

So that's why he's been distant. It wasn't his planned sabotage of NeoElite behind her back; it'd been the fact that he was leaving. The pain built inside her. Once again, everything seemed like a dream. Everything around her faded into the background.

He's leaving. Tonight.

That was all that mattered now. She didn't even care about the championship anymore. She just wanted to be alone with him to figure out what was happening. Vee stared at Cypher's profile, unable to even look at the screens, the teams on either side, or the announcer addressing the fans.

One by one, the top five teams were named.

She vaguely realized that she and Cypher were never called. It wasn't until Deadly Dearest was announced as the winner of this year's game that she tore her gaze from him.

The crowd went wild as Diatrix and her team of women surged onto every screen in the stadium. Fireworks went off, and vibrant lights flashed as Deadly Dearest accepted their win. Tears were in Diatrix's eyes.

Vee reached out and grabbed Cypher's hand, squeezing it. Her eyes trailed back to his face. He didn't squeeze her hand back.

It was over.

Attendees came out and ushered them off the stage. The crowd in the bleachers started to disperse. A few minutes later, she and Cypher were back in their lounge, empty now of her parents. It'd even been cleaned, as if no trace of them or their stay had ever existed.

Her heart squeezed.

It was over, all of it. Over.

Cypher released her hand and went to stand by the window. She remained rooted in place.

"I'm sorry," he said, stunning her. "I'm sorry you didn't win."

"You're sorry?"

He ran his hands through his hair. "You've worked your whole life for this, Vee. Of course I'm sorry. I didn't fucking help at all, it seems. You didn't even place."

"I don't care that we lost."

"Of course you care."

She shook her head. "I… don't." She really didn't care, she realized. At least not about the championship. It'd only been a game after all.

Cypher turned to look at her.

"I care about other things more," she whispered.

Pain flashed across Cypher's face. He knew what she was referring to. A crack formed in her heart.

Vee took a step forward. "You didn't tell me you were leaving."

"You knew I was."

"But not so soon. Not so soon after…"

"Would it have mattered? Would it have changed anything?"

Vee folded her arms around her stomach. "I could've prepared."

"For what? You needed to focus on your dream, and I wasn't about to let that slip away," he groused. "But it has, hasn't it?"

His words only made the crack in her heart bigger. "Stop making decisions for me!" she snapped. "You should've told me."

"You're asking a Cyborg to relinquish control. Impossible. I chose not to hurt you."

Tears beaded her eyes. "But you have."

He took a step toward her, and she turned away, moving to the table. If he touched her, tried to comfort her, she was going to turn into a wrecked puddle. Only threads of her pride remained, and if she was going to survive this, she needed them.

He stopped short, his voice low. "I can't stay here, Vee. You know that."

His words stabbed. "I know."

"But I don't want to leave you either."

Her eyes squeezed shut. "Don't."

"I don't want this to end."

A strangling sensation constricted her chest. She rested her palms on the table when she felt his mechanical heat against her back. "Cypher, please don't." She couldn't bear it.

"Come with me," he said.

"What?"

"Join me."

Vee pivoted to face him. "Join you? Out there?" Shock filled her. "You can't be serious. I don't have interstellar passports or clearance. I don't have the qualifications to work as a crew hand. And even if I did, the paperwork would take months! Women don't just leave Earth's atmosphere on a whim, not even if it's on a restricted space cruise. It's a crime."

"All of that can be bypassed."

"Why? Because you're a Cyborg?"

"Exactly."

She stared at him, her heart quickening. *Leave Earth? Tonight?* Leave everything behind just like that? Everything she knew… Her gut hollowed thinking of it.

She planned to leave it all behind one day, hopefully soon, but this soon… She wasn't prepared. Vee gazed disbelievingly at Cypher.

She loved him so much that she wanted to scream *yes*, forget about her responsibilities, and jump into his arms, but did he love her back? And if he did, would he still love her months from now after being stuck with her out in space?

"How?" she asked because she didn't know what else to say.

"Before I came here, I worked for a place called Ghost, a city ship ruled by Cyborgs, and I was their gatekeeper, their security. I spent all my time inside the machine, rewriting a world ruled by other machines."

"And Nightheart? The EPED?"

"He knows."

Vee licked her lips. Her head swirled.

"What about my life here? Bees? What about Bees? I can't leave without my cat."

Cypher straightened, the chilling distance leaving his eyes. "His habitat's already made in my ship's menagerie. As long as he's within it during landing and take-off, and during warp travel, he'll be fine. He'll have a home on the *Repossessed*. Everything else can be taken care of."

"I—"

His face hardened. "Unless you want to stay."

---

*H*ope blasted his chest, vibrating the wires in and out of his heart. Would Vee come with him willingly? Her questions, even her silence assured him she was considering it.

If she came willingly, he wouldn't have to steal her away.

Cypher forced his hands to unclench. *I won't steal her.*

334

He told himself that again and again over the last week. But he didn't believe it, no matter how hard he tried. He'd already begun the process of breaking the ties she had to this world. Bringing her parents here hadn't been a lucky whim like he'd told her. It was so she could say goodbye.

But more than anything, Cypher wanted her to choose to join *him*.

I'll steal her. He would, but he knew if he did, he'd have to spend a great deal of time rebuilding trust between them. He didn't want to waste any time, greedy bastard that he was.

He'd have to deal with Nightheart's wrath too.

She stared at him mutely, and he waited for her next question. Waited for anything she would give him. An unusual surge of anxiety assaulted his systems.

"If you choose to stay, I'll understand," he lied. *She loves me.* "Nightheart gifted me the stocks of NeoElite. They're yours if you want them." His boss couldn't get rid of them fast enough, sending them to Cypher the moment he'd left earlier. "You can become a part owner of NeoElite."

Why was he convincing her to stay? The bear inside him snarled.

Her eyes widened, but then she shook her head. In disbelief, he realized.

She's in Cyborg territory and has been for months—she should be used to it by now.

"Of course you'd give millions of credits away," she muttered, breaking eye contact with him to look out the window.

She was driving him crazy.

His body threatened to shift from the strain radiating through him as he waited for her answer.

"Vee," he groaned.

She glanced back at him.

"Say yes," he urged. "Just fucking say yes."

Her eyes slanted. "And if I don't?"

A dark, savage noise rose from his throat. His claws extended. "I will make the choice for you as you so damnably hate." He cupped her neck and forced her to look at him. "*I need you.*"

She shook her head. "I need you too."

"Then come. Join me. If you need a job, I'll give you one, any one you want. Just come with me this evening and leave this all behind."

"Cypher…"

"Please." He would beg. He would beg for her. "Please come with me."

She gazed up at him, her dark eyes glistening, her brow creased in confusion. It made him weak, not knowing what was on her mind. He couldn't see why she would ever choose to stay here, especially without him. If she loved him, she'd come, right?

Perhaps he should've told her sooner, given her more time to think about the decision. But several days ago, he hadn't even been sure if it was at all possible. And he didn't want her to think of anything else after all he'd put her through—what Nightheart had put her through—when she was an innocent in all that had happened.

Vee dropped her eyes from his and pulled away.

Worry seized him.

"We should go," she said, refusing to look at him, moving away. He let her go. "They probably want us to leave… Most of the stadium is empty now." There was a numbness to her voice that he didn't like.

Cypher straightened, hardening his heart. He licked the sharp edges of his bear teeth which threatened to come out. It pained him that she wouldn't give him an answer, but logically, he understood.

"Sure," he said, keeping his tone light despite the alien emotions vibrating his systems. He grabbed their stuff, opened the door, and waited for her to pass through. Together they left the stadium behind, and with it, all it had done to them. Cypher helped her into her hovercraft, and they flew back to his ship in silence.

There was only an hour or two left before he departed. His hands gripped the wheel hard.

A short time later, and with Vee still quiet beside him, they landed in the EPED section of the spaceport. His shifter plates opened and closed repeatedly in his chest all the while. On their way to his ship, there were freight vehicles and equipment all around, readying the *Repossessed* for take-off. Several men, dressed in crew gear, saluted Cypher as he walked by.

"Captain Cypher."

He waved his hand. "I'll address everyone later," he told them, opening the hatch. "I take it you know what to do until then? You have a layout of my ship?"

One of the men nodded. "Yes, sir."

"Good. Tell the others to get situated in the crew's quarters first before system checks. I'll meet you on the bridge in an hour."

"Yes, sir!" The men scurried away.

Vee shifted beside him, and he curled his arm around her back, ushering her into his ship. They walked through it together, alone, one last time. Bees greeted them yowling for food. After the cat was fed and watered, he watched as Vee picked him up and pressed her face into his fur.

Hell, if she chose to leave and he managed to let her go, he was going to miss the feline too. Having the cat around his feet and on his lap had been an unexpected comfort to him these last two months.

"Vee," he began.

She cut him off. "Can I have a few minutes alone to think? Is there time?"

"Yeah, there's some time still." He didn't want to leave her. "Come find me when you're ready." He turned to leave but stopped short. "Take all the time you need," he added, meaning it.

The door zipped closed as Cypher left Vee in the captain's quarters. In the distance, the sounds of his new crew prickled his audio. Jaw ticking, he stormed to his bridge.

He didn't want them here, not yet. He wasn't ready for them until he had his answer from Vee. The fear that she wouldn't join him upset his systems. Fear of what he would do if she didn't. Having others nearby wasn't safe.

He fisted his hands and tried to force the tension from his body.

The *Repossessed* had become his den, and a bear didn't take sharing his den lightly. Though he spent time with many crews, great and bad during the war, it'd been a long time since he had so many others close by and in such a small space.

All I want is Vee.

I'm only here because of her.

Heavy, unbridled emotion blazed his chest. It left him breathless and wanting.

Some of his other brethren had crews, some didn't; they chose to work alone or employ androids instead. *I may have to do that in the future.*

The thought didn't stay with him for long; his mind kept returning to Vee and her silence—silence that brought him back to the first days he'd waited endless hours for her to return his comms as he traveled from Ghost City to Earth.

She drives me crazy.

I need her.

Even now, looking around his quiet bridge, the stifling loneliness crept back in as he imagined a life without her in it.

How was he going to convince her to join him if she didn't want to? There was nothing in his databases that would help him with this problem. Before her, his experience with the female gender had been severely limited. His lack of knowledge in that department crippled him.

Cypher scrubbed his face, tugged his hair. The plates in his body expanded and contracted.

Several messages from Mia awaited him, accompanied by retrievals, acquisitions, and itineraries for his first excursion on the job. In seconds, he had them all memorized, but his frustration immediately returned after. There was nothing else to distract him.

Throwing up an image of Vee behind his eyes—a sense of déjà vu hit him from those first days. He pulled out a bottle of whiskey and a grouping of leather seat straps from the bridge's storage, and let the feeling rush through him.

He   sat   heavily   in   his   chair   to   wait.

30

"*M*om?" Vee spoke into her wristcon when she heard a click on the line.

"Vee? Oh, honey, I'm so sorry you didn't place," her mom said. "We wanted to call sooner but thought you might need some time first. How are you doing? They should've picked you and Cypher. You two were amazing!"

Vee frowned. "It's fine. I'm fine with it. I need your help."

"With what? We're at a hotel nearby. Dad and I can meet up with you. Give us thirty to get ready and you can stay with us tonight. We'd love to spend time with you. You still like sushi, right?"

"It's not that. I'd love to spend more time with you too, but I can't tonight. I...don't know what to do." Her voice wavered.

Vee took in the room that had been her home for weeks. Her bag had remained partially packed since that last time she'd tried to leave, but it was still filled with her and Cypher's stuff. Not much, but it was there.

Bees had toys scattered across the floor—fake mice with catnip. Vee's red dress was draped over a chair, always out because Cypher went crazy whenever she wore it.

There was a gun on the table next to the bed, and several other weapons stashed throughout because of Cypher's paranoia and aggressively protective instincts. Then there were her toiletries and papers with her notes about Laprencia and several screenshots of the two of them in virtual Yria hanging on the wall.

She loved it all; they made this room theirs. Whenever she inhaled, she breathed in Cypher. His scent permeated the space like an ever-present drug.

But could she join him offworld? Where, if something should happen, she would have no escape or control of her life?

Vee couldn't bear the thought of joining Cypher only for him to break up with her later. It was too painful to think about. He was her first, and she wanted him to be her last. Was that selfish of her? Or naive?

He hasn't said he loves me.

"What is it, Vee?" her mom asked. "What's wrong?"

"Cypher asked me to join him tonight when he leaves Earth," she said.

There was a short pause. "He did?"

"He leaves soon, and I don't have much time to decide. I'm scared. Really scared, or nervous. I can't get my head straight. I guess I'm both, mom."

"How much time do you have? Why are you scared?"

"Hours, maybe less. I love him but I don't know if he loves me!" Vee burst out.

"Oh, honey… He—"

"I've been dreading saying goodbye for weeks now, but I didn't think it was going to happen so soon. I don't want to say goodbye—it hurts my heart—but to leave? There's so much left to do."

"You love him?"

"I do."

"Then you have your answer, sweetie."

"It's not that simple," Vee whimpered. "You know me. I've never had a boyfriend, never had anything but that damn game. I don't even have any girlfriends. I'm a loser. I'm a loner, independent, always have been, until him. What if I care for him more than he cares for me? What if I'm making a big mistake? I don't know what to do."

Her mom tsked. "I don't think that's true."

"How would you know?"

"Vee, in the short time your dad and I were with you two yesterday and this morning, Cypher couldn't keep his eyes off of you. In person and in the game. I don't know much about him other than what's been relayed to us, but it seems he's put his life on hold for you. He didn't have to, did he? Not only that, but he's also helped keep you safe, helped you get to the championship, and stood by your side the whole way. It's easy to see he cares for you."

Vee sniffled. "You think so?"

"I know so."

"Mom... I love him so much."

"He loves you too. He wouldn't ask you to join him out in the universe if he didn't." Vee's mother chuckled. "Can you imagine?"

"So you think I should go?"

"I think you should follow your heart, and if you don't, you'll regret it for the rest of your life."

Vee's heart hammered at her mom's words. She needed to see Cypher. Now. Excitement and anxiety surged through her veins. "If I go," she said, getting to her feet, "I leave in a couple of hours. I don't know how long I'll be gone. It could be awhile. Months at least."

Her mom chuckled again. "We've never known how long you'll be gone, sweetheart. You left home years ago and never came back. I think your dad and I can handle a few months."

"So you and Dad will be okay?"

"Of course. We'll be here when you get back. Always have, always will be. School will be too—when you get back that is."

"Mom," Vee groaned.

"My baby's going to space!"

"Don't be so sure yet." Vee started to pace. "I need to talk to him first. I can't just follow a guy and give up everything without something in return even if he's offering me the universe."

"Right. You better take tons of pictures and get me and your dad souvenirs from every place you visit! What a dream. Maybe ask him if he can take us along sometime in the future?"

"Mom!" Vee laughed halfheartedly. But it did make her feel better. Maybe all this will be okay after all. Hope bloomed in her chest. If her parents were on board, what was left to stop her? "I'm gonna go. I don't have much time left to talk to him."

"Go get him! And make sure you call me back before you take off."

Vee smiled. "I'll try. Love you."

"Love you too."

After she hung up with her mom, her nerves returned tenfold, but they were good this time. *Good nerves.* She rubbed her arms. Vee dashed into the bathroom to wash her face and change out of her

Terraform suit. She eyed the red dress but ended up opting for jeans and a simple shirt.

She wanted—*needed*—something from Cypher, and she didn't want to manipulate it out of him. She needed to know if he loved her back. Not if he *wanted* her for her body. The red dress had never failed her in that regard. It was sacred.

It pained her to know she'd be putting pressure on him for an answer, but she didn't think she could follow him into the stars without knowing.

Bees nuzzled her leg, and she scritched the cat's head. She took a deep breath to calm her nerves.

This could be the last time we talk, she realized, pursing her lips. *The last time I ever see him.* Her heart thundered.

This is it.

She wiped her palms on her pants and left the room—and heard his voice the moment she entered the corridor. Broody, authoritative, and deep, it came from the bridge and made her skin blaze. Even now, he intimidated her, and she swallowed hard.

As she neared the bridge, she glimpsed the backs of at least a dozen men facing away from her, all in black leather space uniforms. Cypher addressed them. He towered over every one of them, now in a similar uniform himself, with an EPED logo stitched on the right side of his chest.

Her pulse quickened. His hard, piercing eyes looked at each man in turn, his face a mask of unwavering leadership, and it made her core knot tight with want.

Seeing him like this, she could barely believe she had him inside her body again and again, all over this ship. That he'd taken her with such savagery and tenderness each time. *Me, a nerdy gamer girl.* Vee sucked her bottom lip into her mouth.

Cypher glanced up and met her eyes. His jaw tightened, and he quickly looked back at his men. "That'll be all for now. Prepare your stations. I have one last thing to do before we ready for take-off."

Vee shifted from foot to foot, beyond nervous.

The men saluted and scrambled away. Cypher caught her eyes again and headed her way.

Vee straightened as he stopped before her.

"Captain Cypher," she said breathlessly, eyeing his body gloved in his suit. She never wanted to climb him as badly as she did now. He screamed power, and her sex clenched, wanting to feel that power thrusting into her.

"Vee Miles," he responded, his voice heavy.

She licked her lips. "C-can we talk? Captain Cypher."

His eyes flashed—a glimpse of the man she'd known for the past several months. "Yes. Let's go to the lounge."

He moved past her, and she reached out and grabbed his hand. Stopping, he tensed and looked back at her. His face softened. He threaded his fingers through hers, and they made their way together. Some of her nerves vanished.

A team. *We're a team.*

Adrenaline coursed through her.

The moment the lounge door shut behind them, Vee threw herself into his chest, wrapping her arms around him. Her fingers tangled into his tied-back hair. He stiffened for a split second before embracing her back and pulling her against him.

She closed her eyes and took in his scent as though it might be her last time. His heat enveloped her, and she gave in to it. It was heaven, her heaven.

He was heaven.

His hands tangled into her hair, and he pulled her closer. For a minute, neither one of them moved.

"Why do I feel like this is goodbye?" Cypher growled.

She jerked back to look at him. "It's not."

"It isn't?"

She shook her head, dropping her gaze to his chest. "I need…" The words trailed off. She couldn't say them without pain.

"You need what? Tell me what you need? I'll give it to you."

"I need…" She tried again, but her throat squeezed.

"Tell me," he demanded.

Cypher cupped her cheeks and forced her to look at him. Tears prickled her eyes.

"What's holding you back, little spitfire? Let me give it to you. I want to give it to you."

"Love," she burst out. "I need to know that you love me too."

His eyes widened. Vee tried to turn her face away, but he held her fast. She clawed her fingers into his suit. "I don't know if I can give up everything and follow you into the unknown without love. I…I haven't experienced much in my life, and I'm afraid. Really afraid. These last few months have been awful but so incredibly wonderful to me.

"You've made my life, my real life, spark. I want to experience it with you beyond the virtual. I want to explore the universe, but I don't know what you want or where you stand. Are you asking me out of friendship, pity? For sex?" Her lips quivered, but she kept her voice firm. "I don't think that. But I need to hear you say it so I know where I stand with you. Where we stand going forward. I can't give you full control without knowing I'm not more than a girl your bear wants to rut." She blushed, dropping her eyes. "Even saying that hurts."

"Vee—"

"—please be honest with me," she interrupted.

"I love you."

Her heart stopped. "What?"

"I fucking love you. This feeling in my chest, it hurts. It's hot and constricting. If it isn't love, it's adoration. I love and adore you, Vee."

Her eyes met his, and Cypher's thumbs caught the tears under her lashes. She could barely process his words. "You do?" she asked. Her chest threatened to burst.

"More than anything in this universe, past or present. I've loved you since you had the naïve audacity to take my identity and pretend to be me and when you ignored my comms as I raced here to stop you. I didn't ask you to join me out of pity," he spat. "Or out of guilt. I asked you to come with me because I need you like I need my next breath. You want to find your own way, Vee? The only way going forward is *our* way. Understand?"

Her mouth went slack. "Really?"

"Fucking Nightheart knew what he was doing when he sponsored you, that wormy piece of shit."

Her lips twitched to smile. *Is this real? Is this happening?* "Did he know your type?" she teased, still shell-shocked.

He loves me?

"Who the hell knows?" Cypher grumped. "But I love you, Vee Miles, and if you don't join me for takeoff in a few minutes, I'm going to gag your mouth, strap you to a seat, and force you to come against your will." He dropped his arm and pointed to one of the seats in the lounge. Lo and behold, leather straps were resting on the table before it.

Vee stared at the straps, knees weakening. "*Oh.*"

"You may think I'm a good man, little human, but I'm not. I'm a good Cyborg, maybe even a decent bear, but a man? I am not. I've tried to be, but my thoughts and intentions never line up."

He spun her back to face him before she could respond and slammed his mouth down on hers. A groan emanated from his throat as his tongue forced its way between her lips to thrust inside her, mimicking rough sex. His teeth emerged to graze her skin as his arms banded around her back and head, lifting her off the floor.

Vee clutched him hard. She swung her legs up around his hips. His cock pressed into her, and her sex fluttered with need.

Hard and all-consuming, Cypher's kiss stole her heart. He devoured her, and she melted into his feasting, scarcely believing this was happening.

When she managed to pull away, lips raw from his kiss, she moaned. "You really love me?"

"Enough to destroy the reputations of Cyborgs everywhere and so much more. I finally understand why Zeph kidnapped his woman when he did. Are you coming with me this evening, or am I going to have to make you?" he growled. "Either way, at this point, you're not stepping off this ship."

She slid down his chest until her feet touched the ground. She rolled her eyes. "Yeah, I'm coming."

The tension in his body vanished. "Thank the fucking devil."

Vee smiled. "I'm coming," she repeated.

"You sure as hell are."

She grabbed his hand. "I am. I think… Right?"

"Do you want me to hogtie you and bind you to that chair?" he growled. "I'll be inclined to do a hell of a lot more than that once you're at my mercy."

Dirty thoughts shot through her head. Her eyes widened. "Really?"

"A hell of a lot and more," he warned.

She swallowed, imagining the worst, or the best. "Maybe we should wait…"

"After takeoff it is." Cypher turned toward the door, reaching out and grabbing the straps on his way. "Let's get this show on the road." The door zipped open, and he waited for her.

Vee shivered, excitement surging through her.

He loves me.

I'm doing this, I'm leaving Earth.

Finally.

And with him.

She stopped at the threshold before him. "We're a team," she whispered.

Cypher gifted her one of his rare, wicked smiles. "We're a team. Wherever we go, wherever we end up, we'll always be a team, little spitfire." He grabbed her hand and kissed the back of it. "Whether it's in a game or not, we're a team, always."

"I love you, Cypher."

"I love you too, Vee Miles. Obsessively."

A darkness returned to his face, and a shiver coursed through her. With his hand gripping hers—as if she would run, *hah*!—he led her back to the bridge. The floor buzzed under her feet.

A buzzing she was certain came from her. She couldn't be happier, more anxious, or more excited. Her body twitched. All that happened these last weeks was nothing compared to this. To what she now had to look forward to. She turned to Cypher, and her heart burst with warmth.

She'd become an entirely different person over the last few months. A little more steadfast, a little more wayward, and a lot more of a risk-taker.

As if he could read her thoughts, he glanced at her before the bridge doors opened. "You ready to finally see what it's like leaving a planet? To experience the stars?"

"Yes!"

Oh, yes.

He lowered his mouth to her ear. "Then follow me."

EPILOGUE

Cypher docked his ship and headed for the ship's arsenal, letting Bees out of his habitat remotely. The cat had taken to space better than most of the crew.

In the mirror within the weapons room, he pulled up his shirt and checked the wound that was dead center on his chest. It was almost healed from the incision from the night before. A wound he'd inflicted after Vee was sound asleep in his bed.

His systems roiled in his head, telling him to repair himself, but he overrode them whenever they came up. There was time for that later.

Cypher trailed his fingers across the cut once more before placing his shirt back down. Donning his jacket, he returned to the task at hand.

His crew meandered about now that landing was complete, readying to disembark the ship. They had the rest of the day and night off to enjoy themselves. Most would go out into the tropical, glitzy metropolis of Elyria to let off steam.

He wasn't easy to work with. He'd heard them mumbling about his gruff attitude and standoffish ways more than once.

But Elyria had it all. The good and the bad, the beautiful and the downright ugly. Money, drugs, and trafficking ruled the planet, and yet it was seen as a paradise beacon to humans and Trentians alike across the universe. It was enough for any man to reset his mood.

Cypher picked out a laser gun and strapped it to the harness crossed over his chest.

Vee stepped up beside him and grabbed a handgun. "Captain Cypher," she said, smiling.

She wore simple civilian clothes and had her flaming hair tied back. He watched as she tucked the gun into her jeans. He fucking loved it when she called him captain.

During the past month, he'd been teaching her how to defend herself. The virtual Terraform Zero rigs were useful in that department. They continued to play, to learn. And his time with her after hours had become the most important part of his day.

Not to mention, the rigs were great to strap her up in and take her at his pleasure. Another thing he'd learned since they left Earth: Vee liked the straps.

Cypher loved them as well. Life was easier away from Earth.

Everything else, even their first requisition, was dust in his mind compared to Vee. He thought his rut had come to an end before the championship, but it hadn't. He wanted her now more than ever. She was now his completely, and the thought of that stoked his lust.

He handed her a knife, and she slid it under her jacket.

"I'm excited," she chirped.

"You'll like Elyria."

"Our planet was based after it."

Yria, the one she introduced Terraform Zero to him with.

"It's not as beautiful or wild, at least not in the metropolis, but I think you'll like it," he said.

"Oh, I know I'll like it! After we pick up Hysterian, can we see the falls?"

The falls was a tropical Eden where the Farchia River met one of Elyria's oceans. There were ninety-eight waterfalls in total, which spanned for nearly a mile. It was considered one of the wonders of the universe.

"Sure." He rounded his arm over her back. "Business first, though." He guided her down the hallway and to the ship's open hatch that led to Elyria's main spaceport.

"Yeah, yeah, don't want to get angry messages from Nightheart again."

Fuck that Cyborg.

"Don't say his name," he grumbled.

"Nightheart."

He twisted to Vee and pulled her ponytail back, arching her head back and exposing her throat to him. Eyes flaring, he extended his jaw, opening his mouth, and pressed his teeth to her neck. "I will claim you right here out in the open where any one of my crew could see if you continue to goad me," he warned.

"Then they'll see me," she breathed.

"I'll rip out their eyes afterward."

Having Vee being surrounded by men—built men—every day in a confined space like his ship had made him an even more paranoid and jealous ursine.

"I won't continue to goad you, Captain Cypher," she panted as his tongue slid across her throat. "For now."

He released her with a light nip. "Good."

Cypher stormed forward and walked out into the port.

"Cypher!"

He turned, and her wide eyes looked directly at his crotch. "You're tented. You're not going out in public like that, are you?"

He glanced down and shrugged. "Unless you want to take care of it for me real quick, I am."

Vee stuck out her tongue. "I refuse. Show me Elyria. I'm not missing those waterfalls for Cyborg dick." She stomped past him and followed the exit signs to leave the port.

Grinning, he stalked behind her.

A short time later, taking public transport, Vee held his hand tightly—like she normally did—as they made their way deeper into the neon city. They stood gazing out the glass-paned windows as the tropical hub whipped by.

Leaning down, Cypher pressed his nose into Vee's hair.

He listened to her fluttering heart and her gasps of awe—between her constant stream of questions. They were the perfect distraction. That, and he had a surprise planned for her.

"I wish we had more than this afternoon here," she said. "I want to see everything."

"We'll come back," he promised.

"I can't wait. Will we have time to pick up something for my parents?"

Vibrant green, steel chrome, clear glass, and bright blue skies passed them by.

"We'll make time," Cypher said.

"Thanks. Should I be worried about Hysterian?"

He tensed. "No," he said after a moment's thought. "Why?"

"Every Cyborg I've met so far has upended my life." Vee met his gaze in the glass. "I'm kind of happy where I am right now." She laughed. "I don't want things to change."

"Nothing will change," he rasped. "Nothing."

"Good." She laughed some more. "That's all I needed to hear. No more change. Screw change. The only change I like now is when you change your clothes and I get to see all your muscles."

A heated rumble filled his throat as the skytrain came to a stop, entering under the bridge of two skyscrapers. Cypher pulled Vee after him as they disembarked. "This won't take long."

Hysterian's IP and signal suffused Cypher's senses. The other shifter Cyborg was near. Near enough that Cypher could smell the unique aroma of skin, hot metal, and tight-assed alpha anguish. It was a smell they all shared to some degree.

Their signals connected as the other Cyborg came into view.

"Let's get this over with," Cypher muttered. Vee's hand tensed in his.

Hysterian sat at a table outside a bar, lounging with his leg hooked over the other, an untouched drink in front of him. Vee's steps slowed, and he squeezed her hand reassuringly. He knew why she hesitated. No one else looked like Hysterian—and knowing what kind of creature Hysterian shared his DNA with, no one else would ever be like the Cyborg.

They were all unique, but Hysterian especially so. Hysterian was cursed.

Wearing a skin-tight full body suit, he had almost no skin showing. A mask rose over his face from his neck to cover his nose, leaving only his eyes, brow, and hair uncovered. His hair was slicked back, a perfectly cut swathe of white that ran close to his scalp and ended in a point at the back. His skin was almost as pale as the suit and hair, nearly porcelain, and there was no color whatsoever to Hysterian, not even his eyes. His eyes were jet black.

As if the Cyborg had never experienced warmth.

Cypher didn't doubt it. There was a reason Hysterian covered himself up so thoroughly that not even his mouth showed. Like Stryker, he protected himself so he wouldn't hurt others. And it wasn't like Hysterian had the DNA of a creature that preferred the arctic climates of the universe. No shifter Cyborg that thrived in the cold would ever live on a planet like Elyria willingly.

Besides the iciness that Hysterian exuded, he wasn't a loner like Cypher. His latex-suited brethren had been doing business for a powerful crime lord on Elyria for years, working as a well-paid bouncer for a club known as *Dimes*. A club supposedly always filled with people—human, Trentian, or half-breeds.

Now he was Nightheart's latest Monster Hunter.

He scanned the area and the crowds around them. There were no women with Hysterian; the Cyborg had come alone, with nothing more than a duffle bag at his feet.

Good.

As long as Hysterian kept his distance from Vee and respected their space, having his brethren on his ship wouldn't be a problem.

"Hysterian," Cypher greeted.

Hysterian uncrossed his legs and stood. For a split-second, Hysterian's eyes bulged slightly and twitched back and forth. But it was over before even Cypher could capture it in his databases. The white-suited Cyborg was tall—taller than Cypher. But unlike himself, Hysterian was lean and wiry. It made sense for the DNA he harbored.

DNA that Cypher thanked the devil's children that he wasn't spliced with.

"Captain Cypher," Hysterian greeted back.

Their eyes met, and they made a connection. It was the reason he wanted to meet Hysterian first, away from his ship—never trust a being until you look them in the eye. Cypher transferred the *Repossessed's* docking site and access stations to Hysterian, allowing his brethren officer status.

Silence fell between the three of them as the data was transferred.

Around them, bystanders looked on, giving their group a wide berth.

When the codes finished downloading in Hysterian's mind, they stepped away from each other.

Hysterian picked up his bag and hauled it over his shoulder. "I'll head over there now."

Cypher nodded. "We'll meet you there later."

Hysterian nodded back. "Very well." He looked over at Vee.

Cypher stiffened.

"I'm Hysterian, a brother of Cypher's. I'm sure he's told you about me by now, but whatever he might have said, you have nothing to fear from me. Unlike some of my kind, you'll find me honorable."

Vee pulled her hand from Cypher's and offered it to Hysterian. Cypher stiffened further as Hysterian hesitated and stared at it.

"I'm Vee Miles," she said. "Cypher probably hasn't told you anything about me, but I'm honorable too, and you have no reason to fear me. I hope you like cats."

Hysteria looked at Cypher. "Can I touch her?"

Vee sighed.

Cypher growled, "Briefly."

Hysterian's brow arched but he took her hand and shook it. "I do."

Vee smiled. "Great. Bees likes sitting on Cypher's lap due to his heat. He may do the same to you."

"Very well." Their hands dropped, and the tension in Cypher's chest vanished. Hysterian turned back to him. "Later then, Captain Cypher." Hysterian strode past and headed toward the skytrain.

When he was out of sight, Vee turned to Cypher. "He's different."

"We all are."

"Yeah, but where you and Nightheart seem constantly ready to battle over turf and territory, he doesn't. He's a shifter too, right?"

"Yes."

She slanted her eyes up at him. "What kind?"

Cypher tugged her ponytail. He wasn't a fan of Vee's curiosity over another male. "Classified."

"Since when? Classified my ass! What kind?"

He smiled despite his jealousy. "Classified, little spitfire. If you want to know, you'll have to ask him yourself. And it's not your ass anymore." He reached behind her and grabbed it, squeezing with a sudden, unbridled need to touch it. "It's mine."

She squealed and laughed, pushing his hand away. "He's going to be like you, isn't he?"

"Why so many questions about him?" Cypher growled. "You're not thinking about trying to leave me, are you?"

Her mouth parted. "Never."

"Fucking good." He grabbed her hand and led her to a different airtrain terminal. "He's taken the same job I have with the EPED. When we head back to Earth in several months, his ship will be ready and waiting for him."

"Nightheart's hiring a lot of you. Must be expensive. He's got a lot of money."

"He's lost a lot of us recently too."

He'd told Vee about the Retrievers and the recent history of the EPED and his kind. He wanted her to be prepared for the world she was entering, especially since one of their stops would soon be Ghost City— once he found a way to render his crew unconscious first—where he planned to give her the nano transfers she needed to live a long, *long*, healthy life with him.

But that was for another day.

Today, he had another surprise.

"Remember Zeph? How he caused so much of all of this shit we've had to face?" he asked as they entered the train and it sped into action.

"Yeah."

"Hysterian's getting his old EPED ship."

"Hmm."

The city flew past them, the neon lights, giant advertisements, and sandy hills and lush trees between. The buildings spread out over time, and the landscape of the Elyrian Oasis took over. Soon there were more trees, rivers of turquoise water, and cliffs covered in dewy flowers and vines than there were buildings. Long patches of desert spread between them.

He pulled Vee to his side, and she rested her head on his chest as they stared out the window together.

"It's so beautiful here. Are we headed to the falls?" she asked after a while.

"Almost as beautiful as Yria, and no, not yet."

She lifted her head. "Where are we going then?

"It's a surprise."

"A surprise?"

"One you'll like, I promise."

She settled her head back against him. "Humph, I hope so."

Warmth permeated his chest, sparking through his wires and into every fiber of his body. Cypher wrapped his arms around his woman. He still couldn't believe after a month of being confined with her in his ship that she was there at all. That she was his. And that his new den had a den-mate.

That she chose to follow him into the stars and trust him with her life.

He tangled his fingers into Vee's hair until her hairband fell out. He only wished he could've helped her win the championship and see her reign as the champion he knew she was.

But there was always next year...

And the year after that.

She didn't know it yet, but he was already making plans for them to compete again.

Then there were the planets he'd begun to gather intelligence on to take her to that did not yet have a colony but were reserved for future research. When Vee declined the Terraform Zero NeoElite stock shares, he'd begun to funnel them into colony and much-needed expansion supply and development organizations to help fund a better future for humankind.

The airtrain came to a stop amidst a rocky plateau with a view of a forest below that stretched to the ocean.

Vee's gasp delighted him as they left the train behind and stood with the sevcral others nearby looking over the sight.

"It's so beautiful," she whispered. "So much more than anything I've ever seen, simulation or not. And it's real, really real."

He kissed the top of her head. "Is that so?"

"Thank you for bringing me here."

He loved the wonder in her voice. "I must confess it's my first time on Elyria too, seeing this, all of this." Cypher glanced over the vast landscape and the water far beyond. It took his breath away too. "I would've missed this if it weren't for you," he whispered.

"I love you." She smiled. "Thank you for this surprise."

"This isn't the surprise."

"It isn't?" She glanced up at him.

"No, follow me."

Renting a hovercraft, he flew them down the plateau to a lower one, closer to the ocean. Amongst the trees, there was a building made of sandstone with large open terraces. A private place he rented. Crystalline water trickled into pools so perfectly blended in with the environment, it looked like the epitome of paradise's entryway.

Cypher listened to Vee's racing heart.

A man in a beige suit met them out front. "Mr. and Mrs. Miles?"

"Uh—" Vee began.

"That's us," Cypher said.

The man smiled. "Come this way."

Inside the building, it was just as beautiful, if not more so, with a panoramic view of the ocean where the forest below split away and curled inward.

Vee hesitated beside him.

"Don't worry," he reassured.

Their usher led them to the back terrace. There were a large spread of exotic foods and drinks on a crystal table, brilliantly colored flowers spilling out from all sides, and a lilting harp sounded somewhere behind the blooms.

Vee tensed as Cypher moved to the middle of it, letting go of her hand. She stopped, staring at him, a mask of confusion over her face.

This is how a man proposes to a woman, is it not?

He may have been inept with the opposite sex, but he did research this at great length.

Marriage, the sacrament was an act of love, the ultimate union. He had no plans to ever let Vee go, and thought nothing of it as 'jumping the gun.' He wanted her, forever, and that was it.

Cyborgs didn't have any traditions, he found. Not a single one. There was nothing his kind had in the way of history and culture, and it saddened him. *Him.* The Cyborg who hibernated on Ghost for the last several generations because of his job, and because he couldn't be bothered.

Besides that, those of his kind who were partnered with their mates—the very, very few—had done it in a variety of ways.

He detested that Nightheart had been right all along. He'd allow the Cyborg to live for a while longer—a short while. Long enough to see his boss fall to his knees in worship when he finally found a woman he couldn't live without. Cypher looked forward to that glorious day of revenge. Whether it was tomorrow or a hundred years from now, he would be there to enjoy it.

He turned to Vee and got down on one knee.

"Cypher…" Vee whispered, sucking her lower lip into her mouth and wiping her palms on her pants. "What are you doing?"

"Vee Miles," he started, pulling out the priceless pyrizian metal band from his pocket. It sparkled in the suns' light. "Will you marry me?"

Her jaw dropped open, and her lovely dark eyes widened. "What?"

"You heard me," he scoffed. "Will you marry me?"

"Oh my God." She looked around wildly. "This is happening—you're proposing. You didn't knock me out and set me up in a simulation, right? Are we in the game?"

His brow knitted together, and he hardened his lips. "What else do you think I'm doing? And no, we are not in the game."

She pressed her hands to her chest. "Oh my God, oh my God, oh hell! You even have a ring! Where did you get a ring?"

"Vee," he growled. "Don't make me force an answer from you." Was this how proposals were supposed to go? Maybe he shouldn't have kept it a secret. "The ring is from the metal plates protecting my heart. I took it out and fashioned it last night while you were sleeping."

"You did *what*!?"

Was the location, the flowers, the food, and the music not enough?

"For fuck's sake, Vee, yes or no?" He got to his feet and strode up to her before she had a panic attack and ran.

"But you're a heroic, legendary Cyborg, and I'm—I'm just…"

"Just what? My partner? My teammate?" He cupped her cheeks. "Answer. Now."

"Partners…" she whispered, the shock slowly leaving her gaze. "We are that, aren't we?"

"Answer! I'm growing impatient." Always, *always* with her, the wait killed him. He should've known it wasn't going to be easy. He wouldn't have it any other way.

A smile crept over her lips.

His lips followed.

"Yes," she said.

Cypher tugged her hand between them and slipped his ring onto her finger. Though devoid of gems, it was priceless. Holding her hand up with his, a thrill filled him seeing the metal encircling her finger. He liked it. He liked it a little too much. Fuck that, he loved it. Vee closed her hand into a fist and pressed it to her heart.

He covered it with his own. "You're mine now. Forever," he warned.

"And you're mine now forever, too. Don't ever forget that."

The heat coursing through his body blazed hot. He leaned down and pressed his brow to hers. This was one non-negotiable contract. One game they'd win. He slid his lips over her forehead and down her cheek.

Who knew he'd fall for the woman who practically catfished him? Cypher found Vee's willing lips and claimed them.

He was awake now, and would always be.

Because   of   her.

AUTHOR'S NOTE

Thank you for reading *Ursa Major: Cyborg Shifters* book seven. If you liked the story or have a comment, please leave a review! I love reviews!

What's next on my plate, you ask? The eighth book in *Cyborg Shifters* (Hysterian), the third book for the *Bestial Tribe* (Thyrius!!), and another *Venys Needs Men* dragon book. Yay!

If you love cyborgs, aliens, anti-heroes, and adventure, follow me on Facebook or through my blog online for information on new releases and updates.

Join my newsletter for the same information.

Naomi Lucas

Turn the page to read the blurb for my next book!

TO WAKE A DRAGON

(Venys Needs Men)

It's been eight years since the red comet flew across our skies. Eight years since the blood moon. No dragon has been seen or heard from since.

Until now.

As one of the guardians of my tribe, I'm known as Milaye, a Protector of the Mermaid Coast. I've never had the honor of consideration as a future matriarch, or a match for one of the rare-born males born near the Forbidden Jungle. Because of this, I've kept my grief hidden—despite my envy for my fellow tribes mates who are happily mated.

I've lost hope for such a life long ago. My duty to protect those I cherish is all I have now.

But one day, my ward flees into a cave deep beneath the jungle brush. A cave, I soon realize, that holds a giant, long dead monster.

A *dragon.*

I touch him and find he isn't dead after all...

Printed in Great Britain
by Amazon